~ A Disney PRINCE NOVEL ~

Prince of Song & Sea

~ A DISNEY PRINCE NOVEL ~

Prince of Song & Sea

LINSEY MILLER

DISNEY PRESS

Los Angeles • New York

For information address Disney Press, 1200 Grand Central Avenue,
Glendale, California 91201.
Printed in the United States of America

First Hardcover Edition, October 2022
10 9 8 7 6 5 4 3 2 1
FAC-004510-22231

Library of Congress Control Number: 2021949319
ISBN 978-1-368-06911-3
Designed by Margie Peng

Visit disneybooks.com

To everyone who ever wished they
could be part of another world. ~L. M.

Overture

*P*AIN washed over Eric in waves, salt sticking to every scratch. Water lapped at his legs, and a bone-deep cold shuddered down his spine. He tried to turn his head and groaned. He couldn't move. Why couldn't he move?

The ship! He had been on the ship. A storm, worse than any he had ever weathered, had swept over them faster than lightning. They'd caught fire and crashed, the powder kegs exploding, and he had been thrown into the sea. Eric tried to call out and choked. Each breath stung, the acrid taste of ash prickling across his tongue. His chest ached.

But all of it meant he was alive. He had survived.

A soft hum broke through the pain. It started low and sad, like far-off whale calls. Fingers stroked his face, brushing salt and sand from his sore skin. The melody, the tender touch, became a pinpoint of light in the dark, and he struggled to hold on to it. The gentle voice grew louder and stronger. Sunlight burned through his eyelids. Eric forced his eyes open and gasped.

She was breathtaking, a backlit shadow glittering with seawater. Her features were as distorted as her words, but the hand against his cheek was so tender that he knew she meant no harm. He reached for her, and she eased him back into the sand. A warm, fluttering feeling flowed over him.

Safety, he thought. This was safety.

She must have been strong to drag him from the wreckage and kind, too, to risk her life for his. The sweet lilt of her song filled his head.

She and her voice were the only things between him and death at sea.

And they slipped through his fingers like sand.

I

Fathoms Above

*T*HE SUN hung high and hot above the white-washed, red-roofed homes nestled in the kingdom of Vellona's Cloud Break Bay. Warm winds whipped through the cobblestone streets and canals, and voices called out across the rippling waves. The soft notes of a song, as cheerful as it was distant, drifted through the piers. Eric turned his ear toward the tune and shuffled his feet back in time with it. A sword sliced through the air where he'd stood.

"Too slow!" Eric shouted, sweeping one leg back and bowing.

The crowd hollered. The dock above them rattled, salt peppering down like snow. Eric dunked his stinging hands into the low tide. Across from him, Gabriella, his childhood friend and the only person who regularly outmatched him, paced along the edges of the fighting ring, and her gaze flicked from his hands to his face. She grinned, brown skin gleaming with sweat and seawater. Seaweed clung to her sword.

These weekly bouts had been small at first, an easy way to help train folks who might otherwise never see a sword. They had only started using live blades this week. Eric had gathered his friends into the little nook on the beach beneath the last dock and strung up an old canvas sheet between the posts to hide them away from curious eyes. It hadn't worked, and these last three months had seen their numbers swell. This little fighting ring beneath the docks was all Eric could do to make up for the ever-present fear of pirates that infused Vellona these days with more towns being raided and razed every week.

"You're too cocky," Gabriella said and shoved her damp sleeves up to her elbows. "If I were a pirate, you'd be dead."

Gabriella was the only one here who'd lived through a pirate raid. The sparring had been fun at first, but now there was too sharp an edge to it.

"If you were a pirate, we'd have bigger problems than—"

She struck out and nicked his arm. He reared back.

"You always give in to the urge to chat," said Gabriella, lunging for him. "Real fights aren't fairy tales. No one will stop so you can monologue."

"Then stop me." He met her in the middle, both of his knives blocking the thrust, and locked them together at the center of the ring. "And don't worry about my breaking."

"Never." She grinned. "Princeling."

Eric laughed. This was why he liked the morning fights. These bouts were a good way to relax and find out what people needed help with before heading to work. Would these spars fix all of Vellona's problems? Never. Would they help a few survive? Maybe. Did they make Eric feel like part of the crowd, just another soul living in the bay instead of a prince always held at arm's length? Absolutely.

"Every time you call me that," he said, "I'll hit harder."

"I'm quivering," she said, and fluttered her off hand over her heart. "Come prove it."

Eric reversed his grip on his knives. He feinted for her left, her sword scraping down his blades with a teeth-shuddering grind. She kicked him back, and they circled each other. He slashed at her, but she angled away. The frantic rush of blood in Eric's ears drowned out their sloshing steps.

"You going to hit me?" she asked.

Eric thrust one blade at Gabriella, herding her

right, and aimed a backhanded slash to where she'd have to step. She pivoted and ducked, the knife catching only her sleeve. The crowd roared.

Someone behind Gabriella shouted, "Trounce him!"

"His right side's weaker!" yelled Vanni, Eric's best friend and, in this moment, worst enemy.

Gabriella shifted to attack his right. Eric pretended to stumble, windmilling his right arm back. She lunged, and he swept his knife up. Their blades collided.

His riposte sent her sword flying. It splashed behind her, sinking beneath the murky tide. Eric rushed toward her, expecting Gabriella to chase after her sword, but she crouched down and met his charge. Her shoulder slammed into his stomach and knocked the wind out of him. His arms went limp, the edge of his knife bouncing uselessly off her collar. Gabriella's hands grasped his ankles.

She tugged at his boots. Eric pressed his shaking knife to her neck. She froze.

"Well," said Gabriella, her odd crouch muffling her words against his wet shirt, "I've lost in more embarrassing ways."

Eric couldn't recall any. The raid that had driven Gabriella to move to the bay as a child had killed her sister, Mila, and now Gabriella trained with her aunt almost every day. Once she'd gotten over Eric's being the prince, she had always had the decency to leave Eric with far more bruises than his tutors did when sparring.

No part of this loss was embarrassing.

"If you insist," he said, and cleared his throat, moving his knives away from her.

"Princeling!" A pair of arms looped around Eric's neck and pulled him into a tight hug. "You lost me supper, so I expect some compensation."

Vanni—far more interested in swords and sailing than his baker of a father would have liked—clapped Eric on the shoulder and spun him around.

"Stop betting against me, then." Eric bowed to him, glaring the whole way down. "Keeping you and your ego fed is my only goal in life."

"Obviously," Vanni said, tossing his flaxen hair from his face. He didn't sweat in the stifling heat beneath the docks so much as gleam, looking far more princely than Eric ever did. "Who's up next?"

"You," Gabriella said, and dragged him to the center of the crowd. "I want a real fight."

Vanni laughed, and Eric let out an uncomfortable chuckle.

"Rude of you to say it wasn't a real fight," he muttered, and Gabriella flinched.

Vanni and Gabriella didn't bow to each other. Vanni fought with a single sword, and Gabriella switched to a dagger. He was limber enough to dodge her strikes, and Eric had assumed she would be too exhausted to match Vanni's intensity given how she had lost. Each of her strikes was as strong as the last, though, and Vanni was gasping in the humid air after only three minutes. He swung wide, and she dropped to one knee.

Vanni smiled like he'd already won, but an uneasy revelation wormed its way through Eric's chest. Gabriella wasn't shaking or out of breath, and when Vanni lunged, she plunged her off hand into the water. Quick as lightning, she yanked his foot out from under him. Vanni collapsed with a splash.

"You've got the balance of a fish on land," said Gabriella, holding up his leg like a trophy.

The crowd applauded, and she dropped him. Vanni coughed up mouthfuls of water and peeled seaweed from his face. Gabriella handed Eric Vanni's sword, and Eric mumbled in response. All the joy of finally doing something useful and fun with friends condensed onto a single memory.

Gabriella's hands had been on Eric's boots, and she could have taken him down. Or up, as it was.

"Eric?" Vanni called, shaking out his sopping shirt with a smile. "Your head's in the clouds."

Eric forced himself to smile.

"Bit overcast," muttered Eric, "but I'm fine."

Vanni snorted and patted his shoulder. "Least you won and won't be wearing sand all day."

He shook some from his hair and onto Eric and Gabriella. Eric jerked away. Gabriella shrugged.

"I work outside," she said, and checked the knot of the kerchief covering her black curls. "You needed a bath anyway."

"Gabriella," Eric said, and leaned down slightly so that Vanni wouldn't hear. "You let me win."

Gabriella stilled. "I did."

"Why?" he asked. "Why let me win now?"

"We've been using training swords for months, and the sharp edges drew a crowd. It's better if they don't see their prince flipped head over heels," said Gabriella. "Isn't that what Grimsby is always going on about—the crown is an idea, not only a person? Seeing you getting dunked would be bad for morale."

"If Grim keeps giving you ideas like that, I'll dunk him," Eric said. Of course Eric's status was seeping into his one escape from the castle.

The crowd milled around them, people kissing cheeks and comparing bruises while they said goodbye. Sparring was a fine way to pass the morning, but now the day had begun and there was plenty of work to be done in the bay. Vanni wrung out his shirt, muttering under his breath. Eric slapped his shoulder.

"You're getting better," said Eric.

"Damper, more like." Vanni shook out his hair. "I'm going to be squishing about all day."

"You're improving, though. You both are." Gabriella glanced up at Eric and grinned. "Do you know why I always beat you?"

"Because you're better than me?" Eric asked, and Vanni laughed.

"You lean on your training too much. You never go for a hit or kick when you start the fight with blades," she said and punched his arm. "You've got better form with a sword and stick, and you can disarm me a dozen times. If we were dueling, you'd beat me—I can't fence to save my life—but we're not dueling. You fight in the same order you run drills, and one day you're going to have to make the choice of what to do on your own. Get dirty."

Eric bit back a grimace. He couldn't choose anything. That was the problem. Politics and circumstance within the last ten years had made sure that he had no choices that wouldn't lead either to a battle with the neighboring kingdom Sait, destruction at the sword points of the pirates, or a civil war over his throne. One wrong move, whether it was an impolite look or a strike back at the wrong pirate ship, could get Vellona destroyed.

Once most of the crowd had scattered, the trio emerged from their makeshift meeting place, squinting in the bright morning light as they walked along the beach. Cloud Break Bay was the largest city in the small kingdom of Vellona, and the pale green waters were as much a home to Eric as the castle tucked into the cliffs. Masts listed across the harbor, their ships rolling unevenly as cargo shifted. Summer rose in humid spirals of steam from the decks, and voices called out across the waves as people basked beneath the first warm, clear sky in weeks. Vanni squinted up at the sun.

"We went long today," he said, and turned to Gabriella. "Won't get you in trouble with your aunt, will it?"

"No, we're doing repairs this week before taking off," she said. "She doesn't even really need me for those."

Carpentry was one of the few things she didn't excel at. Still a touch too young to take over her grandfather's fishing ship and too needed at home to take off and join her aunt's crew, she had spent more time at sea than Eric and dreamed of captaining her own merchant ship like her aunt.

"I could help with repairs," said Eric, eager to stay with his friends. That way, he could be Eric, just Eric, for a little while longer. "Does your aunt need the extra hands?"

"Not really," Gabriella said, and made a face. "That last storm did a number on the ship, and we'd be in the way of the good shipwrights. Hopefully we'll be able to pay them. We're getting wrecked by storms every time we leave the docks."

"Those hurricanes aren't normal," said Vanni. "That last one came out of nowhere."

"It's magic. Got to be," Gabriella said.

Magic was uncommon but not unheard of. It was limited to reclusive sorcerers and old tales swapped over pints. Small magics, like tonics and whistling up a wind, were alive and well, and Eric knew there were stories about witches in the old days who could call down lightning or manipulate souls like puppets. Grimsby wouldn't hear of it, but Eric agreed with Gabriella. Sait, the large kingdom to the north dead set on expanding, had almost certainly found itself a witch.

"Even your mother, bless her, would be struggling

these days." Gabriella nudged Eric. "Especially with Sait in the mix. Can you prove it's them organizing the pirates?"

The pirate attacks, suspiciously well organized and as regular as the storms, had started up eight years ago once Vellona's money was nearly drained by the near constant squalls and droughts that had plagued the kingdom for as long as Eric could remember. It was then that Sait, with a navy as flush as its coffers, had started poking at Vellona's defenses. When Eric's mother, Queen Eleanora, had died in a shipwreck up north two years ago, Sait had gotten bolder and Vellona had gotten desperate. Eric had been left with a floundering kingdom and dozens of others eager to take his throne.

He shook his head. "Grimsby calls it a long game, weakening us before striking, but accusing them outright would start a war we can't afford."

Eric suspected that was exactly what they wanted—justification to conquer Vellona.

"Is there not some rich old widow with a flair for dramatics you could wed to get us out of this mess?" Gabriella asked.

Vellona had exhausted every avenue that led to money save for one, and only Eric could take it.

"Sadly, no," he said, pulling his flute from his pocket.

He always had it on him. He played a quick tune, taking the moment to calm himself. The familiar motion of his fingers eased his worries.

"I thought Grimsby wanted you married before your birthday?" Vanni asked. He glanced around and lowered his voice. "You'll have to kiss them at the wedding, but how can you when—"

Eric froze, song dying off, and Gabriella grabbed Vanni by the collar.

"Shut it!" she hissed. "Sait finds out about that, it'll be the easiest assassination in the world."

A shock of panic shuddered through Eric. Here, on the docks with people working around them, no one was paying attention, but they had never discussed his secret in public before. He pocketed his flute. "Grimsby wants me to marry well and figure it out after. Personal feelings cannot trump convenience and duty, he says, but I refuse to hand over control of Vellona to someone I don't trust."

Vanni and Gabriella shared a look.

"Is Grimsby still angry about Glowerhaven?" asked Vanni.

"Incandescent," Eric said. "The only reason he didn't force it was because she loathed me as much as I loathed her."

She hated music and dogs, and he couldn't stand the scent of the paints she treasured. Looking at art? Fine. Living in a miasma of paint fumes and odd alchemical mixtures? Not for him.

Gabriella laughed. "Wasn't your fault Max didn't appreciate her trying to glaze him. When's your next marriage proposal?"

His next proposal? Never again. His next entrapment? The lunch with—

Eric's blood rushed in his ears, drowning out Gabriella and Vanni's chatter, and he wiped suddenly sweaty palms on his trousers. He took a deep breath.

"Grimsby's going to kill me." Eric looked around, trying to figure out what time it was, and groaned. It had been ages since he had forgotten a meeting, and he had no excuse today. "Lord Brackenridge arrived this morning, and I'm supposed to have lunch with him and his daughters."

Gabriella's eyes widened. "Run."

"How do I look?" Eric asked. "I won't have time to bathe."

"Like you were running late because you were sparring," said Vanni. "It's almost like—"

"Don't you say it," muttered Gabriella.

Vanni ignored her. "You're cursed."

"I'm letting that one slide," Eric shouted over his shoulder as he started running. "You only get one."

"A day?"

"A lifetime!"

"Ignore him," said Gabriella over the sound of Vanni's laughter. "Enjoy your prince-ing."

Eric rarely did. He was always Prince Eric first, a citizen second, and—secretly, terribly, through no fault of his own—cursed third.

2
Son of Vellona

$\mathcal{I}$T WASN'T Eric's fault, the curse. His mother had stressed that so often that he had circled back around to "definitely my fault" a few times growing up. Eleanora had told him little of the curse but that if he felt the need to blame anyone, to blame her. It had been laid upon him before he was even born.

"If you kiss anyone or they kiss you, and they are not your true love," she had repeated whenever he asked about the curse, "then you will die."

The vagueness of it haunted him. If his mother had known more details, she hadn't shared them before she died. Eleanora had told the story of the curse's origins only once, and that was when Eric was old enough to comprehend the seriousness of it. The curse was cast the winter a bad fever swept through the kingdom, right after Marcello, Eric's father, died. Five months pregnant with Eric, the queen had treated her grief with a journey up the coast, stopping in the smaller towns to see how they had fared once the sickness had passed. In one of them, she had run afoul of a witch.

"Hair as white as bone, lips red as dawn, and as beautiful as the sea can be terrible," Eleanora had said one night when her son was asking about it again. "She cursed my child to die if they ever kissed someone who wasn't their true love, and I could never even learn the witch's name. I'm sorry, Eric."

The only people now who knew that Vellona's leadership was so precarious—another reason Eric should marry as soon as possible—were Grimsby; Carlotta, his maid; Gabriella; and Vanni.

"Prince Eric!" someone called in a familiar disapproving voice the moment Eric stepped onto the castle's grounds.

Eric skidded to a stop and rubbed the stitch in his side. "Eric," he corrected.

"The heat is getting to you, Your Highness." A tall, pale man with the face of a jagged cliffside and more patience than the sea had salt, Grimsby had been an adviser for Vellona longer than Eric could remember. He had fought under Eleanora during the war with Sait twenty-five years ago and lived in Cloud Break ever since, keeping his cravat tightly knotted on even the hottest of days. Sweat beaded above his smirk. "You are Prince Eric of Vellona, not I."

"I know who you are, you—"

A hairy white blur slammed into Eric's chest, sending him sprawling across the dirt, and a slobbering tongue lapped at his face.

"Whoa, boy!" Eric wrapped his arms around the dog atop him and pressed a quick kiss to Max's head. "Glad to see you, too."

At least Eric could kiss Max without dying. His mother had been fairly sure the curse only counted people, but she had still shrieked the first time she saw Eric kiss Max. It had been the only time he had forgotten about the curse.

"You would have seen him earlier if you were preparing for your luncheon with Lord Brackenridge with me as you should have been," said Grimsby. "You also neglected to make note of what you thought of my plans for your birthday celebrations."

Eric groaned. His eighteenth birthday was only two weeks away, and his coronation would be one week after his birthday. The court had ruled for the last two years as regents with Eric's input, a necessity while Eric was too grief-stricken to lead and still on the young side of sixteen. Now several of the nobles were loath to give up that power.

Eric opened his mouth to argue, and Grimsby rolled his eyes skyward.

"Come," he said. "You smell like a week-old fish, and Brackenridge was a friend of your mother's. He is not above mocking you for it."

"It's hard to cheerfully plan a coronation when it's only happening because my mother died, Grim." Eric rose and rested one hand on Max's head, letting the familiar warmth calm him. "It's barely two hours after dawn. The entire day is left to work."

"Don't speak to me of work." He took Eric by the shoulders. "First of all, it's nearly noon. Second, you are privileged beyond belief, and suffering through the boring aspects of statehood is not true suffering."

"Fine." Eric took a deep breath and rolled his shoulder back. "What do I need to do?"

"Good lad," said Grimsby. They both ignored Max's answering bark. "Lord Brackenridge is here to discuss the pirate attacks up north and the assistance"— he arched both brows at Eric—"he is prepared to offer."

It was another marriage proposal, then.

"Is he offering, or is his daughter?" asked Eric.

"I have no idea what you mean." Grimsby sniffed and took off toward Eric's quarters. "Let's get you changed, and I'll have Louis serve something more fragrant than you."

"Anyone who can't stand the smell of the sea is hardly suited for a life here," said Eric, jogging after Grimsby. "My partner should be able to live in the bay, at least. I want romance and trust and intimacy. I want to know my partner."

"Kissing isn't—"

"I'm not talking about that," said Eric. "Stop assuming I mean physical intimacy when I say *intimacy*. I mean closeness. Knowing your partner. A relationship built on a business transaction is a rocky start for fully trusting a spouse. We would begin on uneven footing."

"I will grant you that marriages of convenience have fallen out of fashion, but they are currently Vellona's best hope." Grimsby herded Eric into his quarters and shoved him behind the changing screen. "You need an heir—a well-positioned spouse or a child. Marrying would provide someone to rule in the event of your death or the promise of an heir in the future. The old nobles like security and tradition. If there is no clear line of succession when you are crowned, then any of your distant relatives with a clearer line can and will challenge your claim to the throne."

Eric stripped off his damp shirt and sighed. "I wish you lived up to your name less."

"Forgive me, Your Highness, but one of us must live up to theirs."

"That is a low blow, Grim." Eric washed his face, letting the chilled water calm him down. "You know my feelings on this. Not telling my potential spouse I'm cursed is a matter of life and death, but marrying purely for business? Glowerhaven may have offered the most, but she would've killed Max and me within the first week."

Eric's curse might not have told him how to identify his true love, but he had known it wasn't her the moment the princess of Glowerhaven turned up her nose at Max and the scent of the bay. He wanted to be struck by true love—a meeting of eyes, a touch of hands, a breathless gasp—as quickly and surely as he had been cursed, not trapped in a marriage no one wanted.

Grimsby threw a clean shirt over the screen separating them. "Frankly, I would leap for joy if you married anyone at this point. Lady Angelina is one of the last eligible potential partners in Vellona or the surrounding small kingdoms. If tonight goes poorly, I fear you'll be out luck and unable to marry before your coronation."

"Don't tempt me," said Eric. "Vanni and Gabriella are free if you're that desperate."

He came out from behind in the screen once he was done dressing and held up his arms.

"You're not Gabriella's type, and Vanni isn't yours," Grimsby said, frowning. He held open Eric's coat and nodded for him to put it on. "You have done well with what was left to you, you know."

Eric slipped into the coat, putting on Prince Eric like an ill-fitting skin. He traced the symbol of Vellona—a sparrow clutching a sword and scepter in its beak—sewn onto the chest.

"I'll have Carlotta note the day," muttered Eric. "'Grimsby finally admits Prince Eric not useless.' There'll be parades."

"Hilarious," said Grimsby. "Come along."

They made for the hall, Max at their heels. The castle was bare these days, and Eric spent the quiet walk preparing himself. He slowed to a stop near an open window outside the dining hall, shook out his shoulders, and ignored Grimsby's tapping foot. It was time to be Prince Eric again.

"All right," Eric said, and raised his chin, lungs full of Cloud Break's clean, salted scent. "Anything else?"

"There is a perfectly nice girl here today, and you will behave. And you," Grimsby said, rounding on Max. He wagged his finger at the dog. "No eating any shoes this time."

Max whined, and Grimsby narrowed his eyes.

"No. Shoes."

Grimsby swept into the dining hall ahead of them, and Eric knelt down next to Max.

"Grim can't help finding problems everywhere." Eric kissed Max's nose and stood. "No shoes, though. He's right about that."

The dining hall was one of Eric's favorite rooms, the ceiling-high windows catching the sunlight in glittery bursts. The glass was so clear he felt as if he could reach out and touch the sea, pluck the white smear of a distant ship from the waves and hold it up to the noonday sun. Grimsby introduced Lord Brackenridge and his two daughters, Angelina and Luna, to Eric, and made sure that Eric sat across from Lady Angelina. The bright light filtering through the cherry trees behind her warmed her black skin and brought out the brown in her eyes. The branches outside curled above her black braids like a blushing crown.

"Lady Angelina," Eric said once they had all settled down and quenched their thirsts, "are you enjoying the bay?"

"According to my father, I love it here," she said, and glanced at her father. He was speaking with Grimsby and not paying attention. She adjusted her dress, the deep red fabric rustling. "And he would say I would love even more to live here."

Eric hid a laugh behind his cup. Maybe this wouldn't be so bad.

The meal began with the usual niceties—Eric asking how the travel was, Brackenridge updating Eric on his holdings and the quality of the roads he used, several unprompted explanations as to why his daughter was an excellent and unmarried leader, and Eric nodding and smiling whenever Grimsby kicked him under the table. It was a blessing and a curse that Grimsby sat in on all these meals.

To Brackenridge's credit, he kept pulling Angelina into the conversation instead of speaking for her like a few other parents had done. The small talk gave Eric time to nibble on a swordfish roll and consider her. As tall and plump as her father, she cut a striking figure against bright blue sky. She was a far better conversationalist than Brackenridge, though.

"Do you play an instrument, Your Highness?" Angelina asked, shifting so that she could meet his gaze.

Several of the windows were open, letting a gull perch on the narrow sill. It ruffled its feathers when her chair squeaked, and Max growled from under the table. Eric nudged him with a foot.

"I play several," he said, "but I can't say anything about the quality."

She smiled at him, and lightning didn't strike. His heart didn't skip. Much. Eric had asked himself how he was supposed to know that someone was his true love each time he sat down to one of Grimsby's setups. He'd never figured out the answer. Angelina, at least, felt more like a confidante than an offering.

"Ah," said Angelina delicately. "I prefer the quiet. Plays I quite like, though."

"I'm more of an opera person," Eric said, and turned to Angelina's younger sister. "What about you, Lady Luna?"

"Me?" The nine-year-old's fork slipped through her fingers, clattered against the table, and tumbled over the edge.

Angelina sighed.

"Percussion is a lovely area of study," Eric said, and winked. "Do you have a favorite song?"

"No." Luna looked to Angelina, who nodded. "Angelina says I'm a danger to ears everywhere."

That sounded like something Vanni would say, and Eric couldn't imagine not getting along with someone like Vanni.

"So was I as a boy," said Eric. "It's why practice is important."

Luna beamed at him

"She plays well but tends to think louder means better," Angelina said, grinning at Luna's thrilled look. "Her mathematics, though, is exceptional."

Luna puffed up her chest. "I'm better at playing than Angelina is singing."

"Luna," Brackenridge said, but not unkindly. "Now, my Angelina has taken up navigation of late, which has proved more useful than any song."

Angelina shrugged slightly, and Eric smiled into his cup. In addition to attempting to arrange a marriage between his daughter and the crown prince, Brackenridge was supposed to be stopping in Cloud Break to speak to Eric about the recent damage to his holdings. The coastal area up north had been hit badly by a storm last month, and now they were traveling south to check on his late wife's land, which had suffered the same fate recently. Surely Eric could make some deal with him that didn't involve matrimony. Maybe then any relationship he had with Angelina could grow normally, unburdened by financial entanglements.

"Have the storms been worse than usual?" Eric asked. "I'm sure we could assist with repairing the damage."

"Well," Brackenridge said and leaned back. "I wouldn't call them worse, and as for what we can do—"

"They're odd," said Angelina quickly, gesturing with a soup spoon. "Most storms bloom, but these don't. My telescopes are designed for astronomy, but they let me observe the storms well enough."

Luna, who had been trying to slip oysters from her plate to Max with no one noticing, said, "She saw the pirates first."

"Pirates?" Eric asked.

Even Grimsby perked up at that.

"Two pirate ships," Angelina said with a glance at her father. "They were spotted three weeks apart. The first raided a town and razed the fields. They destroyed the stores instead of taking from them."

"Odd behavior for pirates," said Eric, and he set his utensils aside. It wasn't odd at all if they were following Sait's orders to weaken Vellona. "And the second?"

"Captain Sauer from Altfeld," she said.

Grimsby startled. "Sauer? You're sure?"

"They've got this hat," said Brackenridge, gesturing to his head. "Big red thing. Can't miss it. They robbed one of our smaller towns and made off with fresh water and some food."

"It wasn't that bad." Angelina raised one shoulder. "No one was hurt, and they didn't damage more than a door or two. It certainly was a contrast to the other attack."

Eric leaned back in his chair. Sauer had been around since Grimsby's days, their ship adored by every child who had ever dreamed of being a dashing rogue. They weren't known for viciousness, but they weren't renowned for their mercy, either. Sauer had never been seen as far south as Vellona, though.

"Better than the other pirates. That lot was carrying Sait steel and powder, and I'd bet my life on that." Brackenridge sat up straighter, lacing his fingers beneath his chin. He pointed at Eric. "Angelina, tell him about the other ship."

"What other ship?" Eric asked, and looked at her.

Angelina dabbed at her lips and gathered herself. Her fingers shook. "Every morning before the storms hit, a ship comes near shore. It flies no flags, bears no crew, and never stays long after dawn. The sails are rotted through, but it sails nonetheless. I thought it was a hallucination at first—one of those false ships on the horizon."

"Ships lost in the storms, surely," said Grimsby, finishing off the last bites of his meal.

Eric pushed his plate away, anxiety writhing in his gut. "Is it the same ship every time?"

"I'm sure it is. Others have seen it, too," said Angelina. "I'm not mistaken."

Brackenridge nodded. "It's a ghost ship. An ill omen for terrible times. My Angelina can pick out those sorts of things. She would be an asset to a bay like this."

"It's a real ship," said Angelina, hands clenched. "I don't know what it is, but it isn't normal."

"Of course," Eric said quickly. "Does it have a figurehead? Is it a Vellonian ship?"

"It's an old galleon, but the figurehead has been worn down," she said, and shook her head. "It might have been a merfolk once."

"Every town has stories like that one." Grimsby shared a look with Lord Brackenridge. "Perhaps it is time we retire and give you two time to speak and the ladies a chance to rest?"

"Can't wait, lad," said Brackenridge. "Though I'm happy to leave you and Angelina to talk more if you would like."

He made a slight gesture toward Angelina, as if sweeping her toward the prince, and Eric pretended not to have noticed. Angelina smiled, but it looked forced.

"You came to discuss business, so let's get that out of the way first," said Eric. They had been dining for over an hour, and the family was staying only until dawn. "You must be exhausted from traveling."

"Of course," Angelina said, mouth tense.

"I'll look into what you said about the ships," said Eric, rising to help Angelina up. As he leaned down, he whispered, "Before I'm trapped in a study with your father—what do *you* want?"

"To not marry someone I just met," she whispered back. "Maybe slow him down?"

"Can do." Eric nodded to the windows. "We have fairly clear skies, and the northern tower is the highest. I can't say it will inspire poetry, but it's there if you want to stargaze when it gets dark."

"Thank you," she said.

If Eric had never been cursed, he would have held on to Angelina's hand for maybe a second longer than necessary. Perhaps he would have kissed it, but the familiar fear, cold and creeping, took hold of him. He did neither.

Angelina moved away from him, looking disappointed, and he opened his mouth to explain. A hand tugged at his coat.

"Can I say goodbye to Max?" Luna asked.

A warm, bubbling sort of joy burst to life in Eric, and he knelt down before her.

"Forgive my youngest daughter," said Brackenridge. His dark eyes glittered with a grief Eric recognized from his mirror. "I haven't had the heart to cull her more childish qualities since their mother passed."

"There's nothing to forgive," Eric said. "Max has been with me for years, and I fear any family I hope to gain must meet with his approval first."

Brackenridge smiled at that, and Grimsby looked far too pleased with himself.

"Now, I think a proper goodbye is in order." Eric lured Max out from under the table with a piece of pasta, held out one hand, and winked at Luna. "Goodbye, Max."

At the word, Max lifted one paw and shook Eric's hand with all the solemnity a dog with oyster on his face could summon. Eric mimed kissing Max's paw, and Max licked his hand. Luna gasped.

"Max, say goodbye to Luna." Eric shifted Max until he was facing the small girl and gestured for her to hold out her hand. "You'll have to say goodbye first."

"Goodbye, Max," Luna said.

Max stuck his paw below her hand and licked it as if giving it a kiss goodbye. Even Grimsby and Brackenridge broke into smiles at her wide-eyed look up at Eric.

"I'll teach you his other tricks if you paint me a picture before you return," he said, and smiled. "Do we have a deal, Lady Luna Brackenridge?"

She glanced at his offered hand and then at Angelina, who nodded.

"Of course, Your Highness," said Luna.

Eric bowed over her hand. She drew up her narrow nine-year-old shoulders and mimicked his bow. She moved to kiss his hand just as Max had pretended to kiss hers. Panic gripped Eric, and he ripped his hand away, throwing himself back. He slammed into the table and toppled it. The dishes clattered to the floor.

Max leapt to Eric's defense, hackles raised and a growl low in his throat, and Luna stumbled back. She tripped over the upturned table and landed hard on her back. Cold soup splashed across her face. She yelped.

"Max, down!" Eric yelled, struggling to his feet. He moved to help Luna.

Brackenridge shoved him away. He dunked the corner of his coat into a puddle of water and wiped Luna's eyes clean. She sat up, burying her face in her hands. An onion sprig and fork had tangled in her hair. Angelina gathered up Luna in her arms.

"I'm so sorry," Eric said, and twisted his hands together, scraping the ghost of the touch from his skin. One kiss, a single touch of a person's lips to his skin, and he would die. "Grimsby, please—"

But Grimsby was next to Brackenridge and not listening. The gull in the window squawked and flapped along the edge of the room. Max lurched toward it, and Eric yanked him back. He looked to Angelina, hoping that she might listen, but she only stared at him with narrowed eyes. Even the blasted gull glared at him.

A rushing filled his ears, and panic trembled down his hands. Tugging Max with him, he hurried toward the door.

3
Part of Their World

$\mathcal{E}$MBARRASSMENT burned in Eric's chest, and Max let out a low whine as he fled. He could still see the embarrassment and confusion on Angelina's face, Luna's red eyes, and their father's anger. The memory carried him through the quiet hallways of the castle until he was far away from the dining hall. It had been too much to hope for a normal meal.

Even if Grimsby offered a good enough explanation and Angelina and Eric came to an agreement, any hope for a friendship was strained. It wasn't as if he could blame the curse; they had no idea about it. Angelina would want nothing to do with him now.

No, now there was simply another noble on the council who thought Eric was an odd one. Too odd to rule, certainly.

Eric finally came to a stop. He looked around, spied no one, and let his forehead *thunk* onto the wall.

"Go find Carlotta. Go." Eric nudged Max, but the dog didn't budge. Eric sighed.

He wasn't even sure what part of the castle he was in, but he needed to be alone.

His mother had been scared of someone finding out about his curse, but wasn't that why he was in this situation? He was so afraid of letting anyone near that he could barely handle normal situations. What was the point of anything if he didn't have anyone to share it with?

It wasn't fair. He had liked the dinner with Angelina more than any of the others and enjoyed her company. His curse had ruined any hopes he had of getting to know her.

Eric laid his head against the door in the hall and brought his hand to the bronze plate upon the door.

ELEANORA OF VELLONA

It was his mother's old study. He hadn't touched it. Not since—

"What would you do?" Eric asked, staring at his mother's familiar name.

Not be afraid to enter a study. Well, he had probably

ruined his last chance at finding a queen. If he had ever needed his mother, now was the time.

He pushed open the door and braced himself for the heavy wave of grief, but it didn't hit. Only a dull ache flared in his chest. Eric rubbed his heart.

It still smelled like her, tuberose and plum with ambergris beneath. He shut the door, taking a deep breath, and made his way to her desk. Grimsby had retrieved all of Eleanora's important notes on ruling Vellona, leaving the top of the desk nearly empty.

His fingers skimmed the edges of the wood, feeling the slight dents from her chair and scratches from constant use. Here she had nicked a drawer with her pen-knife, and there she had banged her staff against the edge when sparring with him. His mother had never let anyone clean or repair this desk; it had been his father's. Carlotta even kept the little bowl of licorice full.

Eric took one of the licorice candies and sucked on it, sinking into her old chair. His knees shook.

"How could you leave?" he asked his mother's empty desk. "Some nonsense journey to verify reports about Sait, and a storm kills you? After everything, a storm?"

A few half-finished letters stuck out of the top

drawer. Eric ripped the drawer from its slot and dumped out the contents. None of the letters were for him and most were reports made irrelevant by the last two years. He tore the second drawer from its place, pocketing a bundle of notes from his father to his mother, and tossed it aside. He moved on to the third. Two old forks with the tines bent to make them look like dog ears and painted-on eyes courtesy of four-year-old Eric. Dozens of old drawings from Eric to his mother over the years. A quill with the tip nearly chewed off.

"Nothing."

Max let out a low huff and wiggled his way beneath the desk. Eric patted his head.

"Not that I expected anything, but it would've been nice," he said. His fingers traced the lines of the desk. The shutters clattered in the breeze, and gulls cried from the towers. Waves crashed against the cliffs below. He felt as worn as the rocks.

"She was checking on the northern holdings and trying to spy on the ships attacking them," he told Max. "You remember her talk?"

Eric hadn't been paying attention the last time he'd spoken with his mother. It had been a normal day, and Eleanora had moved as if to hug him but held back.

"She said she'd be back," Eric told Max. "I don't

know if I can do this. I couldn't even get through a meal. How am I supposed to be king?

It had never been fair, and it wasn't now. He didn't want a crown and responsibilities; he wanted to remember his father's voice and wake up to breakfast with his mother still here, alive and well. He wanted a coronation only when his mother was old and ready to step aside. He wanted and wanted, and it was never enough. He had so much.

Guilt gnawed at his stomach. He had everything. He shouldn't want.

"Why couldn't you have left me something to help?" The licorice left a bittersweet taste in his mouth, and Eric leaned his forehead against her desk. "Anything would've done."

Lightning flashed outside, and Max yelped, leaping up. He smacked his head against the bottom of the desk and scrambled away. Something thunked against the floor.

"Max," Eric grumbled and peeked under the desk, "if you broke anything . . ."

A needle was on the floor that hadn't been there before. The wrinkled corner of a scrap of paper hung down from the underside of the desk, and Eric knelt for a better look. Pinned underneath the desk by three other needles, far away from prying eyes, was a piece of paper with his name written across it. Eric ran his hand over his mother's slanted script.

"You're joking," he whispered.

Eric yanked the needles free and caught the letter. His breath hitched.

"Mother," he whispered, eyes burning.

Oh, he was so thoughtless. Of course she had left something. Secrets were as common to her as breathing. He should've known she had saved one more.

With a deep, steadying breath, he opened the letter and began to read.

Eric,

I'm so sorry. If you're reading this, I am almost certainly dead. I promise that I intended to return from my voyage, but I knew it was dangerous. I hope the risk, however, was worth it.

Now, darling, I have so much I wish to tell you that cannot be placed within a letter, but I have urgent matters I must relay to you. I know I have never been forthcoming with the events surrounding your curse. I always hoped that I would break you of your enchantment myself and that you would never find out what I am about

to reveal to you. If I have failed, though, you will
have to finish what I started, and to do that, you
will have to know everything.

As you are already aware, you were cursed
before you were even born, but here is how it
happened. A month into my journey across the seas
after your father's death, I was walking on a beach
at dawn, no one in sight, and saw a body floating
in the surf. It was a child, small and chilled to
the bone, and when I pulled them to shore, they
weren't breathing. I breathed for them, and eventually they coughed up the water from their lungs and
lived. It was then a woman appeared.

"It's mine," she said. "It is owed to me."

I don't exactly know why, but in that moment
I did not believe her. I refused to hand them over.
The woman grew angry. She revealed herself to be
a witch. She claimed I had taken a soul from her,
and that she would steal a soul from me in return.

"If that thing in your belly ever kisses someone
without a voice as pure as their spotless soul,
someone who isn't its true love, then it will die,
and I will drag its soul to the bottom of the sea."

I know I never mentioned anything about a
pure voice. Please forgive me my lie of omission.

I feared if I told you all of what the witch had said that day, you would think of nothing but f inding this person. I dreaded your obsessing over someone's singing voice rather than their heart.

I have spent every moment since that day trying to uncover more about the witch who cursed you and how to break her enchantment. I am afraid her curse was frustratingly vague, and the details of her existence are even more murky. I have found many stories of her appearance through-out history, but never have any of these tales called her by name.

According to some, she was a princess who sunk into dark magic. She was a commoner who used it to break free. She was the lost child of an old sea god. She was the old sea god who gifted weather magic to humans. She was denied her throne, her freedom, her godhood, and when deprived of what she had earned, she took it by force. In one story, she snuck into the heart of the sea and stole magic from the gods. In another, her brother was gifted a kingdom and she was gifted nothing, so she instead learned forbidden magic. Most tales involved her making deals that favored

*her, unbeknownst to the person she made the deal
with. Regardless of which stories are true, I do not
trust those who believe children are things that can
be owned.*

*Recently I have found one promising lead,
a mention of a home she keeps called the Isle of
Serein. There are few details about this place. All
I know for sure about it is that it is an island in
the seas to the northwest of us, protected by storms
and something called the Blood Tide. But it is the
closest thing to a clue that I have, and I will be
going on this voyage to try to find it.*

*I do not want to ask this of you—I could
hardly ask it of anyone—but this witch is a threat
to not only you and Vellona but to people everywhere. Once you read through my research you will
see that her stance on others is clear—they are
tools to be used and discarded. She makes deals
and takes the souls of those who break them. Worse,
there are signs she is hoarding power for reasons I
don't yet fully understand, and knowing that her
might comes from the souls she steals, I fear there
is only one way forward. She must be imprisoned
or killed.*

If the stories I have read about magic are

true, killing her will break your curse, save the souls she has stolen, and free anyone trapped in one of her deals. Even if the deals aren't unfair, she plays games with souls, Eric, and we cannot let that stand. Whatever her ultimate aim, it is not peaceful.

Uncover what the Blood Tide is, find the Isle of Serein, and kill the witch. If you can find a less murderous way to undo her wrongs, so be it. She must be stopped whatever the costs.

There is a compartment in the back of the bottom drawer. Inside is everything I've collected about your curse and the witch who enchanted you, including the potential locations of Serein that I hoped to check with this journey.

And I am so, so sorry to leave this duty to you. I wish I could be there with you now. I wish I could have fixed everything on my own.

Whatever happens, I love you.

Eric traced the looping lines of her handwriting. The ink was smeared near the bottom, water damage marring the paper. He buried his face in his hands.

He wasn't sure if her traveling to find the witch and kill her made him feel worse or better. His curse had taken so much from him, and now he knew it had taken his mother, too. But this was the most he had ever known about it—a pure voice and the name of the witch's home.

"Thank you," he whispered, and tucked the paper into his chest pocket. "Thank you."

Lightning flashed again outside, and rain pattered against the windows. Max whined.

"It's all right, boy." Eric dragged his hands from his face. "Better, really."

A pure voice wasn't a lot to go on, but it was more than nothing. Eric had never had even a hint of how to find his true love, but now he knew two things about them—they had a good soul and a good voice. Both attributes he could find out about someone with enough effort.

In the hidden compartment his mother had mentioned, he found maps pocked with patches of corrections. There was even a list of the greatest singers around Eric's age. He found a journal full of stories about sea witches, weather witches, and magical dealmakers. There were dozens of legends and rumors about people being forced to do terrible things against their wills, and that terrified Eric. In one, a mermaid implied the witch was beautiful but not as lovely as the mermaid's wife, so the witch took her wife's beauty for her own and then took her soul. The sheer needless cruelty of it made Eric shudder.

With every story, this witch degraded people's very sense of self until they were unrecognizable. Apathetic. Wretched. More like sea grass caught in the current than people. She ruined them.

And the area around Vellona was her hunting ground. If she was so cruel and so active to have all of these stories about her, then some of the missing and dead had to be her fault. Many people from Vellona had been lost in pirate attacks and storms recently, but many of them were just *assumed* to have been lost to them. If the witch was responsible, it might have been even worse than his mother had thought.

"Mother is right," Eric said aloud, trying to sound braver than he felt. He tucked several of the stories into his pocket to make sure he always remembered why he had to finish what she had started. It wasn't just for him. "She has to be killed."

Grimsby was going to hate it, but without his curse, Eric would be free. He could befriend people without fear and let his feelings take him where they might. He could marry without having to worry about his true love. Or he could find his true love, this person with a pure voice and soul who *was* somewhere out there.

Intimacy and falling in love had always terrified him, and he had resisted it for so long to save himself from other's expectations—how could he prove to friends, families, and lovers he loved them if he couldn't express it in a way they wanted? If he did this, he wouldn't have to be afraid anymore.

"The Isle of Serein," Eric said. He took Max's face in his hands and kissed his nose. "You ready to go on a trip?"

Max licked Eric's mouth.

"Gross," he said, "but I'll take that as a yes."

4
Across the Sea

*B*Y THE next dawn, a small carrack with a crew of sixty-four was ready to set out. They set sail as the first peachy rays of the day spilled out across the shore. The ship, the *Laughing Dove*, was small, agile, and—unless pirates got desperate or sneaky—able to outrun anything thrown at it.

After leaving his mother's study, Eric had gone straight to Vanni and Gabriella and told them everything—why he was cursed, that his true love had a voice as pure as their soul, and that his mother had hidden everything. Explaining the details helped Eric come to terms with it all, and his friends agreed to join him on his quest.

Grimsby had been harder to convince. Eric knew that he definitely couldn't tell his adviser he wanted to hunt down a witch. The man would chain him to his desk. So Eric told Grimsby what his mother had revealed about the language of the curse and said he wanted to find the Isle of Serein to learn more about the witch responsible in hopes of reversing his enchantment without the need of a kiss. Even then Grimsby had protests, but he eventually conceded. Eric would be king soon and would not have time to search for answers; if there was a chance they could figure out how to break his curse now, everything would be easier.

"I'm telling you, it's empty sea. I've been there before, and there's no island," said Gabriella, wrapping her hair up for sleep. Eric, Vanni, and Gabriella were preparing to rest in the captain's quarters. It was a small room plastered with various maps and taken up almost entirely by a bed, a table, and chairs.

It was Gabriella's first outing as a captain—and seeing her face when he offered her the position had been priceless. She was the obvious choice; she already knew about Eric's curse, so he wouldn't have to lie to his captain. The crew knew the voyage had something to do with Queen Eleanora's disappearance but that the details of the trip had to be kept a secret. "These waters aren't a mystery. If there was some big area encircled by storms, we'd know."

"My mother wouldn't have marked it if it was nothing," Eric insisted.

During their first few days out at sea, Eric had not had much time to speak with his friends. They were busy working on the ship while Eric struggled to keep a sea-sick Grimsby watered and fed. Fortunately, Grimsby had retired to his quarters early in the evening, giving the trio some time to talk.

Eric and Gabriella had spent the day before setting sail poring over his mother's maps and notes, and they had gleaned from it the path of his mother's last voyage. They had decided to sail to her ship's last known location and search for the isle from there.

"It's a witch. I doubt she lets people just sail up to her home. I bet there's some trick to it," Vanni said, still reading one of the queen's notes. He gagged and threw down the papers. "It says here that she trapped a merfolk in a dam because they refused to deal with her and let humans keep them like a pet?"

Eric nodded.

"Petty and cruel," muttered Vanni. "If all of these are true, she's been torturing and killing folks for decades."

"That's why if we do find her, losing the fight isn't an option," Eric said, and covered a yawn. "Weird no one's heard about the Blood Tide."

They had planned on following his mother's map to wherever it led and then worrying about the Blood Tide later, but it was still on his mind.

Across the Sea

"Okay, hear me out," said Vanni, and held up his hands. "Instead of looking for some mysterious island, we hold a singing competition and tell everyone the winner gets to be your wife. No more curse!"

Eric glared at him, and Vanni shrugged. Maybe telling them *everything* had been a mistake.

"What? We're riding off into the sunset in search of a powerful witch. Let me find joy in small things."

"Finding my true love can wait until after the witch is dealt with. My mother made it clear that was what was most important," Eric said, and sighed. He marked off one of the maps and sat on the bed next to Vanni. "I always wanted to be the hero in a story, but I thought it would be a comedy, not a tragedy."

"How does one fight a witch?" Gabriella asked, and flopped backward on the bed.

"I'm guessing we won't get more than one chance. But she's not immortal. The stories would mention it if she were, and they only go back so far," said Eric. He swallowed and rubbed his hands together. "Speaking of her, you two don't even really need to meet the sea witch or deal with her. I'm the only one who needs to face her, so—"

He stopped. Without a word, Gabriella was pulling a purse from her pocket and then tossing Vanni five small coins. He caught them and winked at Eric.

"Knew you'd try to princeling out of it," he said. "We don't need you to be our savior."

"You're stuck with us." Gabriella nudged Eric with a foot. "If you think we're letting you hunt down a witch alone, I'm insulted. You should have more faith in us than that."

And, like a well-placed fist, that hit the part of him holding on to his fear.

"Fine," Eric said. "I won't play savior if you two won't."

"More importantly," said Gabriella, "have you figured out where the Isle of Serein might be other than 'northwest'?"

"Deciphering some of her notes is harder than keeping Max away from the ship cats," Eric said. Max was currently asleep beneath the table, exhausted from chasing cats up and down the deck. "I know plenty of stories—the river dragon down south, the Valley of the Seven Men, Scylla and Charybdis, the sack man, the Nain of Sait—and I have never heard of the Isle of Serein."

True or not, Eric had clung to stories as a child. Distant places, new people, and exciting lives so unlike his own. The dashing princes in those stories were sure of themselves and always saved the day. They were what people expected when they looked at Eric.

"But how many languages do you know?" Vanni asked.

"Quite a few," said Eric flatly. "What do you think I spent my childhood doing?"

"Counting your money?" Gabriella shrugged. "I thought of it often while dragging in nets and getting slapped in the face by fish. 'That Eric. I bet he's on five thousand vali by now.'"

"Please," Eric muttered. "I count much faster than that."

He pulled his flute from his shirt pocket and twirled it like a baton. Legends, like merfolk or striges, were common enough, and most superstitions were based in fact. Gabriella had tipped a full bottle of wine into the sea before they left the bay as tribute to King Triton of the Sea, and there had been clear skies since. Those were the oldest stories along the coast—an immortal king with skin as blue as the sea and hair green as grass beneath the waves who lived in a golden palace and blew a magical conch to calm the weather. Or, if displeased by sailors, to call down storms and whirlpools.

"Plenty of mysterious islands in history," Gabriella said. "I like that one rumored to be up in Sait surrounded by water so clear the seafloor looks like fields and you can pluck fish from the waves like oranges from a tree. They say merfolk tend to them like gardens."

"They say they talk to animals, too." Vanni laughed.

"None of those stories help us find Serein, though," said Eric.

"Sleep on it, then." Gabriella rolled over and pulled the blanket over her head. "But on your cot. You can have the bed tomorrow."

"Fine," said Eric with a laugh. He settled down on the small cot wedged between the table and the bed and covered his face with an arm. "Tomorrow it is then, but—"

The clang of warning bells outside interrupted Eric. Gabriella shot up, lurching out of the bed with a gasp. Vanni and Eric grabbed their swords and knives, and Gabriella ripped the scarf from her head. Eric tossed her a pair of boots, bracing his shoulder against the door to the quarters. Vanni came up beside him.

"What do you think it is?" Vanni asked.

The bells chimed so loudly that Eric's teeth ached. He opened the door a crack.

"On deck!" screamed one of the crew. "Cut their lines!"

"Is there any point in asking you to hide?" Gabriella joined them at the door and glanced at Eric. "Just asking so I can tell Grimsby I tried."

Eric shook his head and peeked out the door. Light flickered off blades, and water washed the boards in an inky black. The striped shirts of the five dozen *Laughing Dove* crew members were easy to spot in the dim light, and it was clear they were outnumbered. Pirates were climbing over the sides of the ship faster than the ropes could be cut and overpowering anyone in their paths.

A stout pirate crossed before the door. Eric shoved it open, knocking the pirate to the deck, and quickly took their two knives and pistol.

"No bullets," said Eric, tossing it aside. "Let's hope they're all out of ammunition."

Gabriella startled and swept her foot across Eric's ankles. He toppled, landing hard on his knees. A blade whistled just over his head, tearing a few hairs free, and Eric threw an arm back at his attacker. He caught them in the thigh, and they stumbled away. Gabriella dove after them and planted a foot in their back. She kicked them against the taffrail. Eric leapt up and grabbed the pirate's ankles, tipping them over the side of the ship. Gabriella darted away to help Vanni fight off a woman with an ax.

A rope had been tied over the rail, and Eric sawed through it with his sword. It fell with a loud splash. Curses echoed in the dark below.

A footstep cracked behind Eric. He twisted away, the blade of a short sword piercing the railing where he had been. It stuck in the wood, the pirate holding the hilt let out a curse, and Eric rammed his hilt into their temple. They fell aside and groaned. Eric leapt into the fight.

There must have been eighty pirates on the deck, crowding the ship so that each step resulted in knocked elbows and barely dodged hits. Eric edged along the taffrail and cut as many ropes and ladders as he could. If any more climbed on board, they would lose for sure. A pirate turned as he cut one last rope. She lunged at him with a dagger.

Eric pushed it away with a drag of his sword across his chest. She struck out with a heavy staff, and Eric moved to block it without a thought. His feet slid into place on their own as a sharp calmness settled over him. Eric parried her next attack.

A yellow blur shot past and rammed into the pirate, falling in a tangle of limbs.

"Vanni!" Eric shouted, but another pirate lunged for Eric. They forced him away from Vanni, and Eric dodged their attacks. He disarmed them with a twist of his knife and kicked their legs out from under them.

Gabriella helped Eric heave the pirate over the side of the ship. Vanni had wrestled his opponent to her stomach and pinned her with a knee to the back, but another had caught sight of him. She lunged for Vanni with a metal club.

"Vanni!" Eric screamed. "Left."

Vanni dove left. The attacking pirate tripped over her prone companion, tumbling to the deck. Vanni yanked the club from her hands.

"This is easier than on the sand," Vanni said breathlessly.

Eric snorted, parrying a slash from a knife. Red swirled in the corner of his sight, and Eric spun. He fought on instinct as he watched the scuffle across the ship at the bow.

Grimsby fought with a wide-bladed, single-edged sword. He moved faster than Eric had ever seen, sweeping the one-handed sword in quick, deadly attacks. His opponent was a tall white-skinned pirate in a long red coat and broad red hat, and they moved with the same grace as Grimsby. A dark metal cuirass beneath their coat blocked a slash from Grimsby, and a hawk's feather bobbed as they leapt back. They fought like Eric's mother once had, wielding a long sword with one hand and resting their gloved off hand halfway up the blade. They thrust at Grimsby's left side, and he stumbled away. The red-coated pirate grinned.

And even in the dim light of the moon, Eric recognized them.

"Surrender. You're severely outnumbered," said Captain Sauer—one of the oldest and most prolific pirates on the seas. "In terms of people, not years, of course."

The boards shifted behind Eric. He spun, sword coming up to guard his ribs. The pirate who attacked him was no older than him. Like the one fighting Grimsby, she wore a feather pinned to her straw hat and a cuirass beneath her coat. Starlight glittered deep in her black eyes as she lunged again. Eric sidestepped the blow from her staff.

Eric glanced around—most of the pirates were using batons and staffs instead of knives. The only one fighting for real was Sauer, and that was because Grimsby was more vicious than he looked.

The girl was fast, far faster than Eric. Each attack came quicker than the last until Eric's heels hit a barrel. She smacked him in the temple.

Eric stumbled. Gabriella raced from behind him and knocked aside the girl's attack. The girl fell back.

"Nora," Sauer shouted. "Quit playing."

The girl—Nora—rolled her eyes and lunged. Gabriella dodged, glancing at Eric.

"You alive?" she asked Eric.

He nodded and shook his aching head. "Only ringing."

The rattle of his teeth still echoed in his ears. He didn't want to see what this girl was like when she fought with a blade. Gabriella parried Nora's next broadside attack.

Around them, *Laughing Dove* was losing the fight. Eric forced himself to his feet.

"Afraid of blood?" Gabriella asked the girl.

"Afraid of what comes after," said Nora. "Scarier things than you on the sea."

Gabriella lunged forward, meeting the girl blow for blow.

She was taller than Nora by a head and took a wide slash at her legs. Nora slid back, a smile on her full lips, and swung at Gabriella's chest. She moved with a confidence Gabriella didn't have, gliding from block to attack with ease.

"Eric!" Gabriella took two quick steps back and held out her off hand.

Eric tossed her his dagger. She caught it without looking and went on the offensive. Eric tried to get to Grimsby.

At the bow, Grimsby crumbled to his knees, and Captain Sauer, gasping and disarmed, kicked him back.

Sauer reached for their sword and leaned in close. Eric's stomach dropped.

Grimsby plunged his hand into his coat. A shot rang out. Sauer fell backward, blood splattered across the rail. They steadied themself, blood dripping down their badly grazed cheek, and covered their face with a hand. It was the first shot Eric had heard all night. Smoke curled out of the bullet hole in Grimsby's coat. The whole ship came to a stop.

"That," said Sauer loudly, "is a single-shot pistol and the single mistake I'll allow you."

Grimsby sneered. "How magnanimous of you."

"Now, Captain, wherever you are," said Sauer, taking Grimsby by the throat and pulling a thin knife from their belt. The blade bit into his neck. "Have everyone drop their weapons and kneel, or I'll kill him."

A thin line of blood beaded up along the knife.

Eric stepped forward, and Grimsby's head whipped to him. Even in the dark, Eric could feel Grimsby's gaze on him.

Don't you dare draw attention to yourself, it seemed to say. *You're the prince, not a distraction.*

Eric swallowed, heart fluttering in his throat. "You've avoided spilling blood so far."

Sauer turned to him. "And it's too late for that now, isn't it?"

The tip of the blade pressed into Grimsby's wind-pipe, and Gabriella nodded.

"You all heard them," said Gabriella. "Weapons down and kneel."

In no time, Sauer's group had them tied up in neat little lines between the masts. A purple welt marred Vanni's cheek, and Gabriella's bottom lip was busted. Not a single person had died, but neither were they unharmed. Grimsby was the worst off, breathing harder than he did in Vellona's summers and oozing blood, but he still kept his eyes on Sauer. The pirate was standing at the bow and signaling with a lantern to a far-off ship in the dark. They hadn't even taken the time to bandage their wound.

"Pick it up!" Nora said, her deep black skin taking on a gray cast in the lantern light as she raced up and down the ship. Tension kept her shoulders ramrod straight. "Blood in the water—that means five minutes. If you're not in your boats by then, you're on your own."

Eric had thought they were trying not to kill anyone, but that sounded like something else.

"What happens when blood gets in the water?" Eric asked a nearby pirate, but they ignored him.

Grimsby tossed his pocket watch into the ocean rather than hand it over, having the audacity to glare at Eric the whole time, and Sauer rolled their eyes. Nora tried to take Gabriella's sword, but Gabriella had looped the rope binding her hands through the hilt.

"Proud of yourself?" Nora asked. "Pity. Sword like that deserves a good swordswoman."

Gabriella, completely at her mercy, rolled her eyes and said, "That's why it's so attached to me."

Nora's lip twitched. She turned out Gabriella's pockets, finding nothing, and pulled a silk scarf from her own coat. Gently, Nora draped the green scarf over Gabriella's hair and tied it behind her neck. Nora patted her cheek.

"In case it rains," she said with a wink that made Gabriella swallow. "Can't leave you out here to rust with your sword."

"For Triton's sake, Nora," Sauer muttered as they passed. "Stop flirting. It's a robbery."

"Why are you in a rush?" asked Eric, letting Sauer take the few vali he had on him. With the threat of death by pirates gone, Eric's panic had faded. "What's so scary out at sea other than you, Sauer?"

They stopped over Eric, head tilted so that their hat covered half their face, and grinned. "Not much, but nothing I care to encounter tonight."

"You'll find out soon enough," said Nora. "Blood Tide's coming in."

"What?" Eric felt cold and hot all at once, his skin tingling with unease. "You know what the Blood—"

Sauer stuffed a discarded glove into Eric's mouth. "Enough talk."

"Unhand him!" Grimsby's voice cracked from the other side of Vanni. "No matter how much you man-handle us—"

"Which I have no intention of doing," drawled Sauer.

"Or how much you steal," Grimsby continued and ignored them, "you will not be able to escape justice, you cowards."

"Listen here, you stick-in-the-mud that sprouted legs," Sauer said, rounding on Grimsby. "You are bound, you are unfortunately not gagged, and you are moments away from meeting the monsters most do not live to talk about. We could leave you here to their shallow mercy, but instead are risking our own lives to ensure your lives. So what if I gag a boy and take his gold? What will you do?"

Grimsby opened his mouth again, and Vanni kicked him.

"Thought we were in a rush," Nora mumbled.

Sauer made a cutting motion at her.

Most of the pirates had already left the deck and were rowing back to Sauer's ship. A pale fog swept unnaturally fast over the sea, swallowing up the boats and the flashing lantern from Sauer's ship. Nora cursed.

"Everyone out now," she cried.

"Wait," Eric said, spitting out the glove. "What monsters? What's the Blood Tide?"

"The worst sort of monster," she said, twisting one of her locs back and forth. Her gaze never left the horizon. "The one you love the most."

Eric sat back on his heels. "What?"

Whispers rose up across the deck. Sauer's head snapped up, looking every which way in the dark. Eric followed their gaze but saw nothing. Nora peered over the edge of the ship.

"Sauer," she said, "you ready?"

No one was looking at Sauer. Worse, the whispering was louder now, but no one's mouth was moving. The *Laughing Dove* crew searched the horizon anxiously, testing their bonds. Vanni stared at the fog as if he had never seen anything like it.

"Eric?" a voice called across the ship, and Eric turned to it, but no one was looking at him.

Tears rolled down Vanni's cheeks, and Gabriella

tried to unknot the rope around her hands with her teeth.

"Gab—"

"Shut up," hissed Gabriella, peering out over the water. "I can't hear her."

"Who?" asked Eric. He smacked his boots against the deck. "Sauer, get back here! What is this?"

Gabriella lunged toward the edge of the ship, bonds and skin in tatters from her teeth and nails. A wide, glassy grief lit her eyes, and she choked back a sob. She howled a name Eric rarely heard her mention.

"Mila!"

5
Siren Song

*N*ORA FLUNG Gabriella back in line with the others. The people who had been tied with her were yanked back and forth. Gabriella bit again at the ropes binding her hands, and other sailors up and down the ship began to call out and tug at the ropes. Nora started tying Gabriella more securely against the mast, looking over her shoulder into the dark horizon the whole time. Eric used the slack in his line to crawl nearer to Gabriella.

"Mila can't be here," he said, but Gabriella didn't hear him. Her watery eyes darted around the ship. Her nails tore at her bound arms. Eric stretched until he could lay a leg over her arms to stop her. "Vanni, help—"

"It won't work," said Sauer, coming to stand above Eric. "Go back to your place. Nora will tighten their ropes, and with any luck, we'll all make it out of here alive."

Gabriella threw Eric's leg off her.

"Bad luck, Captain," Nora said, and patted

Gabriella's shoulder as she passed, but Gabriella only continued working at her ropes.

Vanni, too, was struggling now, muttering under his breath and straining against the ropes. Sauer tightened Vanni's bonds and quickly checked the rest of the line. Nora paced up and down the deck, pressing something into the hands of each pirate. They shoved whatever it was into their ears.

"Eric?"

He turned, but behind him were only struggling crew members.

"Sauer!" Eric got to his knees and pleaded. "Please— what is happening?"

Someone called out in the fog, but Eric couldn't decipher what they were saying. A few steps away, Grimsby rose to his knees so that he could see the ocean, and he raised a hand as if waving. Sauer clucked their tongue.

"The Blood Tide is an old tale," Sauer said, sitting down on the deck before Eric. They rolled a small ball of wax in their hands. "There were always rumors of ghost ships, but this ghost ship is nothing like those rumors. Vellona's farther south than they usually tread. Once you acknowledge the ghosts are there, they ensnare you and force you to make a deal with them. Used to be they just offered. Now you have no choice."

An itch burned on the back of Eric's neck, beneath his skin and beyond any part of him that he could scratch. He needed to move, to turn and look at what was coming. He made to turn.

"Don't." Nora laid a hand on Eric's head. "When they call out to you, if you answer, they can control you. When they appear, if you look at them, they can control you. When they wave to you, if you wave back, they can control you. Any response is enough for their enchantment to take hold. Cover your eyes when we do, and don't answer their calls. It will slow them down."

"The Blood Tide is what comes for the desperate." Sauer divided the wax into two pieces and took off their hat. "When blood is spilled on the waves and desperation is in the air, the ghost ship appears. It doesn't sail. It arrives in a bank of fog no matter where you are. The Blood Tide leads the ghosts to you."

Angelina was right—there was a ghost ship in Vellona's waters.

"The ghosts offer you whatever you want most in the world," said Nora, sitting next to Sauer. "If you accept and go with them, you're never seen again. If we're lucky, they'll get bored and leave within the hour."

The itch on the back of his neck worsened, and Eric

shifted. The creak of old wood filled the air. A watery, rotten scent washed over the ship.

"Please," he said, and rubbed his face against his shoulder. "I've been looking for this place and the Blood Tide—"

"Is here." Sauer pressed the wax into their ears. "Look at your hands."

Eric looked down. His fingers were clawing at the rope, leaving long scratches in his skin. Eric jerked back, horrified that he hadn't noticed, and shoved his hands between his knees. Down the line, Vanni nodded at something, someone, in the fog. Nora pressed the wax into her ears.

"But what is . . ."

Someone called Eric's name from down below the rail, where the water met the wood. The fog crept over the deck, catching the light of the lanterns and glowing a pale yellow. Eric pressed his knees together, trapping his hands, but the deep need to free himself remained. An old ship emerged from the fog-soaked night, its boards the black of octopus ink and its ratty sails dangling in the dead air. It moved as if drifting above the waves, and a sliver of moon hung from the star-speckled dark above its splintered mast. A ghostly form with ruffled black hair and sky blue eyes stood at the bow.

"Mother?" Eric whispered.

A calm he hadn't felt in two years washed over him. She was here. She was alive.

Eric clawed at the rope around his left wrist. It scratched and bruised his skin. His mother was there, only minutes away if they trimmed the sails, and no one was doing anything. He could talk to her again, wrap his arms around her and listen to her complain about how she was supposed to be the tall one, and commit to memory the little things he hadn't thought he would ever need to know. Her voice, her laugh, the little laugh lines at the corners of her eyes. He worked at the knots around his wrists with his teeth. He needed a sword.

It didn't matter what she wanted. So long as he could speak to her now—about his curse, his coronation, anything and everything—he would give anything.

"I can hear you. Where are you?" Gabriella yanked at her ropes, sword smacking against her leg. "Mila!"

Her sharp cry drew his eye. Eric scooted to her and strained until his joints ached. He grabbed her ankle and pulled her close enough to use the sword looped through her knot. The sword cut halfway through his rope, edges fraying, and Eric worked the rest of it undone with his teeth. He needed to turn the ship and have his mother come up along the side. As they were, he'd never be able to reach her. His ropes fell away.

"Hang on!" he called out, and ran for the wheel. He was vaguely aware of Sauer and Nora reaching out to stop him, but they were too slow.

His mother laughed and said, "Take your time, sweetling."

He would do anything to have her stay. She had only to ask, and he would give it.

The *Laughing Dove* and the other ship passed each other, prow to prow. Eric darted to the rail, reaching out until he could touch the figurehead. It was crusted in salt and crumbled beneath his fingers. A splinter stabbed beneath his nail.

Eric hissed and flinched. The pain cut through the haze in his mind, panic replacing his joy. Hand clutched to his chest, he whispered, "Mother?"

"Eric?" she called back.

His mother walked to him. Her footsteps left a trail in the salt coating the old ship. She was pale and shimmery, a veil of frost over glass. All the color save that of her eyes had been sapped from her, and he could see the ship through her. Each movement looked like agony, as if the air were as thick as the sea, and she dragged her long sword along the boards in a rattling scratch. She stopped at the rail of the other ship.

"Eric," she said, and the words were the gentlest sound he had ever heard. Why was he worried at all? She had come back. "Come here."

Grimsby shoved past Eric and threw himself over the railing. Eric grabbed him on instinct.

"Garcin!" Grimsby screamed. "The cliff! The cliff! Watch the rocks!"

A memory rose in the back of Eric's mind. His mother had known a Garcin and rarely spoken of him. He had been a soldier from the same small town as Grimsby.

"Grim," Eric said, throat raw. Had he been screaming? "He's dead."

Like Eric's mother.

"None of this is real," said Eric, tightening his grip on Grimsby. "That's not my mother."

As he said it, the odd tug against the back of his neck urging him to look at his mother eased. He was right. This wasn't real. This was a trick. The ghost ship.

The Blood Tide!

Eric swept his gaze over the *Laughing Dove*—Max, locked in the captain's quarters, clawed and howled at the door; Vanni chewed at the ropes around his wrists; and Gabriella sobbed Mila's name so softly Eric's heart broke.

Siren Song

"Eric? Sweetling?" this replica of his mother asked. This Eleanora had a lilting voice, but in his memories it was smokier. The blue of her eyes was too bright. The scar beneath her eye was gone. "I know where the Isle of Serein is, and I can take you to it."

She wasn't alone on her ship. Dozens upon dozens of ghosts crowded the deck, their pale forms overlapping until the prow was a solid wall of gray. They reached out across the rail with beckoning fingers, and they called out names and promises that sounded flat to Eric. He glanced at his mother, and she offered him the Isle's location again. Eric shook his head and turned back to the rest of the people on the *Laughing Dove*. Sauer and the pirates were curled up tightly on the deck. Nora rocked back and forth, hands shaking against her face.

"Sweetling?"

Eric's mother had never called him that.

"You're not her," he said, fighting the fatigue in his head. It was as if the fog that had borne the ship had slithered into his mind and dulled his senses. The splinter, Grimsby, and Max's howls had weakened the ghost's grip. Her voice was the final straw. "You are not Eleanora of Vellona. You are not my mother."

Eric yanked Grimsby back from the rail and tied him to the ship.

"Grim," Eric said. "Garcin isn't real. None of this is real. It's a trick."

But Grimsby couldn't hear him.

"Mama!" The pirate girl Nora crawled to her feet. A piece of wax had fallen from her ear, and her gaze was glued to one of the ghosts on the ship.

She slipped through Sauer's fingers, and they lunged for her, eyes wild with panic. She threw herself at the railing, but Eric sprinted over and caught her about the waist. He threw himself back, and they hit the deck. Her elbows landed in his stomach, and her head clacked against his.

"Not real," he muttered, keeping a tight hold on Nora despite his aching head.

She groaned and pulled away from him. "What in the world are—"

"You were about to leap over the railing." Eric let her go, and they helped each other to their feet. He nodded to her head. "A shock breaks their spell for a little bit."

"Deal with magic a lot, do you?" she grumbled, but stomped loudly next to a crew member's head and hummed when they seemed to snap out of it. "It'll come back. It takes a while, but if the ghosts don't get anyone, they leave within a half hour."

"How long has this been happening?" Eric asked.

From the corner of his sight, he could see the ghosts slowly crawling over the rail. A few plummeted toward the water. One grabbed the *Laughing Dove*.

She shrugged. "Sauer says it used to be just a scary story parents told kids, but a few years ago ships started washing ashore with no crew in sight. Dozens gone and not a mark on the boat. Sails still trimmed and oars crooked as if dropped midstroke."

"Is that what happens to all of the ships you rob? No robbery, just ghosts?"

"No, we usually rob them and leave them in Riva."

"I'll pretend I didn't hear that," he said, and glanced at the rest of the crew. "Can we escape?"

Sauer, eyes downcast but growing mistier by the minute, grabbed Nora's hand. "What's wrong?"

"They don't give up," Nora told Eric. She wrote out a quick note on the palm of Sauer's hand. "They can still get you even if you can't hear or see them. It just takes longer for them to figure out how to communicate."

"How do we get them to leave?" Eric asked.

"We don't," said Nora.

One of the pirates on the quarterdeck lurched to their feet. They signed something to whoever they saw among the ghosts, tears streaming down their cheek.

Sauer and Nora took off running to stop them, and one of the *Laughing Dove*'s crew tore free of his bonds on the bow. He hit the railing before Eric could get to him, leaning down as if to help someone over the side. A ghastly hand reached over the railing and yanked him into the sea.

"Eric?" called his mother. "Come back."

He peered over the edge of the ship, but the sailor and his ghost were gone. The other ghosts crawled up the side of the ship, hands sticking to the hull like suckers. Seawater washed through them, and salt hemmed each pale silhouette. Eric could see through them to the depths below, and he backed up, tripping over a muttering pirate. A ghost crawled over the side of the boat and left a puddle around its translucent feet. He faced his mother.

"You're not real," he said.

"Oh, sweetling." Her voice trickled over him like warm sand. "I could be."

Eric forced himself to look away. At the center of the ship, Gabriella and Vanni had figured out that they could help each other escape. Fear bubbled up in Eric's chest as he raced toward them, and he laughed. It tumbled out of him before he could stop it; the image of them huddled like toddlers learning how to undo their leading strings made the whole thing fantastical and terrible all at once, and Eric caught Vanni by the wrist. Gabriella didn't even look at her best friends.

"Please," Vanni whispered, and reached for the railing.

Gabriella darted for one of the ghosts, and Nora raised her arm. Gabriella struck it chest-first and collapsed. Nora grabbed her shoulder.

"Gods, she's sturdy," muttered Nora.

Gabriella moaned and struggled to her knees. "Did I get kicked by a horse?"

"Not quite," said Eric.

Vanni tried to tug himself free of Eric. "Let me go! He's right there!"

"We can't go around hitting everyone to wake them up," said Eric, wrapping an arm around Vanni's shoulders. "I don't suppose the folks left on your ship can help?"

"Not without getting close enough to be enthralled as well," said Nora.

Eric felt in his pockets for anything useful. All he found was his flute and a handful of lint-covered licorice candies.

"Better than nothing," he muttered, and pulled the flute free one-handed. "Sorry, Vanni."

Eric let out a sharp note next to Vanni's ear. Vanni

winced and pulled away, and the sound cut through the screams and pleading on the ship. Even the ghosts quieted.

"What was that for?" Vanni smacked a hand over his ear and yanked away from Eric.

Gabriella grabbed him. "Shut up."

The five of them that were awake froze. The ghosts, skittering over the railing, watched Eric with a hollow-eyed fascination. He looked at the others, and none of them gave any indication as to what to do. Slowly, Eric brought his flute back to his lips and played a simple song he'd first learned in the forecastle of an old Vellona ship. He couldn't even remember the words now, only the notes and the way his mother had watched from over the crew's heads. Her ghost shuddered and flickered out of sight. Eric stopped.

She reappeared only two steps from him, her hands outstretched and mouth open in a soundless scream. Eric stumbled back.

"Eric," Gabriella said, "keep playing."

He did and rose, the tune shaky. The notes wafted across the deck, bright and clear in the cold night air, and the ghosts all stepped in time toward Eric. He backed away and played a softer, slower song. They followed him.

Sauer and Nora had a conversation he couldn't hear, and Nora gestured at one of the pirates still shaking off the spell of the ghosts. Now that they were following Eric, people were waking up. The pirate started singing, and the ghosts ambled after them. Eric let his song trail off and moved to join Sauer on the quarterdeck. Grimsby leaned against the mast.

"You alive, Grim?" Eric asked.

"With this headache, I must be," muttered the man.

Eric patted his shoulder as he passed.

"This," Sauer said, "isn't something we've seen before. This is useful."

"Can't blame anyone for not trying this," said Nora. "Who would've expected this to work?"

Eric glanced at the flute in his hands and said, "It is useful, and you know what, Sauer, I'll make a deal with you."

Sauer's brown eyes narrowed. "You?"

"I'm Prince Eric of Vellona."

Nora mumbled, "Crap."

As the future king of Vellona, Eric could do almost anything. Piracy already carried a steep penalty, but attacking the prince would see every member of Sauer's crew hanged.

"You didn't know how to distract them or put an

end to their spell," said Eric. "Now you do. You owe me."

Grimsby, as if sensing Eric was doing something he wouldn't like, shambled over to them.

"And what do you want in return?" Sauer sucked on their teeth. "Your Highness?"

"More information about the Blood Tide. I'm looking for a place called the Isle of Serein, and the Blood Tide was mentioned with it. I want you to help me figure out how they are connected so I can find the Isle." Eric ignored Grimsby's scoffing. "And with any luck, after that, these ghosts will be the next thing I take care of."

If the ghosts came on the Blood Tide and the Blood Tide was related to Serein, then it followed that the witch was probably behind this horror, too.

Sauer glanced around the ship, their gaze lingering on the ghosts. "I wasn't aware Vellona had enough money to throw it around so frivolously."

"Oh, I'm not offering you money in return," said Eric. "I'm offering your crew a pardon, barring any drastic crimes, of course."

They'd be able to travel through Vellona's waters without fear of being arrested.

"You'd pardon pirates?" Nora asked.

"Odder things have happened." Eric gestured around them. "You will need to lead the ghosts away from us so we can escape. Of course, one of your crew will have to travel with us to ensure that you return to Cloud Break Bay and help me find the Isle."

"I will," Nora said.

Eric nodded. "We'll head for Cloud Break immediately, and you can find us there once you escape them as well."

Sauer let out a breath through clenched teeth. "You're taking her hostage."

"You are hardly in a position to argue," said Grimsby.

"I very much am," Sauer said. "You're still outnumbered."

"Stop it." Nora laid a hand on Sauer's arm and nodded to Eric. "I'll go with you. I've got some stories about the Blood Tide, and I want that pardon."

Eric and Sauer shook hands, and Sauer pulled him close.

"We will assist you if we arrive and she is well," they whispered.

Eric nodded. "Deal."

6
Storm at Sea

SAUER AND their crew led the ghost ship north. No one on the *Laughing Dove* spoke until the ghost ship was out of sight, and even then, it was only in cautious whispers. Eric kept his flute in hand, and Gabriella started heading the ship back toward Cloud Break. There they could restock and make sense of everything that had happened. Most of the crew were too shaken to do much other than absentmindedly go through the motions of sailing. Eric couldn't begrudge them returning when they had encountered ghosts.

And Nora's presence made the failed trip feel far less like a failure.

"We can talk in here," Eric said, holding a hand out to Nora and gesturing toward the captain's quarters. Grimsby narrowed his eyes, and Eric shook his head.

"We'll be right outside if you need us," Vanni said quickly. "For anything."

Eric nodded and opened the door. Max shot out. He

leapt onto Eric, paws on his shoulders, and lapped at his face. Eric bundled Max up like a baby against his chest.

"Do you think the ghosts' spell works on dogs?" he asked Nora. The inside of the door was badly marred with claw marks.

She sat on a clear corner of the table and rested her boots on a chair. "It doesn't. They can see the ghosts, though. The ship cats can, too. We've dealt with the ghosts twice, and cats reacted both times. The ghosts didn't seem to notice them."

"Well, that's something at least," said Eric. He looked around the ransacked quarters. "Thank you for not stealing my maps, I suppose."

"It looks like a navigator vomited on the walls," Nora said, and hesitated. "Your Highness."

"It sure felt like that," he said. "I know I said it already, but I am looking for a place called the Isle of Serein. The Blood Tide was mentioned with it, but I thought it might be a metaphor for dawn or dusk. So far as I've been able to learn, the Isle is probably in one of the locations marked on these maps, surrounded by storms, and related to the Blood Tide."

Nora twisted to study one of the maps and whistled. "You know these don't make sense?"

"I'm aware." He collapsed onto the bed and let Max

scramble about the room sniffing at Nora until he was satisfied enough to settle down across Eric's feet. "Now, what do you know about the Blood Tide?"

In the light of the cabin, it was easier to take her in. She was tall and lean, her long black hair cascading over her shoulder in locs. A few dark scars crisscrossed her arms, and her knuckles were wrapped like a boxer's. She nibbled on a green-painted nail.

"Not much," she said, still looking at the maps pinned to the walls. "It's a Rivan tale. They used to tell it to kids to keep them from swimming alone in the sea. 'One single drop of blood spilled in the waves, and the Blood Tide will bring to you someone who will offer you everything you've ever wanted. But it comes with a price, and you must never accept.' One of those tales."

Eric nodded. That didn't help him much. Riva was a kingdom bordering the north of Vellona, and they were in just as rough of a spot.

"Who's the someone?" he asked. "A witch?"

She shrugged and wouldn't meet his gaze. "Maybe. Stories rarely got that far, and if kids asked, they'd tell us whatever seemed scariest at the time."

"So the ghosts we saw are part of the Blood Tide," said Eric. "How do the ghosts work?"

"Their ship's real. We know that much. They're

not, though. Fighting them is worthless because we can't touch them even though they can touch us. Swords, staffs—everything goes right through them. They can climb aboard ships and drag you over before you even notice they're there. They can wield weapons, too, and we can touch the weapons they wield. Means we can only defend ourselves." Nora pointed to a thin scar running along her jaw. "So Sauer made a rule. No blood. Soon as blood hits the water, their fog drags them to wherever the blood is."

"And Sauer is certain it's—"

The splintered door creaked open. Vanni and Gabriella slipped into the quarters and shut the door behind themselves. Vanni sat on the bed with Eric, and Gabriella took the only other chair. Her curls were still covered by Nora's scarf, and her lip had been cleaned. Vanni's bruised cheek was a brilliant purple. With four, the room was far too crowded.

"Sorry." Gabriella held up both hands. "Grimsby was getting anxious about you being in here alone with her. He's fine, by the way. Angry he lost the fight and had to resort to his pistol."

"Yes," drawled Nora, "I'm so likely to assassinate the prince who just offered me a pardon for telling him stories and babysitting him on his way to an island."

Eric held back a laugh and shook his head. "Fine. We're talking about the Blood Tide. Better if you know about it anyway."

"We should get Max to train with a carpenter," said Vanni, studying the ruined door. "Or set him on Sait."

"Don't encourage him," muttered Eric, scratching Max's head. "How is everyone?"

"Shaken up," Gabriella said with a sigh, "but we're on course to be home in two days. You?"

"Well, the Blood Tide's real and grossly literal." Eric inclined his head to Nora. "Old Rivan tale."

"But why does it exist?" Gabriella asked.

"No clue," Nora said. She still wouldn't meet his eyes. "Sorry. I could send some letters to the folks I know in Riva still, but that's all I know about it."

She was holding back, and for all of Eric's charm, he wasn't sure how to approach her. He could call her a guest until he was red in the face, but that wouldn't make her trust him.

"We can talk more once we're in the bay," he said. When they were home, he would figure out what she wasn't telling him. "We can talk about something else— have you encountered the pirates currently ravaging the western coasts?"

Her jaw tightened. "We have."

"Are they being paid by Sait?" asked Eric.

"They're being more than paid." She laughed. "They're not pirates at all. Sait spent a few years rounding up every pirate they could and ran them off or killed them. Those people raiding are mercenaries. The ships, the weapons, the orders they're following—those are all Sait's. Sauer hasn't figured out what to do about them yet."

"Well," Vanni said, "that's one mystery solved."

"And you know the Blood Tide is real." Gabriella wiped her face on her sleeve. "We all saw—"

"Different things," said Eric quickly. "Don't worry. No one knows what you saw. I saw my mother, and I think they show you what you would give the most to have."

"But what are they?" said Vanni. "They can't be ghosts. The person I saw isn't dead."

"My mother certainly is," Eric said.

"Why bother offering us a deal, then? If they want us to go with them, there has to be some aim." Gabriella leaned back in her chair and tapped one of the maps. "I know we said this wasn't a current, but what if it's fog?"

"None of us knows enough about magic to know what the fog is," Nora said. "You don't die when they pull you over, we don't think. You vanish with them.

Maybe to some lair. Maybe to their ship. Maybe you just become part of their crew. No one's been able to resist or distract them long enough to find out."

Eric hummed the song he had played for them, an old one his mother had taught him. "Now we know, though."

They sat in silence for a moment, and Eric could've sworn he heard his mother calling. Vanni shifted and rubbed an ear.

"Speaking of piracy, how are you Sauer's second?" asked Gabriella suddenly. "You're our age, and the north's hurting, but given who's doing most of the hurt, piracy seems like an odd thing to turn to."

"Wasn't the pirates hurting us when I joined Sauer. It was the storms and the starving." Nora fiddled with her hair and squinted at Eric. "You really the prince?"

He nodded.

"Great," she said. "You owe me and most folks up there some money."

"How'd you get so good at fighting, though?" asked Vanni, rubbing his cheek.

She held up her finger and thumb. "Beating people who think they're good," she said, and curled her thumb into her palm. "Necessity." Her finger curled down.

Gabriella snorted, and Nora turned to her.

"Keep my scarf, then, if you can," she said.

Gabriella smiled. "Let's see how good of a thief you are."

Nora laughed, but her eyes darted to Eric.

"It would be hypocritical of me to arrest you for thievery now, I think," said Eric. "You'll like the bay, and we should be there for a few days before heading out again."

"I'll take my quiet north any day," Nora said.

"Where will you take it?" Vanni asked.

Gabriella closed her eyes. "So help me . . ."

"Away from you," said Nora flatly. "I'm a pirate, remember?"

Restlessness infected the ship. They held a funeral for the lost sailor their next full day at sea, no one daring to sing them off. The days passed easily, going by far faster than they had on their way north, and Eric spent too many hours staring at the maps and trying to get information about the Isle and Blood Tide from Nora. She told him plenty of old, gossipy tales about it, but he still felt like she was hiding something from him. The night before they reached Cloud Break, he was too tired to keep thinking about it. He found a quiet spot on the forecastle to relax.

Nearly everyone was on the deck preparing for something. He had stayed too long in the quarters and missed whatever was happening. Interestingly, though, Nora had already stolen back her green scarf and was wearing it like a trophy. Eric watched Gabriella's gaze follow Nora's path up the rigging to the nest, her cheeks unmistakably flushed, and he sighed, equal parts pleased and melancholy.

He had always dreamed of meeting the perfect person atop the waves. Maybe she was a visiting dignitary who preferred sailing to state meetings, or perhaps she would be some runaway noble who sang the sun down each day as they traveled across the world. But whenever Eric wanted to be swept up in the endless, intimate possibilities, he remembered his curse and pushed those desires away.

Footsteps approached Eric from the cabin. "I know you didn't find this isle you were after, but surely that sort of frown isn't warranted?"

"Suppose so," Eric said, and turned toward Grimsby. At least he hadn't found out Eric's true reason for the voyage. "Though it's a real pity you didn't have your swords."

Grimsby had taken every spare moment of the last few days to insist he could have beaten Sauer if he'd had his prized case of rapiers.

"Eleanora and I often considered ourselves family, you know," said Grimsby. He leaned against the rail next to Eric. "And you a terrible, terrible nephew who never does what I ask."

It was nearly dusk, the sun staining the sea a burnt orange, and it sapped the green tint from Grimsby's white skin.

Eric chuckled. "You're defining *nephew*."

"Terrible," Grimsby said one final time. "Your birthday is upon us whether you want to admit it or not."

Barely a week until he turned eighteen and two until he was king. Two weeks to secure the line of succession.

"I know you wanted to celebrate at sea," said Grimsby, "and I thought a celebration would be a nice way to help any heartache in case you failed."

Eric groaned. "You did something, didn't you?"

"Celebrating will do everyone some good. We must relax and recover from our recent peril, and Nora has assured me that the ghosts never travel this far," said Grimsby. "Also, I set this up the moment you insisted on traveling, and I won't let my planning go to waste."

"I don't know what I'd do without you," Eric said with a small laugh.

"Yes, you do, and you know it would be the exact opposite of my suggestions." Grimsby smiled and turned Eric around to face the rest of the ship. "Now, I have done something traditional and kind, which I am sure will go unappreciated, but we'll get it out of the way first."

Vanni and the cook emerged from the galley with baskets of food and a crate of drinks between them. The rest of the crew was struggling to carry something from the hold, and Gabriella hid her laughter behind her hands. It was tall and heavy, a sheet of canvas covering it. The same dread Eric got when asked to give a speech without preparation spread through him.

"You know," said Eric, "let's save the surprise for once everyone's rested from lifting it."

Maybe he could tip it into the sea before then.

Grimsby huffed. Eric grabbed his flute and joined a fiddler, playing a quick, leaping song with them. Vanni and Gabriella stumbled around the deck in a laughter-filled dance, and Max chased after them. The rest of the crew joined in, singing louder once the first minute of music didn't draw any ghosts, and someone at the stern started an arm wrestling contest. Vanni eventually dragged Eric into the dance. The beat of the music rattled through him in looping, unrestrained strides. Eric let himself relax and tried to forget the terror of the Blood Tide.

A low crack echoed across the water, fireworks painting the night sky with brilliant reds and blues. Squawking gulls glided in and out of the smoke in a tangled tarantella, and on the other side of the deck, Max sniffed at a scupper hole in the rail. The white feathers of a gull peeked out from behind the rail.

"Max!" Eric whistled and pulled out his flute. "Here, boy!"

Max let out a quiet *ah-woo*, and Eric answered him with a birdlike song. The old wooden fipple flute was nothing like his fancy concert flute, but the soft sounds were far more comforting. It was like being called home.

Max danced around him, and he rubbed Max's side till his fur stood straight up. "You like the fireworks?"

The boom of the fireworks drowned out Max's bark, and the dog chased after the shadows of the rigging on the deck. Gabriella, re-stolen scarf atop her curls, chased Max around Eric. A familiar clearing throat stopped Max in his tracks.

"Now!" Grimsby strutted to the center of the deck and gestured to the large canvas-covered monstrosity behind him. "It is now my honor and privilege to present our esteemed Prince Eric—"

"Steamed?" muttered Gabriella, stopping next to Eric. "Well, that's why no one will marry you."

"With a very special, very expensive, very large birthday present," continued Grimsby.

"Ah, Grimsby. You old beanpole. You shouldn't have." Eric gently punched Grimsby on the back and smiled. "Why did you drag it out here with us?"

"I imagine that will be clear shortly," said Grimsby. One of the nearby sailors pulled away the canvas.

It was a statue, because of course it was a statue. Eric had avoided sitting for portraits as much as possible, and he had only rejoiced when Grimsby stopped pestering him about it. This massive thing did bear some likeness to him, but it was too tall, too muscular, and too proud.

At least Grimsby had made sure the artist knew he was left-handed.

"No wonder we were riding low," muttered one of the crew.

Eric bit his bottom lip to keep from responding and scrunched up his face. Max growled at it. At least Max wouldn't confuse the two of them.

"Gee, Grim. It's, uh . . ." Eric rubbed his neck and

searched for the words. This was why Grimsby usually did the talking. "It's really something."

He couldn't say it was a waste; that was rude to Grimsby and whichever poor soul had carved it. The statue was beautiful, detailed, and nuanced in its decadence. They'd gotten his face and hair right without ever having seen him, though the expression felt a little too upturned. The brows, too.

Or maybe that was what people meant when they said Eric was expressive. He had always assumed they meant transparent.

"Would you guess that none of us wanted to steal that?" Nora asked, and laughed.

"You couldn't have carried it even if you did," said Gabriella.

Nora raised one arm and flexed. "If it were a statue of me, I'd have found a way."

Grimsby ignored it all. "Yes, I commissioned it myself. Of course, I had hoped it would be a wedding present." He dropped his voice and raised a brow at Eric. "Especially since the king of Glowerhaven insisted on paying for it."

Ah, there it was.

"Come on, Grim, don't start," Eric said, laughing.

"Look, you're not still sore because I didn't fall for the princess of Glowerhaven, are you?"

"Eric, it isn't me alone," said Grimsby. "The entire kingdom wants to see you happily settled down with the right person."

That again. Eric went to the rail and looked out over the sea, the smoke of the fireworks a gray veil over the night. Fireworks cracked and flashed above them.

"She's out there somewhere," he said. Knowing there was someone out there perfect for him was the one beautiful thing his curse had granted him. "I just haven't found her yet.

Grimsby grunted. "Perhaps you haven't been looking hard enough."

"Believe me, Grim, when I find her, I'll know. Without a doubt, it'll just hit me like lightning!" Eric clapped, and a burst of thunder shuddered through the night. He threw his head back.

Clouds—not smoke, but swirling clouds the same inky hue as the night.

"Hurricane a-coming!" shouted a sailor from the crow's nest. "Stand fast! Secure the rigging!"

Stillness blanketed the ship, and then everyone moved. Eric leapt to his feet, grabbing one of the ropes to tie back. Vanni gathered up everything loose on the deck and rushed it to the forecastle, and Gabriella sprinted to the wheel. The wind picked up, tossing gulls from the rigging and rails. A wave smacked the hull. Max whimpered.

"It came out of nowhere!" Nora shouted, yanking hard to keep one of the sails from being ripped away. "Which one of you pissed off Triton?"

Gabriella and the crew shouted instructions. A rogue wave swept over the ship, and Eric barely caught himself on the mast. Water soaked him to the bone, burning his eyes, and tore Gabriella away from the wheel. Her head cracked against the rail, and Eric lunged. She stumbled, clutching her head. The wheel spun wildly.

"Grim!" Eric grabbed the wheel, and the handles dug into his palms. "Gabriella!"

Neither answered.

Another wave washed over the ship, rocking it to its side, and half the crew vanished in a blink. Eric's arms burned with the effort of keeping the wheel steady. This close to Vellona, they could run aground or hit a reef.

"The boats!" Gabriella dragged herself to her feet and waved to Nora. "Ropes in the water now!"

The ship steadied. If Eric could keep the ship upright, they could ride it out. Nora led the way. A squall whipped over the deck, and the ship pitched. Lightning struck the mast, and it burst into flames. The rigging went up, and the wheel yanked against Eric's grip, forcing him to his knees. The fire devoured the mainsail and illuminated the night. A dark shadow broke through the waves ahead of them.

"Rocks!" a sailor at the prow shouted, and threw himself back.

The tiller rope snapped. Eric cursed, and the wheel spun wildly. The ship slammed into the rocks. Eric crashed against the rail and plummeted into the sea.

Darkness and cold pressed into his chest. Eric windmilled his arms and kicked, struggling to break the surface. A strong hand gripped his arm and hauled him into a rowboat. Vanni smacked his back.

"Grim!" Eric leaned over the boat, half standing, to look over the waves. The flickering light of the fire glinted off a state ring. Eric lunged for the hands grasping from beneath the water. "Hang on."

He pulled Grimsby into the boat and fell back. Then, a howl echoed over the water.

"Max!" Eric dove without thinking, hoping everyone else was safe, and climbed up onto the crashed ship. Fire lapped at the deck and had already reduced the forecastle to splintered bones. Max woofed and whimpered at the flames lapping at the high deck he was trapped on. Eric scrambled to him and shouted for anyone else. No one answered.

"Jump, Max!" Eric beckoned to him and winced at the heat searing his skin. The wood under his feet was too warm for comfort. "You can do it."

Eric held out his arms, tapped his chest, and pleaded. Across the deck, the fire crept closer to an overturned barrel of black powder. The boards beneath him creaked.

"Come on, boy," shouted Eric.

The dog woofed and leapt, slamming into Eric's chest with a howl. Eric sprinted toward the taffrail, and the deck cracked. His foot plunged through the wood, and he tossed Max as hard as he could. The dog vanished over the side of the ship.

"Eric!" Grimsby's shout barely reached him.

Eric tried to answer but choked on smoke. Pain shot through his ankle, and his heart stopped with each clunk of the loose barrels rolling across the fiery deck. Eric tugged at his foot, but the broken boards held fast. The ship pitched into the rocks.

And the world exploded.

7
Reprise

She and her voice were the only things between him and death at sea.

And they slipped through his fingers like sand.

ERIC WOKE to confusion. Pain sloshed about behind his eyes, cresting as he opened his mouth. Sand stuck to his lips, and a huge, wet tongue lapped it away. Drool dribbled down his cheek, sticking sand and fur to his face. Eric groaned and bumped Max with his forehead. The dog whined.

"Hey, boy," he muttered, voice a rasp. "I'm happy to see you, too."

Eric prodded Max till the great beast moved and sat up. His ears rang and his throat was on fire, but nothing was broken or gone.

"Hey—" Eric tried to ask the girl who had saved him where they were, but his voice broke.

He groaned again and pushed himself up from the

sand. The sunlight was so bright it burned, and he opened one eye. A swathe of pale sand stretched out before him, the calm sea lapping at his feet. There was no music or girl.

But there had been a girl, hadn't there?

Max sniffed at the ground around Eric and barked at the sea. A single handprint—smaller than Eric's with long, tapered fingers—was pressed into the sand near where his head had been. The beach he'd washed up on was bare and empty save for him and Max. Eric lifted a palm to his cheek, the touch of his savior fading. That couldn't have been a dream. Eric couldn't remember making it to shore.

"Max?" Eric whistled, and the dog came bounding back to him. "I'm glad you're okay, but how did you get here?"

The shore ended only a little ways from the water and was littered with rocks from the cliffs looming above. A familiar shock of gray hair bobbed up behind the rocks.

"Eric!" Grimsby's voice clanked between Eric's ears. "Oh, Eric. You really delight in these sadistic strains on my blood pressure, don't you?"

Grimsby came scrambling around the rocks, and some of Eric's tension eased. The old man was worse for wear but clearly fine. He helped Eric up and squeezed him in a tight hug. Eric shrugged off Grimsby's arm. He stumbled forward, searching the sea.

"A girl rescued me," he said. He knelt and pressed his hand over the print as gently as he could. She was real, and he remembered her. He had felt her. "She was singing. She had the most beautiful voice."

Eric stood and turned, and spots freckled his vision. His knees buckled.

Grimsby caught him. "Ah, Eric, I think you've swallowed a bit too much seawater."

Miraculously, no one had died in the shipwreck. It was the first thing Eric asked upon waking up in his own bed after passing out on the way to the castle. The doctor checking his bruised ribs pulled away long enough for Grimsby to reassure Eric that everyone was fine. It was a little after dawn, and apparently they had been searching the beaches for Eric all night. Grimsby's clothes were ragged and wet, and the scent of smoke still clung to him. Eventually, the doctor declared Eric fit enough and took her leave, insisting Eric rest for several days at least. Grimsby collapsed onto the chair next to Eric's bed.

"You gave us quite the fright, Eric," he said, and

patted Eric's knee. "No more, aye? I don't think my heart can take it."

"I can't believe you thought I was dead," said Eric. His throat hurt, each word digging into him, and he was sore all over but thankfully no more than bruised or scratched.

"You exploded." Grimsby snorted. "Now, when Carlotta comes in fussing, let her."

Eric threw an arm over his eyes. "How worried was she?"

"Inconsolable. Don't know why you would think otherwise."

Carlotta had been his mother's maid and had taken over the role of a valet so that Eric wouldn't have to either tell another soul about his curse or nervously interact with someone new. Carlotta had been a different sort of overbearing than Eleanora, treating him like a child regardless of his age. Sometimes it had been nice, and he had liked it after his mother's death. It wasn't coddling. Carlotta cared far more than most.

"Oh, Eric!" The door flung open and smacked against the wall. "Look at you!"

Eric winced. "I'm fine, Carlotta."

"You look ghastly," said Carlotta, bustling into the room with a tray of food in her arms. She set it down on

Eric's lap and adjusted his perfectly fine pillow. "Poor dear, getting tossed about like that."

"I'm fine," repeated Eric, taking a spoonful of soup.

"You hit your head hard enough to hallucinate," said Grimsby. He frowned as Carlotta caught his gaze. "He said he saw a girl on the beach."

"I did see a girl," Eric said, and set down his spoon. "She's the one who pulled me ashore. She sang."

"Now, Eric." Carlotta rubbed his shoulder and lifted a cup of water to his lips. "You've been through a lot in the last day. It's normal to imagine some things."

"I did see her," Eric mumbled. "I woke up on the beach. Someone had pulled me to shore. There was a flash of red, and she was singing. Then Max came howling across the beach."

"Of course," said Grimsby, arching one brow at Carlotta.

"She saved me, Grim," said Eric. "She had a perfect voice. She was brave. She was so . . ." Panic shot through Eric, and he grabbed Grimsby's hand. "It must be her! The one with the pure voice!"

"Eric." Grimsby gripped his hands tightly. "This is exactly what your mother feared—you are hearing a pure voice where there is none."

"I wasn't hallucinating!" Eric pulled away, and

pain lanced through his head. "It's not like that. I heard her. I felt her. There was a print in the sand where she'd been."

"Then where is she?" Grimsby asked. "She saved the prince of Vellona. Surely she would expect a reward or admiration?"

Eric leaned back against the bed. "I don't know."

Grimsby looked as if he wanted to say more, but Carlotta slid between them and pointed at Eric's soup and bread. Grimsby leaned back and quieted.

"Now," she said, cutting the crust from the bread. "What you need is a few days of good rest without worrying about anything, and I'm sure everything will make more sense then."

Eric flopped back. His soup sloshed a bit, making Carlotta frown, and Grimsby got Eric's attention with a soft snap. He gestured at the food and then Carlotta. Eric chuckled.

"This is delicious, Carlotta," he said after swallowing another sip. Too salty, but that might've been him. "Thank you."

She smoothed his damp hair back from his face. "Of course, dear. Vanni and Gabriella are quite eager to visit you. Do you feel up to seeing them?"

"Please." Eric ate slowly, unpeeling the tortellini in

the broth with his teeth in a way that would have made Vanni gasp. "I want to talk to them about what happened—then I'll rest. I promise."

"You? Rest?" Grimsby asked. "I'll thank the sea for knocking some sense into you."

He rose and his whole body creaked. Carlotta shook her head.

"Off to bed for you as well, I think," Carlotta said, and herded Grimsby to the door. "Eat. I'll send Gabriella and Vanni up."

Eric nodded and nibbled on the bread. After a few minutes, his headache eased. A bright slice of light burned through a crack in his curtains, and the warmth of it helped him relax. The door opened.

"Eric?" Vanni asked and stuck his head in.

"I've never been so happy to see you," said Eric, beckoning him in.

Vanni and Gabriella looked mostly well. A deep purple bruise stood out starkly against Gabriella's brown skin, and scabbed-over cuts freckled Vanni's left side. There was a thick line of stitches curling over Vanni's right ear, and his hair had been shaved down short on the sides and back to match. Max darted inside with them, jumping onto Eric's bed. Eric ruffled his fur.

"How are you doing, buddy?"

Reprise

Max huffed and whined, circling a spot near Eric's feet a few times before settling, and Gabriella sat in the chair Grimsby had abandoned.

"Carlotta gave him a bath," she said, and adjusted the green scarf hiding her hair, "so he's furious."

"Poor baby," Eric said, and leaned down to kiss him. Max smelled better than he ever had before. "How are you?"

"Alive." Vanni ran a hand through the long hair along the top of his head. "Worst part of that wreck was the haircut."

Eric laughed. "Tell folks you fought the sea and lived."

"Yes, I think that will work." Vanni hesitated near Eric's bed and twisted his hands together. "Look, I'll keep my face turned away from you, but you nearly died and I want to hug you. All right?"

"Please," Eric said, and opened his arms. "I'm so glad you're both alive."

Vanni threw his arms around Eric's shoulders, and Gabriella snaked her way around his waist. Her cheek pressed warmly into his side. Vanni tucked Eric's head under his chin.

"You're hugging me like I'm a child," Eric mumbled against his collar.

Vanni dug his chin into Eric's head. "Because you, like a child, went back into a burning ship."

"Like a toddler," added Gabriella, clapping him on the back and pulling away. "One who hasn't learned that touching fire burns you."

"I had to get Max," Eric said.

"And then get rescued by some mystery girl?" asked Vanni, letting him go. "Carlotta said you dreamed some girl saved you, and we weren't to antagonize you about it."

"Fitting," he told them, "that the girl of my dreams is only in my dreams."

"Actually," Gabriella said, "Carlotta told us, 'Poor boy imagined his true love had come to save him and won't hear a word otherwise,' though I guess her tone was sweet."

"Her tone is always sweet." Eric sighed. "I was so certain. I am certain. I was out. If she wasn't real, how did I get to shore?"

Gabriella shrugged. "Stranger things have happened. Plenty of people have done something they normally would never have been able to do when in danger. You might have imagined her to distract from your pain."

"I wasn't in that much pain," he muttered, but it was beginning to feel less and less reasonable. "She sang to me. It was the purest voice I'd ever heard."

Reprise

Gabriella laughed. "Of course it was."

"What was the song?" Vanni asked.

"I couldn't make out the words," said Eric. Eric could hear a piece of music and remember it for years, notations nearly perfect. Most people's eyes went glassy went he talked about it. "Like a chorus of bells out at sea. Sharp and clear."

She had been so cold, but not uncomfortably so. Her voice, too, held the same comforting clarity that felt like waking up to a frosted world. Clear and sharp.

Real.

If anyone had a spotless soul, it was someone selfless enough to risk their life to save a drowning boy. His mystery girl had to be his true love.

Vanni hummed and nodded. Gabriella, though, smiled.

"Here. Look." Eric stuck his arm out at Gabriella. He'd doodled the tune with a pen—there wasn't any paper within reach and Carlotta would've killed him if he'd used a blanket. His savior had a voice as pure as her soul. She had risked herself to save him, and she sang a song with a voice like winter bells. He whistled the tune; the melody was already fading from his mind, and he shuddered at the idea of losing it. "That's it. I think."

"How about this," said Gabriella, rising with a

wince and holding a hand out to Eric. "Vanni and I have work to do—he as usual, and I got roped in to help Nora research the Blood Tide. Grimsby wants me to keep an eye on her. You go for a walk on the beach, stretch everything out, and clear your head. Sauer will probably get here in a few days. There's not much we can do until then, anyway, and walking will help get rid of that soreness."

"Grim will kill me," Eric said. "Carlotta might, too."

"Then don't get caught." Vanni helped Eric to his feet. "You're restless, you've rested, and you need to move to feel better. Come on—I'm covering for my sister while she sleeps after searching for you last night. You can walk us out."

The trio parted at the back stairs of the castle. They carried on to the courtyard, and he descended toward the private dock. Max looped ahead of him with snuffling curiosity, stub of a tail wagging nonstop. Eric let him.

If Max hadn't been too badly affected by the shipwreck, Eric could buck up. No dog was going to outdo him. He navigated the stairs slower than Max, though, and kept one hand on the walls as he paced along the narrow walkway connecting the private dock to the beach.

"Max, leave the crabs alone," Eric called, boots sinking into the sand. "They've done nothing to you.

Keep this up, and they'll rise up against you with the gulls as allies."

Max, already too far ahead for Eric to see, woofed and yelped.

"Max!" Eric sprinted toward the bend in the beach and groaned. "Quiet, boy. What's gotten into . . ."

A girl perched on the rocks, slightly out of Max's slobbering reach. She was a storm of red, like a sunrise spilling across a ship. The sailcloth wrapped around her twisted about like white water, and two dark blue eyes stared out from her tangles of hair. She bundled her hair up out of her face, leaving half to cascade down her back. Max woofed and jumped. He lapped at her face.

Eric hesitated, breath in his throat, and tried to place her. He was sure they had met before.

"Are you okay, miss?" he asked, pulling Max away from her. "I'm sorry if this knucklehead scared you. He's harmless. Really."

She just smiled and nodded, and Eric glanced up at her, close enough to feel her breath on his cheek. Her button nose wiggled.

There was something so familiar about her, but he couldn't place it. From a shop in the bay, perhaps? A ship passing through?

He ruffled Max's fur to avoid staring at her, and she

let out a breathy little laugh. She reached out one tentative hand to pat his snout. Max licked her hand.

"You seem very familiar to me," Eric said slowly, not wanting to admit he couldn't remember who she was. "Have we met?"

The girl nodded and moved to grab his hand, then hesitated. She held out her hand, asking for permission.

"Uh, sure," he said, and she took both of his hands in hers.

The chill of her skin made him shiver. She studied his hands, and he studied her, looking over her slight form. Her hair was tangled and smelled of brine—the open ocean salt, not the week-old stench of the port. The sailcloth tangled around her like a dress was clearly from a recently wrecked ship. Her hair was a beautiful splash of red against it.

Eric's heart fluttered, and he feared he would faint. She was here. His savior was here!

"I knew it!" he said. "You're the one! The one I've been looking for! What's your name?"

Unadulterated joy burst in him, filling his veins with an airy sensation of freedom he had never felt. His true love! He had not made her up after all.

But his hope died as suddenly as it had come upon him as she opened her mouth. All that escaped her was a strangled puff of air, and she clutched her throat. Eric took her by the shoulders.

"What's wrong? What is it?" he asked, clinging to the happiness that founding her had brought him. But then he realized what her gestures meant. "You can't speak?"

She shook her head, and it hit him as hard as the storm had.

"Oh," he said. Everything in him collapsed, the great void of his loneliness leaving him the worst sort of cold. "Then you couldn't be who I thought."

Maybe he had hallucinated his savior. He *had* learned about his true love having a pure voice only a few days ago, so it was on his mind. Not finding his true love immediately was fine, but Grimsby being right? That wasn't fair.

The girl tapped her throat and reached for him, fingers falling shy of his. Her hands flowed with the cadence of speech. It wasn't any sign language Eric recognized, though.

"What is it?" he asked. "You're hurt? No, no. You need help."

She nodded, leaned toward him, and toppled over, tumbling off the rock.

"Whoa, whoa." Eric caught her about the waist and nearly dropped her when her face neared his. She only wrapped her arms around his neck. "Careful. Careful. Easy."

Her legs trembled, and Eric tightened his hold on her to make sure neither of them fell. Her skin was cold even through the sailcloth.

"Gee, you must have really been through something," he said. "Don't worry. I'll help you. Come on. You'll be okay."

She wasn't his soul mate, but she still needed help.

"Let's get you up to the bay and find you some clothes, water, and a real chair," Eric said. "Then we can figure out what to do."

She nodded—so she could understand him; that was good. Max twined between their legs, and the girl made the same gesture she had made earlier. Eric frowned.

"I'm sorry. I don't know what you are trying to say." He nudged Max out of the way and patted her arm apologetically. "I bet we can figure this out together, though."

8
Wildest Dreams

*T*HE GIRL was as wobbly as Eric. He led her down the beach, their arms looped together for balance. They couldn't use the rocky path he had taken down to the beach because of her bare feet, and Eric wasn't strong enough to carry her. Instead, he led her toward the city, trying to corral her and Max every time they spotted something interesting. The girl had nearly lost him when she went chasing after a flower seller.

After he found her staring at a bookshop with a hunger in her eyes Eric usually saw only in scholars, he had asked if she knew how to read and write in Vellonian or any other languages. She didn't, but that didn't make her less interested in the books.

"Here," Eric said once he was able to tear her away from the shop. He helped her down the street, back toward Vanni's. "This should be easier to walk on."

The girl took a few hesitant steps on the flat surface and stumbled into his arms, knocking them both over. She let out a breathy laugh. He held back a sigh.

"Up we get." He struggled to his feet, chest aching, and helped her up. The sailcloth and rope were quickly coming undone. He kept his gaze fixed on her left ear. "So here's my plan—we visit my friend nearby, borrow some clothes from his sister who's about your size, and then figure out what else you need. Sound good?"

She nodded and tightened her grip on his arm. The streets weren't crowded this time of day, and most of the people on them were too busy working to notice Eric rushing past with the girl. She looked at everything with wonder, hesitating in front of a cobbler's and nearly slipping away from him as they passed an apothecary. It took half an hour and three stops to reach Vanni's. Eric had to close his eyes to keep from snapping. His head ached so badly that his teeth felt like they were shifting with each step, and he knew if Grimsby checked on Eric and found him gone, Eric would be dead by sunset. It wasn't the girl's fault, though.

"You can look around Cloud Break later," Eric said, and told Max to stay by the door to Vanni's. He needed to get back to the castle to rest enough for Grimsby not to balk when he started researching the Blood Tide and his curse. "But today's not a great day for it."

But she was too taken with the stalks of wheat in

a large bottle outside the door, touching the kernels and rubbing the leaves between her finger and thumb. She tapped the tall glass bottle with her nails.

"You're not listening to me, are you? If you've never been here before, I can't blame you." He laughed and buried his face in his hands. "All right, definitely going to get murdered by Grim for being away too long."

He touched her elbow and nodded her into the store. Vanni didn't even look up from his cleaning as they entered.

"Vanni," Eric said, "I need a favor."

"I just got here. What trouble could you have possibly found on your walk?"

"I doubt her name is trouble," said Eric. He glanced at her, and she shook her head. "To be fair, I haven't figured out what her name is yet."

"Her name . . ." Vanni's face scrunched, and he looked up to see Eric and the girl. His gaze dropped to her bare feet, took in the sailcloth, and ended on her open-mouthed looked of wonder at the dough on the counter. Vanni dropped the cloth he'd been holding and covered his mouth with a soapy hand. "You found her?"

The full meaning of Vanni's words were like a punch, and Eric was disappointed all over again.

"Ah, no. This isn't *her*," he said. "I found her"—

he gestured at the red-haired girl next to him—"on my walk. She doesn't speak. I was hoping she could borrow some of Lucia's clothes so she didn't have to walk through the bay in a sail."

The girl looked up at him and tugged at her makeshift dress, covering her chest with her arms.

"Ignore him," Vanni said, wiping the soap bubbles from his face. "If it had sleeves, no one would know the difference. Let's get you some more comfortable clothes."

He gestured for her to follow him, and she glanced back at Eric. Eric smiled.

"I'll wait outside the door for you," he said. "Once you're dressed, we can go up to the castle and figure out what to do."

She nodded. Vanni grabbed some clothes from his sister's room and led them to a small storage area separated from the main room by a thick curtain. Eric stayed a good ways down the hall and leaned against the wall while the girl changed.

"I need to be able to call you something," he said. "Any hints as to what your name is?"

She stuck her head out from behind the curtain, scrunched her mouth up to one side, and mouthed something he couldn't make out.

"Emma?" he asked.

She shook her head.

He hummed. "Snow?"

She shook her head so hard her hair smacked the wall, and Eric laughed.

"All right, all right. Change." He whistled a bit, trying to think of a way to make it easier. "We need to figure out a better way for you to say yes and no before you break your neck."

Her breathy laugh was so quiet he nearly missed it, and he smiled.

"Something people can see and hear," he said. "Any ideas?"

There was a rustling of canvas, the scrape of a rope being undone, and a thoughtful little huff. Quietly, she knocked on the wall once.

"You all right?" he asked.

She stuck a bare arm out from the curtain and held up a single finger. Then she knocked on the wall once again.

"Is that a yes?" he asked, relaxing when she did it again. That would work and be easy for others to pick up on. "One for yes and two for no. That's a good system, Ruby."

She slapped his arm twice gently through the curtain, and he nearly choked. He had moved closer to the curtain without realizing it. It didn't seem to bother her, but he was far too close for propriety's sake. Eric backed up a few steps.

"One knock is yes, two is no, and three is I don't know," he said. "That way we have the most pressing answers covered."

She clapped once. He waited in silence after that, letting her change in peace. He hadn't considered that her normal clothing might be different from Vellona's, but she hadn't asked for clarification yet. Eric waited another minute before clearing his throat.

"Regina?" he asked. "Do you need any help? We can get one of Vanni's sisters if you want."

Two knocks rattled the wall.

"Good, good," said Eric. "So, Regina, how did—"

She rapped twice, hard, against the wall directly next to Eric's ear.

"Point taken," said Eric, chuckling.

The curtain rippled. The girl peeked out, blue eyes nervous behind a fringe of red hair. Eric stepped back, curious to see her out of the canvas and realized immediately why it had taken so long. Statuesque Lucia, who was two years younger than Vanni and whom Eric had a hard time picturing as not the little sister he had always seen her as, was far taller than this girl. The collar hung too low on her chest, and she had rolled the top of the trousers too many times to count into a thick band. The rolling, at least, kept the trousers on her waist and the hem off the ground. Her bare toes tapped against the floor.

With the low neckline, Eric couldn't help noticing the freckles—pale, barely-there things—dusting her shoulders. One was even nestled in the hollow of her throat. Eric felt himself blush and looked away.

"Okay," he said, clearing his throat. "One last thing."

Kneeling, Eric pulled the slippers from her hands and gestured to her feet. She held up one of her feet and let him slide the slipper onto it.

"I know everything is a touch too big, but do you think it'll be all right for the walk to the castle? It's about another half hour away." He took her other foot into his hands.

She tapped him on the shoulder once for yes, and he couldn't help leaning into her touch. Looking up, he caught her staring at him, and she flushed. Eric dropped her foot and stepped back. He couldn't quite pull away from her gaze yet.

He was not used to the heat in his chest.

"Good. Great. Let's thank Vanni, and then, ah, then we can head out." Eric swallowed and forced himself to look away. He darted back to the storefront. "Vanni? Thank you, and thank Lucia for us, will you? I'll have the clothes returned tomorrow."

Vanni scoffed. "Don't worry about it."

The girl let out a little breath and darted to the counter, where Vanni was still working. He had finished cleaning and was kneading a spring-green ball of dough on the countertop. Vanni's family sold bread and buns and all sorts of yeasty, tasty things, but it was his grandmother's pasta most people bought. A fine veil of flour glittered in the air, and the girl looked on transfixed as the dough came together. Eric chuckled.

As a child, Eric had watched Vanni's grandmother cook with an ease he usually associated with master artists or fencers, and at some point when Eric wasn't looking, Vanni had taken on the same ethereal quality.

"Never seen pasta before?" he asked, understanding her obsession with Vanni's movements perfectly.

She tapped the counter twice.

"Definitely not from Vellona, then," he said. "Are you rested enough to leave now? I need to get back before Grimsby notices I'm gone."

There wasn't much time left for him to find the Isle of Serein and break his curse.

She nodded slowly, as if she hadn't quite heard him.

Meanwhile, Vanni cut off a small knob of dough and dragged a knife across the top of it, rolling the dough up into a curved shape. A smile spread across her face, and she tore her eyes away from the food long enough to stare up at Eric and touch the rim of his ear before pointing at the dough. Heat pooled along his ribs.

"It does sort of look like an ear," he said, and she turned back to Vanni's work. Eric swallowed, trying not to stare at her. Vanni, hands never missing a beat, smiled at Eric over her head.

"You've got flour in your hair," he said.

Eric smacked the hair near his ear. "Shut up."

"You've got something red on your face, too," Vanni said, wiping his hands on his apron and stretching across the counter. He pinched Eric's cheeks. "Just here."

The girl giggled, and Eric closed his eyes. He should've just carried her to the castle.

"How do you feel about the sea?" Vanni asked the girl.

She broke out into a wide smile and tried to speak. Her hand clutched her throat.

"That's a yes, then," said Vanni. "Want to see Cloud Break's specialty?"

Vanni didn't wait for her answer. He pulled a cloth from a small ball of black dough and showed her one of the wooden stamps. Every town on the coast had its own flag now to let sailors know where they were when they were close to land, and Cloud Break Bay's three-masted ship above a twisting octopus was more exciting than the bird that represented all of Vellona. Eric waited for her to finish fawning over the detailed picture stamped into the dough before he touched her arm. She frowned.

"I'm sorry," Eric said, "but we should really get ba—"

Her stomach rumbled loudly.

He couldn't make her walk across the bay on an empty stomach, not after finding her washed up on the beach. He didn't even know how long it had been since she last ate.

"Okay." Eric laughed and dropped his arm. "Vanni, could I bother you for food?"

"It's hardly a bother. You're watching me cook," said Vanni. He leaned against the counter and eyed the girl. "You like soup?"

She blinked at him and nodded uncertainly.

Eric leaned over to Vanni and said, "Thank you. I'll pay you once we get back."

"If you insist." Vanni left for a moment and returned with two small bowls of soup on a tray with fresh bread and oysters, and he set one before Eric with a stare. "Eat it. I survived a shipwreck. I'm not dying because Carlotta's furious at you for not resting."

Eric laughed and shrugged. "Fair. Thank you."

They could spare another half hour. It wasn't like he was going to solve the mystery of his curse and the Blood Tide within the next hour. The ghosts would still be ghosts and the Isle of Serein would still be in the same place once she had eaten, probably. Nora's information, even, could wait a day.

Especially if Eric had imagined his savior. That definitely meant he should take a day off from thinking about it. He could practically hear Carlotta fussing.

The girl turned to him, stared up at his expression, and tilted her head to the side.

"Sorry. Lost in thought," he said, and groaned. "I keep thinking of you as 'the girl,' but it sounds terrible. Is there a nickname you would like me to use until I figure out your name?"

He glanced at her. She looked up, nodding, and the sun caught her eyes. They glowed a pale bluish gray, like stormy morning light glinting off the sea. They ate in silence, her studying everything around them, and Vanni suggested nicknames every few minutes. The girl mostly swirled her spoon in her soup, nibbling on the pasta as if she'd never had anything like it before. The mussels and oysters on the half shell she avoided.

"How about Sea?" Vanni asked.

She rolled her lips together and shook her head.

"Something to do with the sea?" Eric had finished eating a while back, but rushing her would have been rude. "Or would you prefer something else?"

She knocked twice against the counter, looking around, and then pointed at one of the untouched oysters.

Vanni screwed up his face. "I don't think that's . . ."

It was perfect. And seeing her smile made the waiting worth it.

"Pearl," Eric said and smiled. "You want your nickname to be Pearl until we figure out your real name?"

She clapped once and beamed up at him through the fringes of her mussed red hair. Eric shoved his hands into his pockets to keep from tucking the escaped strands behind her ears.

"Then," said Eric, bowing, "it is lovely to meet you, Pearl." He rose and winked at her. "I'm going to keep guessing, though. Lacey?"

She knocked her knuckles against the back of his hand twice.

"Well, Pearl, I look forward to finding out your name."

9
La Fata Morgana

EING around people was tiresome for Eric. There was something exhausting about having to consider his every little action and word: the tilt of his head as he listened to a dignitary or the toothiness of his smile with the council. Sailing and sparring were never as troublesome, and he had assumed it was because they weren't talking. Entertaining Eric could do, but it brought him no pleasure.

The girl from the sea—Pearl—though, didn't seem to care about his shrugging off tradition or how he held himself apart from others. She didn't demand answers or get offended when he asked her to never kiss him on each cheek as Vanni had done to her when they left. She nodded and moved on.

The only thing that really gave her pause was the first glimpse she got of the castle as they wound their way through the bay.

"It looms," he said, leading her through the main

gate. "I promise everyone inside of it is less imposing. Except Grimsby, but don't tell him I said that. He'd take it as a compliment."

She laughed. He clenched his hands together to keep from smiling back at her.

She wasn't his true love. She couldn't be. She had washed ashore far too late in the day to have been the girl who saved him, and she didn't have a voice as pure as her soul.

And he wasn't feeling any different. Just recovering. His ribs were black and blue, and it was no wonder he felt warm. He might have even had a fever.

"Here. Rest for a little bit." Eric led her to one of the benches in the courtyard. "I'll be back in a moment, all right?"

She nodded and toed off her shoes, testing out the blanket of clover around the bench. Eric took off to find Carlotta, Max at his heels. There was no telling where she might be.

It had taken longer than he expected to cross Cloud Break. Once again, Pearl kept stopping to stare at everything, and this time he hadn't had the heart or strength to drag her away. He had abandoned his worry about Grimsby discovering him gone once it was clear Pearl had never seen some of the things she was so taken by on their walk, and honestly, spending time with her had made him lose track of time. For the first time in ages, he had simply existed and not been worried about Vellona or Grimsby or his curse.

Eric nearly barreled into Carlotta while turning the corner to his own quarters. She yelped.

"Three! Hours!" She smacked him with the cleaning cloth in her hands. "Where have you been? Gabriella said you were going on a short walk, and then no one saw you come back from the beach, and Grimsby—"

"Carlotta," Eric said, taking her by the shoulders, "I am fine. I ran into—"

"Trouble!" She drew herself up to her full height. "I knew it!"

"Why do people keep saying that?" Eric shook his head. "I found a girl washed up on the beach, and we stopped at Vanni's so she could borrow some clothes. She doesn't speak and doesn't read or write Vellonian. Until we can figure out where she's from and what happened, I would like to make her feel welcome."

"Oh, that poor dear," muttered Carlotta. Her tone shifted, and she clutched her rag to her chest as her eyes widened. "On the beach? Where you were? Does this mean you were not imagining your mystery girl after all? Eric, is she—"

"She's not my savior," Eric said. "Her I haven't found yet, and I swear she's real."

Once the witch was dealt with, Eric would find his true love. She had saved him, she had sung to him, and he would prove it.

Carlotta hummed and nodded, her expression skeptical. "Of course. Of course. Until you find her, then, I'll take care of this other girl, and you can rest like you were supposed to be doing."

"Rest?" Eric laughed. "Never even heard of the word."

"A nice, relaxing day," she said, glancing down the hall. "No expectations and no worries. Now take me to your girl."

"She's not my . . ." Eric shrugged and gestured down the hall. "Come on."

He led her back to the courtyard. Pearl wasn't on the bench when they arrived. She was near the high wall, crouching down before a scraggly tree. A trio of baby gulls, still fluffy and black-beaked, squeaked up at her and snatched pieces of Vanni's bread from her fingers. Her shoulders shook with laughter, and one nipped her hand. She wagged her finger at it. The little thing bowed like a courtier on knobby legs.

"You've been making friends," Eric said, careful not to startle her.

She spun and smiled, giving him a little wave. The red indent of the gull's peck sent an unexpected warmth through him. She wasn't angry at the gull like most would be. She was kind in odd little ways, the gestures coming without a second thought.

"Pearl, this is Carlotta," he said, gesturing to the older woman. "If you need anything, she will do everything she can to help. I think a bath, some rest, and new clothes would be best."

Her smile slipped slightly, and he knelt before her.

"Are you all right going with Carlotta and staying at the castle for now?" he asked. "If not, we can find somewhere else for you to go."

She tapped once on the back of his hand.

"Good," he said.

A few strands of hair fell before her face, and Eric had moved before he even thought about it. He brushed the hair behind her ear. He had never done that with anyone. It felt too intimate, a bit too much like a kiss on the corner of the lips.

"We should have dinner tonight," he said, and Carlotta stared openmouthed at him. "We both got shipwrecked, and you don't know anyone."

And even though she wasn't his true love, he wanted to spend a bit more time with her.

Pearl grinned and nodded.

"Now," Carlotta said, slipping between them and taking Pearl's hands in her own. She shot Eric a questioning look over her shoulder. "Let us get you into a nice warm bath and clothes that fit. Eric, go put Grimsby out of his misery. I'll take care of her."

"Pearl's a nickname, by the way. You might have better luck than me figuring out her actual name," he said and avoided her eyes. "Grim in his study?"

"The old study," said Carlotta. "Go on now. Pearl is in good hands."

The study was one of the oldest rooms of the castle, tucked away near its center where the air was chill and the stone walls damp, and Grimsby used it only when tradition demanded it or he didn't want many people stumbling upon the meeting. It was where Eric's mother had made quiet pacts and dealt with folks other nobles or kingdoms would scoff at. It was where he had learned his mother had died. It was where he would sign his name to the list of Vellona's rulers.

"A place for the best and the worst of Vellona's

quirks," he muttered, his mother's description sticking with him still as he turned the final corner.

The hallway was decorated with old portraits and tapestries, and Grimsby paced before them. Eleanora's painted face stared down at him.

"Grim?" Eric said, raising his voice slightly.

The man nearly leapt from his skin. "Where have you been?

Eric explained about his walk and meeting Pearl, and Grimsby's forehead gained a new wrinkle with each word.

"Are you telling me that you found a girl on the beach, showed her around the bay, and welcomed her into the castle?" Grimsby asked. "No questions? No concern for if she's a Sait spy or one of those mercenary pirates raiding up north?"

"Bold strategy, then, stranding herself naked, exhausted, and with few ways to communicate." Eric snorted. "If she is a spy, Sait will soon learn our darkest secret—Vanni's best pasta recipes."

Grimsby groaned. "You are missing the ocean for the waves—you are the cursed prince of a troubled kingdom, and there is far too much going on for you to be bothering with some random girl."

"She's a guest," said Eric sharply. "She is alone

and vulnerable. I don't care what else I am, but I will not be the sort of person who refuses aid to someone in need."

Grimsby drew himself up, shoulders straightening, and his hands clenched by his sides. "There are more important things for you to deal with now. Hand her off to Carlotta, by all means, but you need to focus. You need to marry and secure the line of succession before your court takes matters into their own hands."

Eric ground his teeth together to keep from snapping. Helping someone in need shouldn't have been unimportant or secondary. Vellona had a line of succession if you squinted. Eric had plenty of cousins—the same ones who wouldn't hesitate to challenge his claim if he didn't marry, but still. Eric rubbed his temple and sighed.

"Marrying won't kill the witch or break my curse. Marrying won't instantly bring us money or resources. Marrying won't instantly create an heir. Marrying won't keep the pirates or storms away," said Eric. "I will leave Pearl to Carlotta, but I will be hunting down the Isle of Serein again. You may stay behind and deal with the quandary of marriage if you want."

Grimsby scowled. "You need not go looking for your island so soon—that pirate Sauer has returned, and they dragged who-knows-what back with them. They asked for a wagon to carry something to the castle and to speak with us in private."

Sauer was in Cloud Break? It wasn't impossible for them to have made it back so soon, but Eric hadn't expected them to arrive until tomorrow given the storm.

"Did something happen?" asked Eric, curiosity burning in is stomach. "Come on."

Eric pushed open the door to the hall. The wooden walls were darkened by age and years of cigar smoke, the portraits hung up as serious and monotone as the rest of the room. The long wooden table that usually sat in the center of the room had been pushed to one side, and the leather chairs circling it pushed to the other. Sauer, studying the last portrait Eric's mother had sat for, stood at the back of the room next to a large crate covered in canvas. Eric couldn't bear to look at it.

"Captain Sauer," he said. "You made good time."

They didn't respond. They looked older than they had on the ship. They were still taller than Eric despite their tired slouch, and they stood out in the dour room. Their red coat was as weathered as their face, the bottom hem little more than fringe and most of the buttons missing, and they inclined their head to him. Salt-matted white hair stuck to their neck.

"Circumstances changed, Your Highness," they said, taking off their wide-brimmed hat. "This is your mother, Her Majesty Eleanora of Vellona?"

Eric came to stand next to them and eyed his mother's portrait. "Yes, that was commissioned when she became queen."

"It's an uncanny likeness."

Confusion ran through Eric. The back of his neck prickled.

"I was unaware you ever met my mother," said Eric, "so what could possibly be uncanny?"

Grimsby's footsteps echoed behind Eric, but he didn't take his eyes from Sauer.

"What's happened?" Eric asked.

Sauer scratched at the sunburned skin stretching across their large nose. "There's no easy way to say it, so I'll show you. Brace yourself."

The pulled the canvas from the crate, except it wasn't a crate at all. It was one of the ghosts, standing inside of a hastily built box frame. The bottom of the frame looked as if it had been cut from the deck of an old, rotting ship, and salt flaked from the ghost's form, peppering the floor. The ghost was as tall as Eric, and her short black hair was wild and windswept. She was paler here than she had been on the sea, as translucent as a spiderweb in the wrong light.

"No." Eric took a step back, gaze sweeping over her again. From the slight inward turn of her feet to the broad post of her shoulders, to the way her hands hung closed and fisted at her sides to how her mouth was slightly open, this was his mother exactly as he remembered her. "That's not . . . She's a lure. The light of an anglerfish. Nothing more."

He backed away from her, and next to him, Grimsby fell to his knees. He covered his mouth with shaking hands.

"I've noticed from the three times my crew has encountered the ghost ships that the ghosts, after they lose interest in their target or the target is far enough away, revert to what I can only assume are their original forms," said Sauer. "This is the form that this one reverted to once there was no one around to lure."

"My mother is dead," said Eric, but his voice wavered. He hated it. "My mother has been dead for two years, and we are well within this thing's luring range right now. I see this ghost as my mother because that is who I want."

"And yet I see Eleanora of Vellona, too." Sauer

glanced at the ghost. "She's not in the dress coat and that scar on her cheek isn't visible on the ghost, but she has been Eleanora of Vellona since all the ghosts reverted and left."

Eric swallowed, unable to look away from her face. "How did you catch her?"

"We didn't," they said. "Once they were no longer trying to lure us and far enough away that they were leaving on their own, she came walking back across the waves. Not for my ship, but for yours. She nearly walked right past us on the waves."

Grimsby tensed behind Eric and, with a cracking voice, said, "That cannot be Eleanora."

Hands shaking, Eric reached out to the ghost that couldn't be his mother, and she didn't react at all. His fingers brushed against her form, the pale shimmer of her body dulling for a moment. He passed right through her as if she were smoke.

"It looks like her," Eric said.

Slowly, her eyes rolled to stare at him. Her mouth worked as if she were speaking, but there was no sound at all. Not even breathing.

"Most of her scars aren't visible, but that little notch in her upper lip." Eric gestured to the portrait. On the ghost, it appeared as if a sliver of flesh, or whatever it was made of, was missing. "That's in the right place."

Grimsby came up behind him. "As is her mole."

Dread washed over Eric.

"What if it's not a copy?" he asked.

"She is the only one who left the ghost ship. The only one I have ever seen do that." Sauer bowed their head. "Several times, when the music was at its weakest, she broke free of the group following our singer and looked as if she were searching for someone."

"What are these ghosts?" Eric asked. "She's dead. Why would she . . . What sort of waking nightmare is this?"

Eric couldn't even bring himself to look at Grimsby.

"I don't have that or, honestly, any other answers for you. Only speculations," said Sauer. "I believe that some part of her is here right now. There are not many ghosts, perhaps only four or five dozen, but surely they do not run into people they knew during their lives often. However, she did see you again. The farther she got from the ghost ship, the fainter she became, and she began to sink through the waves."

Eric inhaled, suddenly realizing what they must have done.

"So you lured them back and cut a piece from the ship for her to stand on."

Sauer nodded. "Only me. I rowed a ways off and called them. I was quite desperate to do it, seeing as a pardon for my crew is on the line. But it worked."

"And here she is," whispered Eric.

"Yes," said Sauer. "She kept trying to continue her walk, but she stopped once we traveled in the same direction she was going in for an hour."

A yawning ache opened up in Eric's chest, like missing a step on the stairs, and all the grief he had bottled up within him strained against his heart. He leaned his forehead as close as he could to her ghost without touching her.

"You really think she's here for me?" Eric opened his eyes and found her staring through him. Not seeing him. Not really seeing anything. But his mother's ghost was looking at him, and he couldn't stand it. "Back then, on the ship, there was a moment when she didn't offer me anything. She only said my name. Do you think she's aware of me on some level and that she's waiting for something even now?"

No one answered his question. Grimsby was frozen in place in the center of the room, his gaze on Eleanora and his hands covering his mouth. Eric pulled the man's hands from his face.

"I think marriage can wait," Eric whispered. "Don't you?"

Grimsby stared at him. "Eric—"

Eric spun away from Grimsby to stare at the captain, Nora's words at sea about her time as Sauer's second coming back to him. He took a deep breath, willing himself to stay focused despite the discomfort he felt with his mother's ghost just steps away from him. "I believe I promised you something if you helped me, but I have a question first—why did you turn to piracy?"

"Turn? That's a rather loaded word, isn't it?" They laughed and shook their head, running their long fingers through their hair. "When polite society won't even deign to recognize that you're a part of society, much less be polite to you, why bother trying to fit in? My home wasn't doing anything to ensure people could survive. We had to do it ourselves. I feel no qualms about my work. How do you feel about yours?"

"Better than I feel about this." Eric pointed at his mother's ghost. "Do you still agree to abide by our deal?"

Sauer nodded.

"I want to leave tomorrow for the Isle of Serein. The

same course we took last time," said Eric. "On the Isle is a witch responsible for terrible things. I'm going to kill her. Get me there and back alive, and you and your crew will receive full pardons."

"Eric!" Grimsby reared back as if struck and shook his head. "You cannot go on a mission to face some witch just—"

"Just?" Eric asked, gesturing to the ghost of his mother. "Think about how many we saw on the ghost ship, Grim. How many people have died to the ghosts? How many to this witch? I'm done waiting for life to align itself. Mother died going after this witch, and I'm sorry for not telling you, but I'm doing this whether you like it or not."

Grimsby stared at Eric, skin bone white. "Eleanora went after her?"

"She did," said Eric. "And she died for her troubles."

Grimsby was silent for a moment, staring at Eric with an unreadable expression. Finally, he took a breath and rounded on Sauer. "You will, of course, uphold your end of the deal and escort him?"

Sauer ran their tongue along their teeth and seemed to be going over the time line. "We can be ready tomorrow evening once we've rested and restocked, but I'm giving my crew the option to stay behind. I'm not ordering them to fight a witch. I and any who agree will uphold the deal."

"That's fair," said Eric at the same time Grimsby said, "If he gets so much as a single bruise, I swear you'll never know peace again."

Sauer's eyebrows shot up. "Understood."

"Grimsby, get Sauer whatever they need," said Eric. "If my mother moves, I want to be told immediately. Have two people in here watching her at all times, preferably two who already know about the ghosts. Those sailors we traveled with, perhaps. Tomorrow we're on the hunt again."

Eric took one last look at his mother's ghost, her empty eyes never meeting his, and turned away.

10

Salade de Crabe

*E*RIC FLED the room in a panic. Grimsby found him in the hall a few minutes later, laughing under his breath at the absurdity of his situation. There wasn't anything Eric could do yet, but all of it hinged on finding the Isle of Serein and killing the witch. Grimsby gave Eric a moment to compose himself before dragging him to the dining hall for dinner with Pearl.

"You *just* told me to leave her to Carlotta," muttered Eric as he straightened his clothes outside of the dining hall. "And Sauer's arrival has changed things."

"It has not changed the doctor's instructions for you to rest," Grimsby said. "If Carlotta hasn't come chasing after me about her, she's almost certainly not a spy."

Eric narrowed his eyes. It had been annoying at first, trying to get back to the castle when Pearl didn't seem to know the meaning of the word *urgency*, but then his stress and pain had eased as they ate with Vanni and meandered through the bay. Her company had been a balm.

Salade de Crabe

"Fine," said Eric, and he pushed open the doors to the hall.

Pearl hadn't arrived yet, and the room didn't bear any scars from Eric's last disastrous dinner. Eric went to one of the windows, leaning against it. At the far end of the harbor bobbed Sauer's ship.

"And I think the company of this girl will be a good distraction from your mystery savior," Grimsby said in the same tone he usually reserved for when Max licked his face.

"She *was* real," said Eric. "I would have drowned if someone hadn't saved me."

A woman as compassionate as she was courageous had pulled him from the waves, and she had possessed a pure voice, or pure so far as he could tell. It hadn't been a near-death hallucination or figment of his imagination. She had been his true love.

"Oh, Eric. Be reasonable," Grimsby said with a frantic gesture. "Nice young ladies just don't swim around rescuing people in the middle of the ocean and then flitter off into oblivion like some—"

"I'm telling you, Grim, she was real." Eric ignored Grimsby's scowl at being interrupted. "I'm going to find that girl, and I'm going to marry her."

He would look for his mystery savior after the curse

was broken and none of the fears of his curse hung over him to ruin the joy of having true love, and no one, not a witch or Grimsby or all the long-lost cousins challenging his claim to the throne, could stop him.

Grimsby shook his head.

Laughter echoed from the outside of the hall. Carlotta rarely laughed like that anymore, and even Grimsby looked up from his favorite pipe to the doors. Both were thrown open, and Carlotta paced between them, gesturing for Pearl to follow her. The soft shuffling of her feet, so uncertain, reached Eric first. No doubt Carlotta had gone overboard. Pearl had barely been able to walk without shoes. She would—

"Oh," Eric whispered and swallowed.

Pearl stood in the doorway. Her hair spilled like sweet wine down her back, a small river of it gathered up in the teeth of a white shell comb. In the dimming light of evening, her eyes were darker, blue sapphires plucked from the deepest part of the seas, and the pink dress she wore swirled around her body like high tide at sunset. She dropped into a curtsy, graceful despite the clearly unfamiliar movement. The pearls dangling from her ears glittered.

"Oh, Eric." Even weathered old Grim sounded charmed. "Isn't she a vision?"

Salade de Crabe

"You look . . ." Eric moved toward her, wanting to reach for her hand, but at the last moment, he pulled away. He couldn't. "Wonderful."

Pearl shrugged, smiling up at him, and all the words Eric meant to say fled.

"Come, come, come. You must be famished." Grimsby beckoned Pearl to the table and held out her chair for her. "Let me help you, my dear."

Eric swallowed, squeezing his eyes shut, but the vision of Pearl remained. The heat in his cheeks eased, and he peeked at Pearl again. Grimsby glanced at Eric, one brow raised.

"There we go," said Grimsby to Pearl. He stepped back and let Eric help Pearl with her chair. "Now, quite comfy? It's not often that we have such a lovely dinner guest, is it, Eric?"

He had said that about every dinner guest of marrying age since Eric turned sixteen.

"You're plotting," muttered Eric, leaning in close so that only Grimsby could hear him.

Grimsby shook out his napkin and whispered, "I am picking my battles."

More likely he was trying to get Eric's mind off his true love.

Eric shook his head. Pearl was still inspecting the

place setting, none the wiser to Grimsby. She ran a finger over the fork, and before he could react, she picked it up and ran the tines of it through her hair like a brush. Grimsby froze. Eric tried to think of something to say but couldn't. He hadn't even considered that Vellona's customs might be different from hers, and they hadn't used forks with their soup at Vanni's.

Pearl blushed and ducked, sinking in on herself, and she looked around. Eric's skin burned with her unease. Grimsby, long immune to any embarrassment Eric felt, picked up his pipe and struck a match. The sound and flicker drew Pearl's gaze. She leaned toward it.

"Ah," said Grimsby, drawing from it once. "Do you like it? It is rather a fine one."

Grimsby offered it to her, and Pearl ran her fingers along its neck. She put her lips to the mouthpiece and blew. Tobacco ash spewed out of the bowl, scattering across Grimsby's face. He froze, and laughter exploded from Eric. He pounded his chest to stop.

"Sorry, Grim," he said.

"Oh my!" Carlotta—he had forgotten about her since seeing Pearl entering—came up beside Eric and lightly smacked his shoulder. "Why, Eric, that's the first time I've seen you smile in weeks."

After learning of his mother's fate, or her soul's fate,

he hadn't been sure he would ever smile again. Grimsby was right; Eric felt lighter. Better.

Grimsby ripped the cloth from his chest pocket and wiped his face clean. "Oh, very amusing."

Eric shot Pearl a comforting look. The blush in her cheeks seeped all the way down her neck, speckling her collarbone like fading freckles. Eric laid one hand on the table near hers.

Suddenly, the gulf between them, widened by their difficulties communicating, felt impassable, and he hated that. Their communication was already so limited, and propriety was another unnecessary barrier. It had never really bothered him before; usually, he was pleased by the added layer of protection propriety gave him. Pearl shouldn't have been any different, and he wasn't sure why she was.

"Carlotta, my dear," said Grimsby, interrupting Eric's thoughts, "what's for dinner?"

"You're going to love it," she said, darting past Eric. She squeezed his shoulder. "Chef's been fixing his specialty—stuffed crab."

Eric rested one elbow on the table and blocked Grimsby's view of Pearl with his shoulder.

"Don't feel bad about the fork and the pipe," he whispered to her. "A lot of things here are new to you, and I should have asked. If there's anything else, tell me or Carlotta, and we'll help."

Her smile fell slightly, and Eric reached out for her, not quite touching but leaving his hands open for her on the table. A crash came from the kitchen. Carlotta winced.

"I think I'd better go see what Louis is up to," she said, scurrying off.

A few short minutes later, the little door to the kitchens burst open, and Carlotta hustled out with three plates along her arms.

"You know, Eric," Grimsby said. He took a puff from his pipe, smiling slightly. "Perhaps our young guest might enjoy seeing some of the sights of the kingdom. Something in the way of a tour?"

A tour? While his mother's ghost sat waiting in the castle? Yes, that would provide a distraction and keep Eric out of Grimsby's hair until Sauer and their crew were ready to depart, but that wasn't enough for Grimsby. Eric just had to stay focused on the witch and her isle and ignore Grimsby's quest to find him a spouse.

Eric nearly said as much, but Pearl's hopeful smile made him pause. He *had* offered to give her a tour at Vanni's, and rarely did Eric get to show off Cloud Break to people so excited to see it. He smiled back at her and

Salade de Crabe

imagined how much she would like the markets, given every stop she'd made between Vanni's and the castle. She had enjoyed watching Vanni making pasta, and plenty of vendors would be happy to demonstrate their work to someone. She would almost certainly love the windmills. . . .

"I'm sorry, Grim," said Eric, forcing himself to look away from Pearl. "What was that?"

Carlotta set the plates before each of them, the scents of butter and herbs rising with the steam.

"You can't spend all your time moping about. You need to get out. Do something, have a life." Grimsby lifted the lid from his plate and inhaled so deeply he closed his eyes. The crab on his plate was so fresh, it looked alive. "Get your mind off—"

"Easy, Grim, easy," Eric interrupted to avoid Grimsby going off on another tangent. So it was Grimsby's last-ditch effort to attach Eric to a pretty young bride. He had never looked forward to spending time with his potential spouses, but doing so with Pearl didn't feel like a chore. "It's not a bad idea, if she's interested."

He glanced back at Pearl . "Well, what do you say? Would you like to join me on a tour of my kingdom tomorrow?"

She nodded furiously, arms crossed over the serving lid. Eric smiled.

"Wonderful," said Grimsby, holding up his fork. "Now, let's eat before this crab wanders off my plate."

Metal clanged against ceramic, and Eric turned back to Grimsby. Only a lone piece of lettuce covered his tray.

"Ah, Carlotta, dear," said Grimsby. "I seem to be missing my meal."

After dinner, Max met Eric and Pearl outside of the hall and followed them down to the beach where they had found each other. It had been Eric's suggestion as a way for him to learn more about Pearl and to talk to her somewhere less intimidating than the castle. Grimsby's crab had never reappeared, and Eric had made the horrifying realization that he had overlooked another major thing—what Pearl ate. She hadn't touched the crab, but she had seemed to like the rest of the meal well enough. He suspected she didn't eat meat at all. He didn't want to make the same mistake again.

"If you want anything else to eat or there's something specific you want, ask Carlotta," he told her, helping her navigate the small rocks separating the stairs from the beach.

Pearl nodded, but her head was tilted back and her gaze focused on the stars. Max nudged at her side. Grinning, Pearl toed off her slippers and darted across the sand. Max took off after her.

"Tap your shoulder!" Eric called out and followed after them, laughing as Pearl did as he said and Max stood up on his hind legs.

She took him by the paw and led them round and round in a shaky circle.

"Do you know how to dance?" Eric asked. She shook her head, and he held out his arms. "Do you want to learn?"

Pearl set down Max and joined Eric. He placed her left hand on his shoulder. Her fingers fidgeted against him, a slight chill seeping through his shirt, and she leaned into his hand on her waist. She dug her toes deep into the sand. Eric chuckled.

"Here, this will be perfect." Eric whistled the quick triple meter of the last song he had danced to—in the poorly lit dregs of the sea beneath the docks with Vanni, Gabriella, and the rest of their friends months ago after Vanni disarmed Gabriella for the first time—and let Pearl get used to the rhythm. It was a leaping dance and didn't demand the precision of most formal routines.

He moved his feet slowly at first, speeding up once she started moving with him. Then he leapt.

With his hands on her hips, Eric lifted Pearl until her feet were a few feet off the ground. Her hair flared out behind her like a crown. Joy lit her eyes.

"Fun?" he asked, and brought her back down to the beach.

She nodded, fingers tightly clutching his shoulder.

Eric pulled her close again and led her in another circle. "How about a leap and a spin this time?"

She tapped him once, moonlight sparkling in her eyes as she laughed, and she looked like how bells sounded, bright and delicate with a promise of depth yet unheard. He raised her up once more and leapt himself. She twirled in midair with all the grace of a lifelong dancer.

So many of the popular dances across the kingdoms required close contact and lips within kissing distance. As the only prince of Vellona, Eric had been expected to entertain, but his mother had rarely allowed him to dance outside of his lessons. It was the sensible route and kept him safe.

But he loved dancing and this, the breathless thrill of it all with Pearl. She leapt higher each time, dancing with an abandon Eric couldn't match, but she respected the distance he kept her at.

Though he was too afraid to admit it, there was a part of him that wished she wouldn't.

"I need a break," Eric said, pulling them to a stop. His ribs did ache, but it was the sudden desire to pull her closer that drove him to step away. "That's harder on sand."

Pearl huffed and gathered her hair up out of her face. They sat down, the water lapping at their feet. Max curled up behind them.

"We can try it again tomorrow on stone," he said, and winced. "About tomorrow—I do have to leave in the evening for a while. I'm unsure as to how long I'll be gone, but it's unavoidable. I will still give you a tour of the bay. Unfortunately, you'll be stuck with Carlotta and Grimsby after that. If you need anything, ask. No matter if you want to stay in Cloud Break or find your way home, they'll help."

Panic darkened her gaze, and for the first time since they had met that morning, she looked afraid.

"Carlotta will be thrilled for the company," said Eric. "And we'll have plenty of time to talk tomorrow still. If I could delay it, I would, but I got some bad news today and can't put it off any longer."

Pearl nibbled at her bottom lip.

"It will be fine. I promise," he said. Then, trying to change the topic, he continued, "I know we can't really talk, but what else is different here from your home, if you don't mind answering?"

She held up two fingers—she didn't mind—and tilted her head back, pale neck arched and bare. Eric looked up at the sky.

"The stars look different here?" he asked and glanced back down at her.

She clapped once and sighed, hair rustling with her breath. A few strands stuck to her cheek. Eric tucked his hands into his pockets to keep from brushing her hair aside.

"Are they completely different or just harder to see?" he asked.

She tapped twice and then made a motion as if wiping her eyes.

"Easier to see?"

She nodded.

"I have no idea where you might be from, then," he said, and smiled as she laughed. They sat in silence for a long while, shoulder to shoulder, and watched the distant lights of ships pass by. Slowly, Pearl patted the back of his hand four times.

"So that's not 'I don't know,' is it?" He turned to her and asked, "Are you trying to say another common phrase?"

One pat.

"I can't explain?" he offered, and she shook her head then wiggled her hand. "Explain?"

One pat.

"Explain what?" asked Eric.

Pearl made a rocking motion with her hand, gliding it through the air like a boat over water.

"Why am I leaving? Oh, that's not a happy tale."

Pearl laid her hand on his arm, inclined her head, and rested her other hand over her heart.

"No apologies necessary," he said. He rarely spoke to anyone about his mother, but her ghost was so new and so much was happening. Pearl, though melancholy, wasn't looking at him like he was broken. "My mother died at sea two years ago, and I found out why and where recently. I'm traveling to learn more."

It wasn't everything, but it was enough of the truth that he felt lighter for having shared it.

Pearl gestured to herself and then him, and Eric knew instantly what she meant.

"Absolutely not." Eric shook his head and pulled back. "I cannot ask you to come with me or allow it. There are pirates and other deadly things, and I will be going directly into danger. If you got hurt, who would we even contact?"

Pearl blew a strand of hair from her face. She shrugged.

Eric squinted at her. "Should we contact anyone for you?"

She held up two fingers.

"Your family," he said carefully. "They're not terrible to you, are they? If you wanted to return, it would be safe?"

She nodded and shrugged again. Her hands twisted in her lap. She touched her heart.

"You love them?" Eric asked. "But it's complicated."

She held up one finger and used it to tap her forehead.

"You think . . ."

Pearl threw her hand out and gestured vaguely into the dark.

"You think the sea?"

Two fingers.

"Them?"

One.

"You think they?"

She nodded and smiled. Her right hand tapped her forehead, and then she held it even with her stomach. Her left hand she waved away from herself again and then held over her head. Eric tried to hold back his confusion.

"You think they think," he said, running through possible things he would say about his own family and friends using these gestures. "You think they think they need to take care of you?"

Pearl dropped her hands and shrugged. She tapped her chest again and held her hand over her head, then raised it slowly seven times.

"You're the smallest?"

She shook her head.

"You're the youngest?"

She wiggled her hand—maybe—and huffed. She drew the lines of a family tree and pressed a hand to her chest. Her arms cradled an imaginary baby.

"You're the youngest, and they baby you." Eric nodded and brought his knees up to his chest. "My mother was sort of like that. She always wanted to protect me, and it's even worse now because she was such a good queen and now I have to fill that role. It terrifies me. She wasn't scared of anything. I feel like, no matter what I do, I will never live up to her."

Pearl nodded and grasped his hand, lacing their fingers together.

He couldn't tell her about his curse or his mother's ghost, but some part of him wanted to. He wanted to let all his secrets slip from his lips and ask, *Do I want to save her so badly for her, or so I don't have to bear all these responsibilities yet?*

Instead, he leaned back in the sand and stared up at the stars Pearl didn't recognize. She lay back next to him.

"We should go back," he said. If they stayed any longer, he wasn't sure what all he'd tell her. "Carlotta will kill me if I keep you out all night."

Pearl snorted.

"We'll leave for the tour early, if you don't mind." Eric helped her to her feet. "Cloud Break's best in the morning."

Pearl smiled and nodded. She reached up and untangled a cherry tree sprig from his hair. She tucked it into his shirt pocket. Her fingers tapped his cheek once.

Something pulled at Eric's chest.

Another mystery to solve tomorrow.

11

Kiss the Girl

*T*HE NEXT thing Eric knew, the early morning sun was burning a line across his face. A low ache ground his jaw to a stop as he groaned, and Eric stretched. There was no time to rest. Tonight he'd be leaving for the Isle of Serein again.

He got dressed and went to the courtyard, sure that he would get there before Pearl, but she was standing off to the side near a tree. The baby gulls had found her again, and she was tossing small pieces of whitebait to them, making each wait their turn with a sharp gesture when they hopped and squawked. One waddled toward her, and she held up an empty hand. It fluffed up.

Pearl shook her head and shooed it back.

"Good morning," Eric said, and stepped beside her. "How do you get them to do that?"

Pearl tilted her head up at him. She was in blue today, half her hair pulled up with a large bow. When she turned back to the birds and raised the hand with the last three whitebait pieces up, her dress swirled around her like rain. The gulls bobbed up and down before her.

They screeched, and she tossed them each their fish.

"They're better behaved than Max," he said. If only screaming until someone threw what he wanted at him would work for Eric.

Pearl smiled up at him, nose scrunched up, and Eric turned away.

Eric liked these moments best—the breath before the smile when her eyes crinkled and her teeth peeked out from her lips. She held back sometimes, as if remembering her predicament, and didn't fully smile, but the barely there dent of her dimples made him smile for her. Here she was, lost in a new land and unable to communicate well, and she didn't seem afraid at all. She was brave, and it made him feel brave.

And all those complicated little feelings smoldered in his chest like a coal. She wasn't his true love, so why was he feeling like this?

"Are you ready to go?" Eric asked.

She nodded. Eric led her to the center of the courtyard near the gate where a cart and buggy waited for them. Pearl inhaled at the sight of the horse, and her hands came up to her chest, fingers twisting. She only approached it after Eric demonstrated how to pet the horse, warning her not to go around near its rear, and it nibbled at her shoulder with its lips.

"We'll start outside the bay and work our way in," said Eric. "That way you'll get to see everything."

Finally, they got in the buggy and trotted through the gate. The farms tucked up on the hills away from the shore were pale gold and green, goats wandering idly through the grass and crows resting on slowly turning windmills. There wasn't much to see out in the sprawling edges of Cloud Break Bay, but Pearl stopped them every now and then to stare at deer and smaller foraging creatures. She laughed delightedly at a rabbit, using Eric's shoulder to balance against so she could watch it hop back into the bushes.

"Here," said Eric, helping her sit down again. She pressed closely against him, and he found he didn't mind at all. "You'll like this. Look."

This was the view of Cloud Break those who didn't journey by ship saw first—the pale stone buildings with red-tiled roofs, wooden pavilions shading the streets with ceilings of leafy grapevines, and glittering canals crisscrossing the town like the silvery-blue web of some great spider. She rose in the buggy again to get a better look, her wide-eyed grin contagious, and Eric slowed the horse. Her fingers curled around his shoulder, her thumb brushing his skin absentmindedly.

"Do you like it?" he asked.

She tapped his throat once and then four times, settling her palm flat against his chest.

"I like it at dusk," he said, "when the sea and sky are the same scarlet smear and the world seems to go on forever."

She sunk onto the bench next to him, nestling against his side. Eric, suddenly warm, was aware of every inch of his body that touched hers, and he leaned away slightly. It was only the morning heat. It had to be.

He looped his arm around her, though.

They made their way toward the main street. The center square was bustling with people, stalls lining the edges of the path. People lingered around the fountain, collecting water and gossip, and Eric helped her down from the buggy. Pearl paused before a puppet show and gasped when she caught sight of a group of people dancing. She grabbed Eric and pulled him into the circle of dancers.

It wasn't the leaping dance of last night, but she caught on quickly and with enough enthusiasm to charm even the grouchiest of observers. He led her through a slow dance and carefully untangled the bow holding her hair from the windswept strands. She beamed up at him.

"Maybe slower next time," he said with a laugh, and retied Pearl's bow. "Emily?"

Pearl laughed and held up two fingers. After another three rounds of dancing, Eric was tired of all the eyes on them. It was late morning, nearing noon, and soon they would have an even larger audience. He was a common sight around Cloud Break, but Gabriella or Vanni were usually his companions. This girl from the sea was wholly and obviously new.

"Most of the folks who live here work at the docks," said Eric, leading her past a gaggle of older folks gossiping over the fishing net they were repairing. He paused as she stared at the net. "Does your family fish?"

She dragged her eyes from the net and shook her head.

They walked through Cloud Break's intersections filled with small booths full of various Vellonian delicacies. Eric grabbed spinach and cheese tortellini in herb-flecked broth for lunch, which they ate sitting on the edge of a canal near the outside of the city where the water was cleaner. Pearl tore little fluffs of bread from a fresh loaf and fed them to the fish and birds gathering around them, and Eric asked her why she had wanted to leave home.

Adventure, she finally managed to pantomime after he failed to understand. *Explore. People. Mine.*

"And your family didn't want you to leave?" he asked, remembering their conversation on the beach.

She shook her head. From the sound of it, her family was stricter than Grimsby.

"Then let's adventure." He offered her his hand. "Ever seen a lagoon before? It's where a bit of the sea got trapped inland, so now there's a little land bridge separating the water from the sea. All sort of things live there."

She loved animals, clearly, and the lagoon creatures rarely made their way into the bay.

Pearl nodded. They returned the horse and buggy to the castle before heading out on foot. Their walk to the lagoon was shaded and private, letting them talk more than they had in town. He told her as much as he knew about the stout bushes and plants lining their path, and she got far too close to the cliff's edge for Eric's comfort. He kept one hand on her side and led her down to the small dock in the lagoon. This swampy stretch of the area was part of the castle's hunting and fishing grounds. She trailed her fingers through the water as he rowed.

"I'll be leaving tonight, but you're more than

welcome to come and go from Cloud Break as much as you please," he said. "But, if you leave, make sure someone knows."

Pearl held up two fingers and drew them across her neck.

"I really hope that means you're not leaving and not that you're about to drown me." He pulled the oars into the boat and let them drift.

She rolled her eyes—at least that gesture meant the same in both of their worlds—and leaned her elbows on her knees. She jerked her hand to point at herself.

He got what she meant almost instantly.

"I'm not taking you with me," said Eric. "It is not a safe trip. You would see nothing but open sea. It's less an adventure and more a wild-goose chase."

She tilted her head to the side, and Eric laughed.

"A wild-goose chase is a long, often useless hunt for something," he explained quickly. "Have you ever been on a ship other than the one that wrecked?"

She hesitated. Slowly, she rapped once on the rowboat.

"Not including this boat."

Frowning, she tapped twice.

"Do you know how to sail? How to survive on open

water? There may be pirates, fights. We might be gone for days or for weeks, and storms come out of nowhere this side of Vellona. It's too dangerous."

Pearl reached into the water and splashed him. Her other hand gestured to all of her.

"All right, fair point. You survived a shipwreck, but do you know how to fight?"

Reluctantly, she knocked twice on the boat. A few fish circling it leapt and washed water over his side.

"I'm sorry," he said, and sighed. He hadn't thought she would be able to, but it was only fair to ask. As much as he wanted to trust that she could hold her own, he had only known her for a day. "I really do not want to be responsible for you getting hurt."

He already had far too many responsibilities.

Her mouth thinned into a pink, angry line, and she narrowed her eyes at him.

"I just met you," Eric said. "How could I justify you joining us?"

Pearl curled up, chin on her knees, and wrapped her arms around her legs. She huffed.

"I'm sorry." Eric picked up the oars again and dipped them into the water.

A gull swooped into one of the trees above them and screeched. Eric winced. Not the best serenading the bay had to offer, but Pearl didn't seem to mind too much. Still, she shot the bird an ugly look as they drifted beneath it.

An awkward silence descended over them when the gull quieted, and Eric cleared his throat. He continued rowing, something pinching his finger on the downswing. Eric shook out his hand. Pearl glanced in the water. The gull cried again.

"Wow," Eric muttered, "somebody should find that poor animal and put it out of its misery."

Pearl snorted. Her smile made his chest ache, and Eric rowed them away from the gull's tree. A rippling breeze rattled the grass. A branch brushed Eric's ear. The quiet was suddenly filled with the croaks and chirps of the creatures around them as if they were in a chorus hall and not a lagoon.

"Do you hear that?" Eric asked.

She shook her head, a strand of hair coming free of her bow, and Eric leaned in close. His fingers skimmed her cheek and pushed the strand behind her ear. She pressed against his hand. Her lips parted.

Eric pulled back, rowing harder. Focus. Focus. Focus. Talking was good. People did that.

"You know, I feel really bad not knowing your name," he said. "Maybe I could guess again."

She nodded, leaning on her knees.

"Is it Mildred?"

She stuck out her tongue and shook her head.

"Okay, no. How about Diana?" he asked. "Rachel?"

She slouched. Her eyes rolled up, and she didn't even bother shaking her head.

Were there any other names left? They had gone through a hundred at least in the last day, cycling through all sorts of common names and meanings. The music of the lagoon swelled around them, birds chirping and water dripping. It was an aria without a voice.

Aria . . .

"Ariel?" he asked, voice wavering. Perhaps they should start back at the A's.

She lunged forward and took his hand.

"Ariel?" He grabbed her, taken aback by her reaction. "Your name is Ariel?"

She nodded, nose scrunched up with a chuckling laugh.

"That's kind of pretty," he said. "Okay, Ariel."

He said it slowly, testing out the taste of her name, and smiled. Simple and pretty. Concise.

"Ariel," he whispered and held out his hand to her. "It's wonderful to meet you again."

Ariel closed the distance between them and took his hands in hers. They glided through a veil of willow branches, the leaves freckling her hair, and Eric gave in, the burning ache in his chest too great to ignore. His fingers plucked each leaf free and lingered at the nape of her neck. Fireflies floated through the air.

She was wild and beautiful, hair damp with the sea. As they stared at each other, her tongue wet her lips, and Eric couldn't help wondering what they would feel like against his own. They both leaned closer, her eyes fluttering shut. Eric reached for her, and—

The boat tipped. Eric went flying, tumbling face-first into the water. Cold shocked him, stabbing into his nose and throat, and he sunk to the bottom of the lagoon. He felt something slither by him, and he kicked at the ground. His feet struck silt.

He broke the surface and called out, "Ariel?" Brackish water splashed over his face, and he blinked it out of his burning eyes. Reaching out, he swept his arms across the water. "Ariel!"

She had already surfaced. Strands of red hair stuck to her face in clumps, floating in the water like tentacles around her. Her eyes were only just above the water, and she stared at him over the rippling waves.

"Are you all right?" he asked, swimming to her.

She nodded and bobbed in the water, but she didn't rise.

"Is your skirt weighing you down?" He moved to pick her up and froze.

He had almost kissed her.

He had almost kissed her.

Eric reared back. Ariel drifted toward him, and he couldn't hold back a flinch when she drew near. She stopped, treading water and unable to make any sort of sign, and he shook his head. Nausea bubbled in the back of his throat.

He had almost died, and yet he still wanted to reach out, cross the distance between them, and hold her. What was wrong with him?

"Let me," he said, and instead of pulling her into his arms, he offered her one hand. "Whoa, hang on. I've got you."

Still, his other curled around her waist, and he walked her to the edge of the water. She shook out her clothes and hair, delicate throat bare. She wasn't his true love. He couldn't do this.

"I'm so sorry," he said, pulling away from her the moment she was firmly standing. "Let's get back to the castle. That's probably enough touring for today."

12

Under False Colors

ERIC LEFT Ariel with Carlotta the moment they got back to the castle without even a goodbye. He knew it was rude, but he couldn't calm himself. This was exactly why he kept everyone at a distance, and now he couldn't focus on his upcoming voyage with Sauer and his mother's ghost. He spent the hour before he needed to leave for the ship checking his notes and writing Ariel a letter apologizing for his reaction to the near kiss. He could explain when he returned if she didn't go back home.

The thought of her leaving hit him harder than it should have.

Sauer's ship, *Siebenhaut*—though Sauer laughed at how Grimsby pronounced it—was a three-masted merchant ship outfitted like a frigate. Max padded onto the ship after Eric and nipped at Gabriella's heels as she paced the deck with Nora. The ghost of Eric's mother was tucked safely in the captain's quarters for now, out of sight from the people of Vellona, and Sauer met with Eric near the wheel. Vanni lingered nearby, out of place and unsure of what to do. He and Gabriella had insisted on accompanying him once they learned Sauer was ready to take Eric to find the Isle of Serein.

"I don't fully have a plan yet," Eric told Sauer.

The pirate sucked on their teeth and scowled into the setting sun. "I figured as much. I imagine we're of similar minds: that no matter what we should do, we should get a few hours away from Vellona before doing it?"

"Just so," said Eric, handing over one of his mother's maps. The light cast everything in a shade of scarlet that made his eyes hurt. "I think heading for this area is a good starting point. Then we can see what happens with . . . her."

Sauer nodded as if they regularly dealt in ghosts and witches and mysterious islands.

They set sail without much fanfare. Nora, her arms full of maps, and Gabriella joined them at the helm once they were a ways out. Max padded up and down the ship, sniffing along the rail, and Eric whistled him over. He didn't come.

"Let him roam," said Sauer. "Once we decide how to proceed and get to open ocean, I'd prefer he be below deck in case we need him out of the way."

"All right," Eric said. "Do you think we'll run into to trouble?"

Sauer snorted. "Did you or did you not mention killing a witch?"

Nora whistled, hugging the maps closer to her chest. "That explains a lot. We're not taking soldiers, though? You know, people who actually kill things for a living?"

"There are none to spare." Eric shook his head. "And given what I know of Sauer, I think your crew will be fine."

Max yelped on the other side of the quarterdeck, and Eric called him over.

"Fair," said Nora, glancing up at Sauer. "If you don't bring the prince back alive, his adviser will strangle you."

Sauer muttered something that might have been "couldn't reach my neck," and she elbowed them.

"Forget Grimsby, I'll strangle you." Vanni narrowed his eyes at Sauer. "Not that I think anyone is about to die on this excursion, but just so we're all in the know."

Still ignoring Eric, Max barked again.

"All right, if everyone is done defending my honor, we should discuss where we're going," said Eric.

"I need to talk to you about that." Nora's gaze darted to Sauer, and she braced herself. "I may not have told you everything I know about the Blood Tide."

Eric nodded. "I got that impression last time we spoke."

"Well, I didn't know you then, did I?" Nora said. "I wasn't going to tell you my life's story without getting all the information. Some prince sailing into the unknown and keeping his own secrets? Doesn't even matter. I'll tell you now."

That was more than fair. Max started barking again, and Vanni spun.

"Max!" he called. When he spotted what the dog was barking at, his face blanched. "Oh, well, that's not ideal."

They all turned at once. Max yelped and jumped around a damp Ariel hanging half out of a scupper hole. Ariel shushed Max with a gesture and pat on the head, and Vanni looked at Eric. When Eric didn't move, Vanni helped Ariel up. She beamed at him.

"What are you doing here?" Eric asked, voice pitching, and he paused to hold back his anger. He closed his eyes, took a breath, and opened them again, trying to calm his panicky heart. "I told you it would be best if you stayed."

Her smile fell, and she made several gestures he couldn't decipher.

Eric held up a hand. "I'm sorry. I don't know what that means, and I don't know what to do."

She frowned.

"Usually," Sauer said as Vanni and Ariel joined them near the wheel, "I kill stowaways."

Her frown twisted into such a bitter scowl Eric almost laughed.

"No one's killing anyone," said Eric. "Did you hang on to the hull?"

Ariel nodded.

He stared at her. "How?"

Ariel frowned and grabbed the rail next to her, gripping the wood with her fingers. She shrugged, and Eric had to stifle the warm appreciation that washed over him. That would've required a ridiculous amount of strength.

"That's impressive," Gabriella said. "You're that shipwrecked girl?"

Ariel nodded at Gabriella and waved.

It was too late for them to turn back. Ariel was going to be traveling with them to kill this witch now, and the idea of dragging her into danger terrified Eric. Everything was already happening; Ariel's presence was the last thing this voyage needed.

"All right, all right," he said. "Here's what's going

to happen, if I may?" He looked to Sauer, and the pirate nodded. "Nora and I will discuss the Blood Tide and what we are going to do. Ariel, please stay on the deck with Max until we're done."

She looked confused but nodded. Then she stepped toward him, and Eric stepped away from her. He frowned, all too aware of how ridiculous he looked, and headed for the captain's quarters.

Gabriella and Vanni followed Eric into the captain's quarters. Nora lingered on the deck, telling them she'd join in once she'd talked to Sauer. The room was crowded but lush. There was a bed on one wall draped with a thick quilt, and worn pillows covered the chairs. Eric paced between the table and bed, palms pressed into his eyes.

"What was that about?" Gabriella asked him. "I know Ariel being here isn't ideal, but if she was ship-wrecked, she at least knows her way around a boat."

"I almost kissed her today," Eric said, and threw his hands up. "I don't even know if she's been on a ship. She can swim, I think, but we are heading to kill a witch. This is just another worry, and—"

Vanni held up a hand. "Wait, what was that

first thing you said, because I know it wasn't what I heard?"

"I almost kissed her," whispered Eric.

"What?" Vanni covered his face with his hands and screamed into them. "Why?"

Gabriella collapsed into one of the chairs and dropped her head between her knees. "You nearly kissed a girl who you just met? When'd you even have the time?"

"When I showed her around Cloud Break earlier," said Eric. "We didn't, thankfully, but I was an inch away from dying."

"Kissed her!" Vanni threw up his hands. "Eric! What part of your curse did you not understand?"

"I know!"

He'd nearly died. A pretty face. A beautiful day without worry. A promise of understanding and a confidante in Ariel, and he had nearly kissed her. It made him so anxious he felt sick.

"Well, hold on," Gabriella said. "Calm down. You didn't, and you're aware you're attracted to her now, so don't do it again."

Eric rolled his eyes. "You say it so easily."

"I would hope not kissing people is easy," she said. "I'm more interested in why we're going after this witch when you're dead sure this woman who saved you is real and your true love. Finding her would probably involve less murder!"

Eric tried to find the words and failed. He swallowed and whispered, "What if I'm wrong? How can I ever trust myself enough to even try? It's a certain death. I at least stand a chance at this."

He retreated to the far side of the table and curled up on one of the chairs.

Vanni approached him, hands out, and said gently, "And if we kill the witch first, you won't be afraid, because the curse will be gone. You'll be able to actually fall in love with someone."

Eric nodded. He wouldn't be terrified or have to be as cautious, and he could go out and meet anyone. Everyone. His emotions wouldn't be a knife in the back. He could fall in love with anyone he wanted, even Ariel.

The thought made him feel dizzy.

"And Grimsby wonders why you're afraid to get married." Gabriella scoffed. She stepped next to him and touched his shoulder. "You good to discuss the Blood Tide?"

Eric inhaled through his nose, exhaled with a whistle, and nodded.

Gabriella stuck her head out the door and got Nora, who looked at all of them with narrowed eyes as she entered. Gabriella perched on the back of a chair, and Vanni sat on her feet. Eric tapped the large map pinned to the table.

"So what did you want to share?" he asked.

"I'm going to say what I think, and then I'll explain why I might be right," Nora said, her body stiff. "I think the Blood Tide's a path that will take us to the Isle of Serein."

"You think that the Blood Tide leads to the Isle of Serein?" asked Eric, leaning forward. "Why? How?"

"Look—I can't prove this with anything. I tried to find some information with Gabriella while we were in Cloud Break, but you're going to have to take my word on it," she said, hand tapping frantically against her thigh. "What I didn't tell you before was that I saw the Blood Tide long before anyone else on this ship."

Eric did his best to hide his surprise and waited for her to continue. Nora circled a wide stretch of sea to the north of Cloud Break that touched Vellona, Riva, Altfeld, and Sait on the main map laid out on the table. Her hands shook.

"The Blood Tide's an old bedtime tale in the towns along this coast," she said. "So if the Blood Tide and the Isle of Serein are connected, it is probably here."

"That's a huge swathe of well-explored sea," said

Eric, watching her face shift between panicked and stoic. "We know there is no island there. Not to mention that would be at least ten days' voyage."

"I don't think we'll have to actually travel far to follow the tide," Nora said. "I think it's magic."

"Magic?" Gabriella echoed. Her brows furrowed. Nora nodded.

"Now, so far as I can tell, my mother and I were some of the Blood Tide's first victims," said Nora, and she swallowed before bracing herself against the table. The room fell silent. "I was raised in Riva by this old man named Edo. The Blood Tide was one of those stories adults told to keep kids in line—don't go into the water at dawn or dusk 'cause the Blood Tide will come in and take you away. Don't wish for things only magic could gift you. The way Edo told it, desperate people used to wade out, offer up blood to the sea, and make a deal with something in the depths so that they could live their wildest dreams. The costs, though, were always souls."

"But what is the something?" Eric sat in one of the spare chairs. "The ghosts? A witch?"

"Having lived through the ghosts plenty, I don't think they're behind anything. I think they're fishing lures. No clue who the fisher is, but based on what you've told me, I would bet your witch," said Nora. "The ghost ship takes people with it when it leaves. We don't know where, but we know it comes and goes on the Blood Tide. I think the tide is a path of sorts. That it's how the ghost ship gets to you no matter how far away you are."

Eric, Vanni, and Gabriella looked at each other. Nora's words made sense and would explain how the ghosts were able to come and go across the sea. Gabriella cleared her throat and hesitantly asked, "What did you mean that you and your mother were the first victims?"

"I don't remember it very clearly. I only know for certain what Edo told me, but he reminded me so often it all feels like my own memories."

Eric nodded. He had never met his father, but sometimes he thought he could remember him. He had been told enough stories about him to hear the bark of his laugh and seen enough portraits to picture his face. All of it was wishful thinking that felt far too real.

"I was only five or six, Edo said." Nora paused and closed her eyes. "When the Blood Tide killed my mother and me."

Eric's heart dropped to his stomach. "What?"

"Killed you?" Gabriella said. "But you're right here."

"Wouldn't be if the Blood Tide had its way." Nora ran the back of her hand across her mouth, looking slightly sick. "I don't tell this story often. It's hard to explain."

"Right," said Eric, trying to hide his shock. "Sorry. Continue."

"It was dusk, when the water was red as the sky, and my mother and I were drowning," said Nora. "I don't remember how we got there, but I do remember being underwater and seeing her sinking. She pushed me up to the surface, but I passed out. According to Edo, who was on the shore when it happened, someone pulled me onto the beach and got me breathing again. He always told me that it was the Blood Tide that tried to kill us, and that it would try again if I ever went back into the ocean."

"So," said Gabriella, "you died at sea and then got right back on the sea?"

"I was too important to stay dead," Nora said. "And I didn't join Sauer till a few years ago. Stowed away and annoyed them till they let me stay. I've still never been in the ocean. I learned to swim in a lake, and Triton has been kind enough to spare our ship from any wrecks."

Eric shook his head. It was a wild tale, and if he hadn't already encountered half of it, he wouldn't have believed it. "But why do you think the witch is behind the Blood Tide?"

"Because I have one other memory from that day." Nora took in a breath. "I thought I had imagined it at first or made it up in some nightmare. I saw a woman walking on the blood-red water toward a shimmering isle too pretty to be real."

Eric tried to picture it, his eyes widening in understanding. "You think the water isn't just a path for the ghosts, but that it leads to the island," he said.

"She vanished after the first few steps. I always thought I'd dreamed it, half dead and delirious, but with your talk of a witch and an Isle of Serein, it's what I've got." Nora took a deep breath and then fixed Eric with a stare. "That's why I'm thinking the only way we can find your witch is to make a deal with your mother's ghost and have her lead us to the Isle of Serein using the Blood Tide."

13
One Step Closer

*I*T TOOK some convincing, but it made sense. If the Blood Tide was how the ghost ship traveled, then they would have to follow it themselves to see where they were traveling from. Nora reasoned that the only way to do that was to trigger the Blood Tide, and they had access to one of the ghosts. Eric's greatest desire was to find the Isle. He could spill blood in the water and let his mother's ghost tempt him, and then the crew could follow her—or the ghost ship, if it appeared—to wherever she went after he made the deal. If anything went wrong, Sauer's crew knew how to stop the ghosts. They would simply play music if Eric was in danger.

Although it was far from a perfect plan, Eric was on board. Sauer took longer to talk into it. They weren't so sure their boat could follow the same path as the ghost ship since it wasn't magical. There was only one way to find out, though.

They decided to sail for another hour until they

were far enough away from Cloud Break Bay that there was no risk of the ghost ship heading there. Ariel lingered at the edge of the forecastle as Eric discussed the plan with Sauer. She played fetch with Max, glancing at them every now and then. Eric nearly missed Sauer saying they should go ahead and move his mother's ghost to the deck.

"Ariel." Eric approached her once everyone else around them had dispersed to get ready for what came next. "Can I talk to you?"

She nodded and followed after him, gesturing at Max to sit.

The little traitor did, and Eric couldn't help smiling.

"I'm sorry that I was annoyed by you stowing away, but this is a dangerous voyage." He led her to the crate holding his mother's ghost. "This is going to sound odd, but I am currently attempting to find an isle that is the home of a witch. She's hurt too many people to be allowed to live, and on top of all of that, we think she has been luring people to her using ghosts."

Ariel let out a little squeak and clutched her throat.

"One of the ghosts is my mother," he said, removing the canvas covering the crate, "so, Ariel, may I introduce you to either an illusion or what is left of my mother, Eleanora of Vellona."

Ariel gasped and stepped back. Her eyes swept up and down his mother's translucent form, settling on her expressionless face. Ariel waved a hand before her, but his mother's ghost didn't even flinch. Ariel looked back at him.

"In an hour, we will essentially follow her to the Isle of Serein. Or we will get attacked when the other ghosts show up." He sighed and tossed the canvas aside, his mother's ghost as stoic here as she had been in Cloud Break. "It's a toss-up."

Wiping her eyes, Ariel gestured from his to his mother's face and smiled. His heart lurched, and Eric ducked. Ariel was a threat to him through no fault of her own. He wanted to hold her; he wanted to dunk himself in another lagoon to escape her. He could do neither, though, and knowing more about magic and witches was a necessity.

"We did look alike," he said. "I wish you could've met her before . . ."

He gestured to her ghost, and Ariel moved to touch his shoulder, then pulled back.

The strongest of Sauer's crew came over and moved his mother's crate to the deck. Eric waited for them to finish and then beckoned Ariel toward the prow.

They walked there in silence. The sky before them

was a hazy shade of darkening blue, sun drowning on the horizon. She came to stand beside him, and he took a half step away from her. Ariel glanced down at their feet and then up at him, an eyebrow raised. He shrugged and gestured to the deck. They sat.

"So, the lagoon back home. When we nearly kissed," he said, hoping his voice came out less awkward than he felt. "I know I acted strangely after. It's silly to even say, but it's me, not you. There's simply a lot happening in my life—I don't think I can explain it all yet—but I'm sorry we capsized and then I just left."

Her mouth opened in an *oh* of surprise, and she nodded, setting a small cloth bundle she'd been hiding under her coat between them. From it, she pulled out two slices of hard bread covered in thin slivers of marbled capocollo, halved figs, and honey. She must have gotten them from Vanni while Eric was with Sauer. He sniffed and caught the sharp sting of garlic and peppers in the honey. Eric stared at the food and realized he hadn't eaten since before the lagoon.

"Thank you," he said, suddenly unbearably guilty over dismissing her wanting to go on this voyage, and over letting her stay. "We should've come up with a better way of communicating before trying to have a conversation about complicated things."

She laughed and made the gesture again.

"You're sorry?" Eric asked.

One knock.

She held up a slice of bread to his mouth. He hesitated, leaning away slightly. Embarrassment flashed across her face for a moment, and she instead took a small bite of the bread. He winced and picked up a fig drizzled with honey. She froze.

"Here—try this."

She was trying, despite being an unknown person in an unknown land, and this was as good a time as any for Eric to try, too. Soon they wouldn't have the chance to discuss what had happened and go on delightful dawn tours. Ariel took the fig from him with two fingers and ate it in one bite. Her eyes lit up.

"Well," Eric said, "if dangerous, depressing adventures don't keep you in Vellona, maybe the food will."

She laughed and scrunched up her nose. The daylight continued to leach away, the time to beckon the Blood Tide growing closer. Eric ran his fingers over his arm even though the notes weren't there anymore. He had to be brave.

"I have trouble getting close to people," he said, "and letting them get close to me."

He usually never talked about it. With Vanni

and Gabriella, it felt too much like the little princeling whining. Grimsby would have scoffed at him, and Carlotta, whenever he broached his feelings, got that look in her eyes and patted his head like he was a five-year-old or Max. Even that single sentence to Ariel felt too silly to consider, but she didn't laugh. Ariel let out a long breath through her nose and nodded. She used her hands to draw a circle in the air between them and then rocked her hand like a boat.

"Exactly. At the lagoon, I realized we were getting closer, and I panicked. There is a lot going on in my life. Adding a new person was more than I could handle." He gestured to the ship. "To be honest, I probably won't have time to deal with my issues letting people get to know me for a while yet."

Holding out both of her hands palms up, she let them rest on top of the bundle between them. She didn't touch him, didn't demand an explanation as to why he had trouble, and didn't dismiss it and try to prove she was the exception. Eric hesitantly laid one of his hands atop hers.

"I will try to move past my awkwardness as regards to getting close to people," he said. "To you, really. Everyone else is still exhausting."

She smiled and pointed at herself. One hand lifted to

the sun, and she moved it in an arc as if it were setting. She held out that hand to him.

"You'll give me time to do that?" he asked.

She raised one finger, and he laughed.

"Thank you. I appreciate it," he said, and held out his hand. "Friends?"

She paused for a second. Slowly, she took his hand and mouthed, "Friends."

Ariel gave him a small smile, but Eric couldn't help noticing the disappointment on her face. His heart rate quickened, but he did his best to ignore it.

"Good," said Eric. He leaned against the rail. "I cannot believe you climbed up the side of the ship bare-handed."

Ariel shrugged and flexed one arm. Eric glanced over his shoulder to look out at the sea. It was a good day to sail, the water smooth and the waves small, but he still couldn't image swimming out from the dock and clinging to the side. Beneath them, dolphins glided next to the ship, a few diving deep and breaking the surface in graceful leaps. A speedy yellow and blue fish zigzagged between the dolphins.

"I've never seen one like that," he said, pointing to the little fish. "Have you?"

Ariel smiled at the bright little fish and tossed a dried apricot piece out ahead of the ship. The fish darted for it.

She rapped once against the deck and leaned against the rail, a sad smile on her face.

"Is it one of the fish from where you're from?" he asked. "Or do you have a little school of fish following you everywhere?"

She laughed and made several motions as if teaching a class.

Eric snorted, and Ariel doubled over in silent laughter. She looked livelier at sea. The wind curled her hair around her shoulders and pinkened her cheeks. The reflection of the waves in her deep blue eyes felt fuller. The white crests were whiter. The silver of the dolphins gleamed.

Footsteps approached behind them, and Eric turned. It was Gabriella and Vanni, Nora a few steps behind them and holding a knife.

"It time?" Eric asked.

Gabriella nodded. "No time like the present."

The five of them made their way to his mother's ghost. The crew had dismantled the crate and placed the salty piece of the ghost ship in one of the small rowboats so that they would be able to see her among the waves. Eric stopped before the ghost, and she shimmered. Her eyes focused on him.

"Our plan, so that we are all clear, is for me to offer up some of my blood to trigger the Blood Tide and hope that she leads us down it to the Isle," he said. "And we think she's going to row?"

Nora made a noncommittal sound. "They usually take the fastest option available, and they do sail an entire merchant ship."

"With magic," said Eric.

"And," Sauer said loudly, holding up a gnarled finger, "if the other ghosts don't show up, perhaps she'll take the rowboat."

Eric sighed. Worst came to worst, they would just have to follow his mother walking atop the waves.

"What if my mother's ghost compels me to do something?" asked Eric.

Nora shrugged. "Closest person to you throws a punch. Problem solved."

They lowered the rowboat to the sea. Eric accepted the clean knife from Nora and backed away toward the starboard rail. Still, the eyes of his mother's ghost followed him. Carefully, he nicked the pad of his left finger and let a few drops of blood splash down into the water. A trail of red shot through the darkening sea to the horizon. His mother's ghost turned from inside the boat.

The ghost of Eleanora of Vellona didn't waver. Her hands gripped the oars, forcing them forward and back. She made no sounds of effort, and her expression didn't change. Eric leaned over the ship to keep her in his sight. The scarlet of sunset spread out before her, and the barrelman shouted to Sauer. Most of the crew peered down at her as well, whispering to each other. Gabriella and Vanni flanked him. Even Max poked his head between Eric's legs to see.

His mother followed a path of deep, dark red that cut through the water and led off toward the horizon.

"There's something out there," said Sauer. "My crow's got an eye on it."

The line of Eric's blood, darker and somehow deeper than the rest of the water, seeped out from beneath his mother's boat. She kept an exhausting pace, no wave slowing her down. She didn't look tired or hungry; the only expression he could occasionally glimpse on her face was grief. She rowed as if everything she wanted was just out of reach. Eleanora of Vellona had been a force to be reckoned with. This was her determination reduced to a single, unfathomable focus.

And the sudden, terrible idea that this really was his mother in some way took root in his soul. He had to free her.

"Help us all," said Sauer. "Look at the sky."

Eric did. Heavy gray clouds gathered above them, lightning flickering from storm to storm. The sky was the color of Grimsby after an hour at sea, and the ocean roiled as badly as the old man's stomach. The sickly smear where red water met green skies darkened and blurred, fog white as bone oozing out across the waves. Ariel grabbed Eric's hand and pointed it toward the waters directly beneath them. Max howled.

Eels rose up from the water and twisted around his mother's boat. She rowed another powerful stroke along the blood-red path, and dozens more writhing eels tore through the surface of the red water. They gnawed at the wood of the boat and sunk once she passed. Their presence unnerved something deep in Eric.

Eels didn't swim in open waters like this. They hid in caves and crevices, waiting until their prey came to them.

"The fog has never looked like this before." Nora snatched a monocular from Sauer's pocket and pressed it against her eye. "That's magic if I've ever seen it."

Sauer stomped away from the rail. "Follow her!"

Eric inhaled sharply. How quickly was she rowing to outrun a ship? Ariel leaned so far over the rail he feared she would fall, and she looked between his mother's ghost and the horizon. A worried wrinkle appeared between her brows.

"There was no ship in that fog," said Nora. She looked up at Eric. "We might have done this right."

"She didn't offer me a deal or compel me," said Eric with a shudder. "Why not?"

"My previous guess that her ghost recognizes you still stands," Sauer offered.

Ariel touched Eric's arm and gestured to the fog.

"We'll lose her in the fog," Eric said. "Or bypass her and lose sight of her in our wake."

Ariel's fingers tightened and she tugged his arm.

Eric's mother vanished behind a tall wave, and he moved to get a better look. "We have to do something."

Ariel tapped his shoulder once and grabbed one of the mooring lines on the deck.

Eric turned back to Ariel. His brows furrowed in confusion. "She can't hold on to a—"

But before he could finish his sentence, Ariel backed up, kicked off her boots, and took a running leap over the side of the ship.

Eric threw himself against the rail as the sound of a

splash met his ears. He looked for Ariel among the eels, but he couldn't spot her against the waves. He started taking off his boots.

"There!" Sauer pointed toward the ghost.

Ariel's red hair was a beacon among the eels, and they parted where she swam. Her movements were sloppy at first, her legs flailing behind her as if not used to the water, but in just a few seconds she seemed to grow comfortable and began gliding through the ocean with ease. Heart hammering against his chest, Eric tried to spy any wounds but couldn't spot any from this far away.

Sauer hummed. "What's she doing?"

Ariel waved back at them. His mother's ghost was barely more than a shimmer against the waves. Ariel swam after her, already nearing the rowboat. She pulled herself into the boat next to his mother's ghost and waved to them. She knotted the rope around the seat.

The rope would keep them from losing his mother's ghost.

Sauer let out a low whistle. "She sure has guts."

A flush of affection surged through Eric, and he gripped the rope. The sky turned to a fog-mottled pale green, and a minute later, the fog blanketed the ship. It softened everything till Eric couldn't hear the sails or see Sauer's bright red hat next to him. Eric tugged hard twice on the rope, and two sharp tugs answered him. All he knew was that the ship was moving and the rope was still connecting him to Ariel. A flicker of light lit the fog.

"Sauer!" Eric shouted. "Do you see that?"

The light grew so bright Eric winced. Sauer's answer echoed unnaturally in the fog, incomprehensible and distant.

The bowsprit broke through the wall of fog. Sunlight seared into the wood. They emerged atop a quiet, clear sea, and the warm beams of a noon sun burned away the fog. A few stray wisps clung to the ship.

"Magic," Eric said and brushed a tendril of fog from his shoulder.

Gabriella slammed into the rail next to him. "You all right?"

"I'm good," he said, ruffling Max's fur as the dog whined at his feet. "Everyone else?"

"All good."

"Ariel!" Eric shouted. "You all right?"

From her spot behind his mother's ghost, Ariel lifted one arm and flexed. Gabriella let out a laugh next to him.

"Look," she said, "if she's not your true love, I'm not as picky."

Eric bristled and hated himself for it. "Stick with your thief."

He tugged the green scarf looped around her neck, and she flicked his cheek.

"You're missing the forest for the trees," she said. "Look ahead."

Eric frowned and turned. Beyond Ariel loomed an island. A maelstrom of fog swirling with shadows that might have been ships or storms or ghosts encircled the island and trapped them in this odd, bright noon. A thin trail of red cut through the water before his mother's ghost and ended on the shore of the Isle of Serein.

It was a crescent of lush greens and sandy browns in the middle of the open ocean. The island itself wasn't large; what looked like a glass-green lagoon took up most of its center, but the lagoon was hidden behind tall trees heavy with oranges. They swung in the breeze, littering the ground with ripe fruit. Brambles thick with berries grew all the way down to the rocky shore.

"A paradise," Gabriella whispered.

Not a paradise. Not a coincidence. He was right—it was all connected.

"The Isle of Serein," said Eric, heart soaring. "We found it."

14
The Isle of Serein

*H*IS MOTHER reached the Isle of Serein first. She hesitated for the first time on the shore, water splashing against her feet. She was far more solid now; looking at her was like looking at a frosted window. Ariel waited in the rowboat. Sauer, Gabriella, Vanni, and Eric were the only ones from the crew brave enough to go ashore. Even Max hid down in the hull with his paws over his eyes.

"Don't trust it," one sailor muttered as she helped lower the shore boat to the water. "No birds."

She was right—there wasn't a single bird on the island or gliding overhead. The thick wall of fog and wind probably kept them out.

Eric couldn't sit still, tapping out his savior's tune on his leg as they rowed the small boat toward the isle. Gabriella grabbed his hand.

"It'll be fine," she murmured, but she still nervously tugged at Nora's green scarf holding back her curls.

"It's beautiful," Eric said, still shaking despite her grip. "There might be anything in those trees, though."

As they got closer to the island, they reached where Ariel and his mother's ghost had stopped. Ariel slipped from the other boat and climbed in next to Eric. He held up a dry coat he had brought for her.

"Are you all right?" he asked.

She held up one finger and bundled her soaked hair onto the top of her head.

"We couldn't see anyone on the island from our ship," he told her, "but the witch might be hiding in the lagoon or on the other side."

Sauer's crew was still readying for a fight and turning the ship for a broadside, and even Gabriella had borrowed a rifle for their trip to the isle's shores. Ariel eyed it.

"She's ruined a lot of lives," Eric said. "I want to make sure she can't ruin any more."

The sword sheathed at his side felt heavier than it ever had before. He had been in plenty of fights, sparring and serious, but never had he killed anyone. This witch couldn't be left alive. He knew that. She had killed. Worse than killed, even.

But the idea of plunging a sword through her chest

filled him with dread instead of triumph. Even now, thinking about it felt like some distant nightmare, not reality.

"Let's go." Sauer checked their pistol and straightened their hat. "Stay vigilant. I know we're here to fight, but first sign of trouble, remember that our firepower is on the ship."

They barely had to row anymore. The currents around the island beached them on the white sand that formed the outer side of the crescent. When they reached the shore, the unnaturally warm water rippled around Eric as he climbed out of the boat. Seagrass greener than he had ever seen grew in the shallow water, tangling around his legs. Ariel trudged out of the surf with him.

The moment his feet left the water and landed on the dry sand, Eric turned to look at where they had left his mother's ghost in the other rowboat, but her form had vanished. He took in a shaky breath, and Ariel took his hand.

"I'm fine, but thank you," Eric whispered to her. "Are you all right?"

A few bruises were blooming across one shoulder where an eel must have hit her during her swim toward the rowboat, but she waved off his concern.

"And thank you for that." Eric wrapped the coat around her and buttoned it beneath her chin. "Please don't do it again, though. I couldn't . . . I don't want you to get hurt because I'm hung up on ghosts."

It had been a brave, irresponsible thing to do. If they had lost track of his mother, would they have been in the fog forever? Would they have ended up on some other isle? Would the magic have spat them out? Would nothing have happened? It was better not knowing.

"I guess I should have let you come with us from the beginning," he said. "You're clearly at home on the sea and know what you're doing. I am sorry for not believing in you."

Ariel smiled up at him and pointed into the narrow line of trees. He took her hand. She was brave, and it made him feel braver.

"Stay close," he said, and looked at the others. Gabriella and Sauer were inspecting the rocks a few steps from the water. Vanni had set up in the boat with a spyglass and a pistol. "Let's go find this witch."

Vanni stayed in the boat to watch their backs and start rowing if they needed to make a quick getaway. Gabriella followed Eric and Ariel, and Sauer brought up the rear, leaving a trail of stones behind them despite the island's small size. Ariel peered up at the trees and raised a hand to Eric. He stopped beneath one of the larger fruit trees.

"Everything seems normal." Eric shuddered. His quiet voice only made the lifeless silence of the island more noticeable. "We were definitely transported here by magic. Given how long we sailed and where we started, we're too close to Vellona for this island to be undiscovered, but every map marks this place as open ocean."

"It looks like a regular island, and I don't hear anything that sounds like a witch," Gabriella whispered.

Sauer swept the isle with their pistol. "Silence is worse. How do we know if she's here or not?"

"We keep going," said Eric.

The trees followed the crescent shape of the Isle. The little wood wasn't too thick, but it still felt dark and deep. Eric glanced over his shoulder, and the shore seemed farther away than he would have thought. Ariel ran her fingers over a grapevine braided into the branches of the trees, plucking a single grape and sniffing it. She dropped it to the ground and shrugged at him. A normal enough grape, then.

"Apples wouldn't grow here naturally," said Gabriella, tapping a fallen one with her boot.

Sauer twisted an apple from one of the trees, peeled

the flesh back, and sunk their thumb through the meat of the fruit. They tossed it aside and wiped their hand clean. "This isle seems more like a pantry than a home, but I think it would be best if we didn't partake."

"Agreed," Gabriella muttered, crouching next to a rosemary bush. She picked up a crab's leg that was as long as her arm. "This one had to have been caught in deeper waters. It would've been huge. Bigger than any I've seen near Vellona."

It was cracked and twisted at the joints like how Chef Louis prepared them for supper. Dozens more crab husks littered the ground beneath the overgrowth, and empty oyster shells glittered in the sunlight. Eric prodded the pile.

"Lots of shells," he said, "but nothing alive here."

"Not even bugs," said Sauer.

They came to a veil of twisted branches and thick green leaves that separated the small fruit grove from the lagoon. Sauer pushed Eric behind them and readied their pistol. They held up three fingers and dropped one. Ariel gripped Eric's hand. The second finger dropped. Gabriella brought her rifle to her shoulder.

Sauer shoved through the branches. The lagoon was still and empty, water lapping at the sand. No people, animals, or witches appeared. Only junk rested in it.

A sharp, bitter disappointment filled Eric. He took a deep breath and tried to calm himself.

"Let's check the whole place," he said. "Just in case."

Surely she was here and hiding. But they crossed the Isle of Serein once more, even checking back in with Vanni, and found nothing other than an abandoned lagoon. There was no trace of the witch.

Eric had been so certain she would be here, that this would be the answer to all of his problems. She was supposed to be here. The disappointing silence of the Isle pressed in on him until all he could hear was the endless rush of waves and the pounding of his own heart. This was what Grimsby must have felt each time he set foot on a ship.

Uneasy, sickening dismay.

Eric had failed.

"Forgive me, Your Highness," said Sauer as they all came to rest near the grove of trees after their third pass, "but I'll consider finding the island and not dying to a witch a win. What now?"

Eric sighed. Even now, upset by his inability to complete the task his mother had left for him, the lack of a fight made him breathe easier. There was less danger and less of a chance anyone would get hurt. He laughed and opened his eyes. Nothing was ever easy.

Happy to kill her. Unhappy to kill.

Were all his emotions contradictory and confusing?

"It'll be all right," said Gabriella, coming up alongside him. "If not today, then we'll try again. There's still a chance that this isle can tell us more about her."

Ariel patted Eric's shoulder and nodded.

"But where is she?" Eric asked. "What's she doing? Does she even still come here? How are we—"

"You know I don't have the answers to those questions, right?" Gabriella swept one arm up and around. "We're working with the same information, Eric, and all we can deal with is what we have."

Waving to the lagoon, Ariel beckoned for them to explore it more thoroughly.

Eric slumped. "You're right. I guess let's see what we can figure out about her from what's here."

"That's the spirit." Gabriella clapped him on the back. "Maybe she keeps a diary of all of her weaknesses."

Eric snorted and walked with her to the lagoon. It was wide and deep, and a giant rock rose up out of the middle. He had seen it during their initial scouring of the Isle, but now he was close enough to see the damp stains on it as if something sat there often. Sauer and Eric rolled up their trousers to their knees, took off their boots, and waded into the crystal clear pool. The bottom of it was carpeted in emerald seagrass, urns, and antique pistols, none of it organized in any discernible way. Ariel and Gabriella walked around the edges of the pool.

"Something over here." Sauer trudged to the deepest part of the lagoon and paused. "Huh. Well, the witch has taste, even if she is keeping it all submerged."

Eric walked past a driftwood shelf of various cosmetics from every country and hesitated when he saw the little collection of art Sauer was standing over. It was in a small nook of rocks half-submerged in the water and shaded by a tall plum tree. A bench was underwater at the center of the nook, perfectly placed for lounging in the warm water and studying the pieces. Sauer pointed to a statue of a reclining god holding a shepherd's crook and torn-open pomegranate in their hands.

"That was stolen decades ago," they said. "Same as this."

They tapped a cracked stone tablet sitting in the water like a gravestone next to the bench. A ring, as if from a cold cup, stained the top of it. Eric tilted his head to the side to study the slightly lopsided carving of a bound, bearded figure.

"It's one of the northern gods, I think," said Sauer. "I have a print similar to it."

"This is from Sait," Eric said, and pointed to a large

portrait. The figure in it was an opera singer and fencer who had vanished into the countryside after her wife passed. "What's it covered in?"

He touched the cloudy white coating covering the picture and caught part of it under his nails.

"Wax," he muttered. The other portraits were covered in it, too. "Well, this witch likes her art."

"Same here." Sauer ran their fingers along a small statuette of two men, one in the ancient armor of the kingdom to the southeast of Vellona carrying the limp form of the other.

Eric cleared his throat. "Maybe steal it after she's dead."

"There's an idea," muttered Sauer.

"Eric?" Gabriella called, and got his attention. She used a stick to prod a rock near the narrowest part of the island, where only a reef white as teeth separated the sea from the lagoon. "I think there's a cave under here."

"Is there an entrance?" Eric waded back toward her.

Gabriella shook her head and tossed the stick aside. "Under the rock, I think, but it's too big to move. It looks like it was placed here on purpose, and the ground beneath it is scratched."

From the other side of the pool, Ariel waved her

arms. Eric met her at the edge of the lagoon. Her damp skirts made it hard for her to walk in the loose sand, and the green fabric stuck to her legs and looked like a tail. Eric offered her his arm.

"What's wrong?" he asked, leading her away from the water.

She held up two fingers and pointed to the opposite side of the pool, where he hadn't searched yet. There was no art displayed there, but there was a large, flat rock near the water. Eric circled the lagoon to it and laughed. Set into the rock was an old sea glass bottle of ink, and a fish skeleton rested next to it, the spine whittled down like a nib. A leaf of fish skin thinned and smoothed like vellum with the words *where is she?* seared into it fluttered on the rock. Eric touched the bone nib.

"The ink's still wet," he said. "Whoever wrote this was here recently."

Sauer looked up from their inspection of the driftwood shelf. "Then they might return even more quickly or be gone for ages. I understand wanting to wait to see if it is her, but the idea of remaining on a powerful witch's island overnight does not fill me with confidence."

"That's fair," said Eric. He rubbed his face. "All right—I don't know how close my mother got to finding and killing her, but I doubt she made it this far or knew what the Blood Tide was before she died since she didn't leave it in her note. We know how to find the Isle and avoid the ghosts now. That is more than we knew before. We can leave, lure the ghost ship to us, and trigger the Blood Tide again tomorrow, or something. Let's make this as worthwhile as possible for now and figure out everything we can about her."

Sauer nodded and used a mirror and hooded lantern to flash some sort of light signal at the ship, and they hummed happily at the quick flash of light that came in response. It wasn't any code Eric knew, but he guessed the three long flashes and three short meant "all clear." From this distance, Eric could barely make out Nora holding a large lantern aloft on deck.

"Sea's clear," they said. "Nothing approaching and no changes on the island except for us."

"Well, we know she's made other people angry, at least." Gabriella leaned down and read the note again. "People she knows well enough that they don't sign their names."

Ariel sniffed the ink, wiggled her fingers, and pointed at the sea. It took Eric a moment and some more gestures to get it.

"That's squid ink?" he asked, and she nodded. "Why would someone use pure squid ink?"

The Isle of Serein

He circled around the rock and nearly tripped over a chest half-buried in the sand. It was an old thing, thick wood carved so carefully that the pieces slotted together and there was no need for metal hinges. Eric touched the lid and came away with wax under his nails. It was thickest around the lid.

"I think I found something." Eric tried not to let his hope leak into his voice. This was the sort of chest people kept important documents and supplies in on ships. Watertight and buoyant, it would survive anything. Surely this was full of documents too fragile to be left in the elements. "It's covered in wax, too."

Gabriella, Sauer, and Ariel joined him. Eric got on his knees, running his hand along the whole of the chest. It was as wide as his wingspan and would have reached his thighs if it hadn't been buried.

"There's a sigil," he said, feeling the edges of an indention in the wax. It covered where a lock would have been. It was a series of odd circles in a pattern he didn't recognize. "I can't tell what it is."

Ariel leaned down next to him, her chin near his shoulder. She touched the indentation.

"Do you recognize it?" he asked.

Nodding, she drew an octopus in the sand. Eric chuckled.

"The suckers. Of course," he said. "It's the imprint of an octopus tentacle."

"She'll know it's been opened," said Sauer.

Gabriella shrugged. "Our original plan was to kill her. Does it matter if we break into a chest?"

"Brace yourselves in case it's magic." Eric dug his fingers into the wax and cracked open the lid. It stank of salt and stagnant water. A shiver washed over him, small and quick like the air before a storm, and the ground shuddered. Stone ground against stone, and the lagoon rippled. Something large and swift slammed into the reef separating the water from the sea, breaking free. A tail broke the surface and vanished. The lid to the chest popped open.

Ariel shot to her feet.

"What was that?" Sauer asked, pistol raised.

Ariel carefully pushed the barrel toward the ground. She drew a fish in the sand with her toe.

"If you're sure," said Sauer, but they kept their pistol in hand and swept their gaze around the Isle.

"I don't see anything." Gabriella climbed on top of the rock to look around. "Whatever is in there, look at it quickly."

The chest was stuffed with letters and maps. Eric shuffled through the top few and pulled out one with his mother's name on it.

"'We have no desire to see our world descend into war once again and possess neither the resource nor the stomach to engage in such a bargain,'" Eric read aloud. "The next part is smeared out—the ink got wet—but it says, 'We will not disregard our deal with Her Majesty, Queen Eleanora' here and there's a signature at the bottom. Benjamin Huntington, Duke of Wright."

Wright was up north in the kingdom of Imber, on the other side of Sait, and it had kept its deal with Eric's mother to not call in Vellona's debts until the storms let up. That had to be what this letter meant.

Sauer whistled. "Bold of Imber to refuse an offer from a witch like this."

"These must be all of the deals she's made or tried to make. Dozens of letters from different kingdoms," Eric said, picking up a different one. "Some offered her holdings in exchange for favorable weather. Some money. A lot of them are from Sait. They're giving her a title once her duty is done—one guess as to what her duty is."

This witch wasn't just the cause of his curse, but of every problem plaguing Vellona. Eric had been right— Sait had allied itself with a witch—but the idea of telling Grimsby *I told you so* had lost some of its appeal since finding the Isle and losing his mother's ghost.

"She's the reason all of Vellona is suffering." Eric's

hands shook, and he pocketed the letters from Sait thanking the witch for her work with the storms. "The date they sent this means the storm they're talking about is the one from last spring in Brackenridge. Forty-seven people died in the storm alone, and they're thanking her."

Ariel laid a hand on his shoulder and squeezed, but the touch only set him more on edge.

"I didn't realize I could hate someone this much," he whispered.

Ariel's hand slid from his shoulder, and she took the letters from his hands, handing what Eric hadn't read yet to Gabriella.

"For a sea witch," muttered Gabriella, rifling through the papers, "she isn't offering any of the kingdoms better sailing conditions or fishing. I wonder if the sea doesn't care for her much."

Ariel snorted.

"Why does she even want a title, though?" Eric asked. "She's a witch."

"It's a different kind of power." Gabriella stepped down from the rock. "To be recognized as noble isn't the same as being skilled enough at something to put fear into people."

"She'll have land in Altfeld, too," said Sauer, tapping

a letter Eric hadn't read. "They're giving her a holding on the coast once she gives them Riva."

Eric looked up at Sauer. "You see anything about the ghosts or curses?"

Knowing why Vellona was being targeted was all well and good, but it didn't help Eric or the kingdom. He needed a way to stop her.

He rifled through the rest of the letters and maps, and Sauer read the ones written in Altfeld's language.

"It looks like she was getting ready to send this one out," they said. "'The harvest has been bountiful, and the beauty of souls is that they require no maintenance other than a space to store them before use. My fields are full and lovely this time of year and far more valuable than your gold and coins. Call on me again once you know the true value of souls, handsome.'"

"Let's take the letters back with us," said Eric. "They're proof of who's been working with her and why. Gabriella, can you carry them?"

She nodded and gathered up the letters and contracts. Eleanora's name at the bottom of the chest caught his eye. Eric pulled the paperlike fish skin free from the pile. At the very top was his mother's name, and beneath it was his. There were only three others on the list, each one a ruler in another kingdom. His mother's name was crossed out.

"This is—"

The scent of rot choked him. Ariel gagged, covering her mouth with her shirt. A loud *thunk* echoed on the Isle, and a series of sickly splattering sounds followed it. Eric leapt to his feet. The trees were withering and their fruit browning in seconds. Sauer grabbed Eric's shirt.

"Time to go," they said. "Kill her later."

Eric nodded. They couldn't fight whatever was happening here.

The four of them ran back across the island. Vanni waved from the rowboat, face white with fear. Before their eyes, the Isle of Serein died. Green mold grew across gnarled trees, letting out puffs of sickly gray spores. Swathes of flies and beetles scurried over the sand, splashing into the rising tide. The group made it to their rowboat as the weakened trees behind them fell over. The seagrass was brown and wilted.

"Get in!" Sauer yelled, waving to Nora on the prow of the ship. "Row."

But Vanni was already rowing the boat frantically. Eric had one foot inside when something made him pause, and he pulled his foot out of the boat. He heard a familiar voice calling his name. It tugged at his heart and awoke a desperation so deep in him it hurt.

"My mother," Eric said, voice wavering. The world blurred and quieted until there was only the voice and his need to find her. "I forgot about my mother."

"What?" said Gabriella. "She's not here."

"Don't you hear her?" he asked, turning away from the boat. "There."

A ghostly figure rose from the sea. Grass as green as young wheat rippled around her, blades twisting about her legs. The sea boiled where it touched her, and Eric struggled to race through the water to her. A headache picked away at Eric's focus. She held out her hand to him, and Eric reached out to her.

"You have to save me, Eric." Her fingers passed through his. "Please. Help. A deal. She'll give me back for—"

A body slammed into his back. Red hair spilled over his shoulder and arms locked around his chest. Ariel's check pressed against his shoulder.

No, no, no, she tapped against his chest. *No.*

The shock, the pain, the memories—this wasn't his mother. It was a lure.

"You're not her," he said to the ghost. "You're not her and you don't know anything about me."

"Don't be ridiculous, sweetling," his mother's ghost said. "Please. Help me."

Eric took a step back. "My mother never called me that."

The ghost cocked her head to the side and froze.

"Well, then," she said in a voice so unlike Eric's mother's it chilled him to the bone. "You're a rude one, aren't you? I was curious as to what would happen if one of my little ghosts encountered someone they knew before I got ahold of them. Disappointing that it lets them fight my control, but here we are, face to face at last. I suppose her leading you here was good in that regard, at least."

"You!"

Glorious, terrible clarity cut through every thought in Eric's mind, and he threw himself forward. He barely felt Ariel slip from his shoulders. His fingers tore through the ghost, catching nothing. The ghost laughed.

"Give her back," Eric forced out through gritted teeth. "Let my mother's soul go!"

His fist passed through her again, and Ariel's hands gripped his other arm

"Give her back. Let her go," the ghost said, rolling her head back and forth. "So contradictory. Do you even know what you want?"

"Shut up, you monster!"

Here she was, the witch, before him finally, and he couldn't even touch her. The rage of uselessness burned in him. His heart thundered in his chest.

He had found her, and he could do nothing. No matter how much he wanted to kill her, he couldn't.

Weak. Inadequate. Powerless.

"If you wanted a monster, all you had to do was ask." Suddenly, her eyes were black as pitch and her mouth was a slash of red. The form wavered. "So hurtful."

"Hurtful? I'll show you hurtful!" He yanked away from Ariel and splashed toward the ghost again. "Where are you, you coward? Face me as yourself instead of using my mother's face for your sick games!"

"Oh, I would, sweetling, but I'm a bit tied up with more important business. Politics—you know how it goes," she said, and rolled her eyes. "But I should be in Vellona soon, and I would hate to get there before you. I mean, what would I even do?"

Fear froze him in place. She laughed at his horrified expression and shrugged, peering at him over a raised shoulder.

"So help me, if you do anything else to Vellona, I will kill you."

The witch wearing his mother's face laughed. "Anything else? But I've already done so much for it, and I have so much more planned since you're gone. See you soon, lover boy. I think I'll retire this ghost. Back in the bank with her, so to speak."

The ghost winked at him. Her face shimmered, fading back to Eleanora's stoic form. A ribbon of seagrass grew around her, coiling like a tentacle, and it burrowed into her chest. Her form spun and shrunk, bones cracking and mouth open in a silent scream. She condensed into a single smear of bright white light beneath the water. When it dimmed, all that was left in her place was a ragged brown blade of grass with two branches like flailing arms. It shimmered with trapped magic.

The fear and fury holding him in place snapped. Disappointment washed over him, and suddenly, he was exhausted. This trip had done nothing but turn the witch's attention toward Vellona, and there was no point in having gone after her if she hurt anyone else. What good was he if he had put Vellona in danger? His vengeance wasn't more important than his people.

A new dread gripped Eric.

"We have to go!" He grabbed Ariel and ran back to the boat. "She's heading to Vellona. We have to get there first."

I 5
Poor Unfortunate Souls

RIC AND Ariel threw themselves into the row-boat. There was a whine in Eric's ears, the squeal of a distant storm or swords scraping together. It was high and low at once, audible despite Sauer's loud questions in his ear.

"What was that?" they asked.

"It was the witch," Eric said, gripping the side of the boat with aching hands. "She spoke through my mother's ghost. She threatened Vellona. Said she might get there before me. She's heading for the bay. We have to beat her."

She was the curse. She was the storms. She was every pain and trouble that had struck Vellona in the last two decades, and she was heading for his home.

"Great." Vanni groaned and rowed faster, the oars slapping against the choppy waves. "Did we find anything useful?"

"More or less," said Gabriella.

Eric bowed over his legs and took several deep, slow breaths. Ariel gently touched his shoulder, the gesture more question than comfort. He snaked one hand between them and tapped her side. Her fingers curled around his shoulder and then moved to his hair, brushing the wet strands off his forehead. She was real and present and not some trick thought up by the ghosts. No; the witch, not the ghosts.

This was real.

It hadn't felt like he was being controlled. Good manipulation probably didn't feel like anything at all, but he remembered the odd haze that had taken him over last time. This time, it had felt natural. The drive to chase his mother's ghost had felt like *him*.

And that was terrifying.

"She called me lover boy, of all things," he said and straightened up. "Why would she do that?"

Gabriella blew him a kiss, and Ariel made a face.

"Get ready for the ropes." Panting, Vanni pulled them up alongside *Siebenhaut*. "We can be disgusted once we're on our way back home."

Two crew members tossed down the ropes and helped them up. The deck was in calculated disarray, people preparing to leave as fast as possible. Nora was halfway up the main mast, a twin to Sauer's spyglass in her hands, and the captain darted to her the moment their feet hit the deck. Vanni held Eric and Gabriella back once they were all on deck again.

"What happened?" Vanni asked.

"Nothing much beyond what you saw," said Eric. "She's the one behind the storms. Sait and other places are working with her, giving her titles in exchange for magic. She's been targeting Vellona for years."

"At least we know for sure now," muttered Vanni.

Ariel raced passed them to the other side of the ship. Eric slipped away from Vanni and followed her. She was leaning against the rail, ear tilted out of the wind and down toward the sea. Eric stopped beside her.

"What is it?"

Ariel tapped her ear.

"I don't hear anything," said Eric. "Hey! Nora, you see or hear anything out there?"

The girl shook her head and pressed the spyglass harder against her face.

Suddenly, something rammed them. The ship rolled dangerously low, people sliding across the deck and water sloshing over them. Ariel latched her arms around Eric, and they slipped down the deck to the rail. Eric could've kissed the waves, they were so close. Ariel braced and pointed into the depths. A dark shadow unfurled beneath the ship.

"Sauer!" Eric scrambled up the deck as the ship righted. "Sauer! There's something beneath us."

"You don't say," they said, dragging crew members to safety. "Brace! Who has it in their sights?"

"Port side," called Nora. "It's coming again!"

The ship rocked again, but the blow was weaker. Gabriella and Vanni skidded down the slant of the deck to Eric and passed him a sword. Gabriella offered Ariel a knife. Ariel wrinkled her nose.

Vanni snorted. "Fair point. What are we going to do—stab a whale?"

"No laughing," muttered Gabriella, "because we're all about to try shooting something the size of a whale."

Nora screamed. A slimy, slobbering sound surrounded them. She slid down the ropes, shouting words Eric couldn't comprehend. Sauer blanched, and a shadow rose up from under the ship. It blotted out the sun and oozed salt water onto the deck, the stench of the deep filling the air. Vanni gagged, and Ariel's breath escaped in a voiceless shriek. Eric's eyes finally focused on the writhing silhouette above them.

It was a malformed tentacle made up of eels. Hundreds of them were knotted together in one monstrous mass, the tangles so tight that blood rained. Mouths snapped open and closed every few feet, and a single eel worked its way free of the tentacle and fell, smacking onto the deck next to Vanni.

"I would rather fight a whale," he mumbled, nudging the thing out of the way.

The tentacle curled over the ship, snapping ropes and ripping away part of the sails, and gripped two of the masts tight. The wood creaked and groaned. The ship stopped turning away from the Isle.

"It's trying to keep us here," said Eric.

He leapt forward and sliced at the tentacle. He tore through the yellow belly of one of the eels, and it collapsed to the deck, dead. Gabriella and Vanni moved to help.

"Easier than the ghosts," Gabriella said, and cut away at a tangle of them.

The knot of three smashed against the deck, and Ariel picked up two by the tails, flinging both back into the sea. Her hands came away covered in a gray, gelatinous slime. All across the deck, people were kicking and throwing eels into the water, shaking the slime from their hands, or cutting away at the large tentacle wrapping from port to starboard.

Eric ran to the port-side rail, and a light caught his eye. Beneath the ship, a spark of electricity flashed from the depths. It jumped from eel to eel and grew in size as it neared the eels on the deck of the ship. Eric stumbled back.

"Get away from it!" he shouted. "Metal down. Quick!"

The crew members attacking the tentacle moved back, and a bolt bright as the sun shot across the eels. It struck the deck with a deafening crack and left a smoldering black spot. More eels tore through the ropes and sails. The ship started turning again.

"Get us out of here," someone screamed.

More eels fell to the deck and were kicked away by angry crew members.

Electricity gathered across the eels again. A terrible crack split the air, making Eric cover his ears. A new sound rumbled up the hull, putting Eric's teeth on edge, and suddenly the eels along the tentacle bared their teeth. Eric lunged at it, cutting through one of the small eels. It fell to the deck and snapped at his ankles. He kicked it off the deck.

All around him, people wove in and out of the fight, dodging teeth and tails. Ariel ran back and forth across the deck and threw the untangled eels back into the sea. One hissed at her, and she hissed right back.

"Nora!" Sauer yelled from the wheel. "You know what to—"

"I do not know what to do!" Stabbing into the thin tentacle of eels and clicking teeth, Nora whipped around to them. "No one knows what to do. This is absurd."

A large eel rose up behind her and bit at her neck. Gabriella grabbed her collar, yanking her back. The pair fell against the rail.

"Are you kidding me?" Gabriella carried an eel and yelped as it shocked her. "Eric, if we survive this, you owe me!"

"Deal." He helped her cut through the eel's thick neck.

Vanni hollered from across the deck and wiped the eels' ooze away from his face. "Figure out how to stop it, Princeling, or forget owing me. I'll kill you!"

Ariel was the closest to the rail.

"Can you see where it's coming from?" Eric shouted at her, ducking under a branch of eels. He hacked it free of the main mass.

She swept a puddle of eels and ooze through a scupper hole with her feet and leaned over the rail. She held up one finger, running to the side of the ship the tentacle had come from. She waved him over.

A thick knot of eels twisted beneath the surface near the ship. It extended underneath, completely encircling the hull. Electricity sparked to life right beneath the surface of the water, and two eels as long as horses writhed at the center of the mass. They seemed to control the tentacle, twisting to direct it this way and that. Two pairs of mismatched eyes—one white and one gold—glared up at them.

"Brilliant," he said, and squeezed her hand. "Gabriella, I need that rifle."

She passed it down the line of people fighting the eels. The weight was familiar and strange all at once. Eric knew how to shoot, but he didn't care for it and avoided it when he could. He tried to take aim, and the tentacle whipped to protect the two eels. Ariel picked up his knife and prodded the tentacle aside. Eric took the shot.

It grazed the head of one of the eels, drawing blood as it passed between them. They hissed, and the injured one's golden eye dimmed to black. They untangled themselves from the knot of eels, and the electricity fizzled out. Without the two leaders, the tentacle of eels fell apart and dropped back into the sea and to the deck. One smacked into Gabriella, and she stumbled to her knees. Eric kicked another off the deck.

Relief, overpowering and exhausting, flooded him, and he dropped the rifle.

"How," he said breathlessly, "have I survived this long without you?"

Ariel smiled at him. She wiped the leftover ooze from his shoulders and patted his cheek.

"No more deals like this," one of Sauer's crew told Nora. "If Sauer gets some high and mighty idea about helping folks with witches again, I'm shoving them overboard and you can be captain."

Nora saluted them and collapsed onto the deck. "Thank you for your support."

"I always wanted a funeral at sea," said Sauer, limping over. "Your Highness, all right?"

"I think?" Eric glanced at Ariel, and she nodded. Gabriella and Vanni looked no worse for wear. The eels still slithering around the deck were too small to do much damage. "Let's get out of here."

"Let's get these eels off my ship first," Sauer said.

"Come on, eel slayer." Gabriella used the taffrail to pull herself up and offered a hand to Nora. "To your fee—"

A newly formed tentacle of eels and dying lightning whipped over the rail and grabbed Gabriella. She shrieked and clawed at the eels, but it yanked her over the rail. She vanished. Nora leapt to her feet.

"No!" She dove over the rail and into the sea before anyone could protest.

"Nora!" Sauer threw themself at the rail. "No, no, no."

Ariel grabbed a rope and tossed it over the side. Vanni came running from across the deck, dragging one of the rope ladders, and he hauled it over, too. It tumbled into the water, hitting the surface where Nora's entry still bubbled. Neither Nora nor Gabriella emerged.

"I'm going after them," said Eric.

Sauer toed off their boots. "I'll get Nora. She shouldn't be in the water. Not if all that nonsense about the Blood Tide and her mother is true."

Eric had forgotten about that.

But before either of them could jump, Gabriella and Nora surfaced. Nora was in a panic, flailing in the calming waves. Gabriella drifted away from her and grasped for the ropes without looking, but missed. Nora vanished beneath the surface again.

"What's happened?" Sauer heaved themself over the rail and started climbing down the ladder. "What happened to Nora?"

"I don't know," said Gabriella. She opened her mouth a few times and swallowed. She stared unblinking into the water. "Eric, the eels are gone, but we've got another problem."

Sauer growled, and Eric grabbed their arm.

"Gabriella," he said, "please explain what's happening."

Sauer pulled their arm free and continued down the rope ladder. Nora surfaced again, breathing hard and choking on water.

"She is drowning," said Sauer. "Help her."

"I don't think she could drown if she tried," said Gabriella.

Sauer smacked the hull of the ship. "Then what's wrong?"

"This!" Nora leaned back as Gabriella had, but instead of legs kicking up out of the water there was a shimmering dark blue tail.

16
Dear, Lost Children

*I*T WAS a tail. A fish tail. A tail on Nora. Who was a merfolk? Human? Was this something to do with the Blood Tide, or—

"Nora, so help me, you can have a tantrum later, but we're getting out of here now, and I will haul you onto this ship no matter how many limbs you've got," screamed Sauer.

"Tantrum?" She thrashed and smacked her tail against the ocean's surface, soaking Sauer, who was halfway down the hull. "Tantrum!"

Nora twisted in the water. Her tail was the same deep blue of the ocean or evening skies, its scales shimmering like stars. It looked longer than her legs had been, and the wide fins were hemmed in an opalescent membrane that trailed through the water like a train. She stayed afloat without even trying, and the waves seemed to lift her instead of ram into her as they did Gabriella. She touched the tip of her tail with a shaking hand.

Vanni walked away from the rail, hands on his head, and flinched away from an eel, muttering about witches and magic under his breath. Around them, crew members were peering down at Nora with shock and interest.

"See?" one was saying to the barrelman who'd climbed down to get a better look. "This is why storms never hit us. King Triton's blessing."

"That's the cats," said another.

"No, no, no. I've seen that girl swim. Two legs the whole time."

"But that was in a lake, not the sea."

Eric shook his head and looked back down at Nora and Gabriella. Nora was still turning in the water, her fingers inspecting the sides of her neck.

"Do I have gills?" she asked Gabriella, rounding on the other girl with a frown.

Gabriella was slowly regaining her composure, and she cupped Nora's neck with her hands. They exchanged a few quiet words. Nora's tail cut through the water behind her, glittering with each ripple of water. Gabriella drifted slightly back from her. Nora nodded.

"Sauer?" she asked. "What if I can't get on the ship?"

"If you can't climb, I'll carry you," they said, reaching down to her. "Come here. If you need to stay submerged, I'll rig a net behind the boat or fill a barrel with seawater. We'll figure it out. Let's just get out of here."

Eric crawled back to his feet and looked down at them. "Maybe whatever's happened will end once we're away from the Isle."

Nora groaned.

Gabriella floated closer to Nora and studied her tail. "Nothing hurts, right?"

"No," said Nora, "but it feels weird. Different."

"First time in the sea since you died, and that man who raised you said you shouldn't ever return." Gabriella swam behind Nora and nudged her toward the ropes. "Maybe once you're out, you'll change back."

Nora nodded unhappily and moved to Sauer.

"Hey, Nora!" one of the crew called over the rail. "Can I have your green boots?"

"Over my dead body," she shouted.

Sauer whipped their head around and glared up at the deck. "Shouldn't you all be getting us ready to leave?"

The crew on the deck scattered.

Nora covered her face with her hands, her tail flicking nervously beneath her, and nodded. "All right. I'm going to climb up, and then we can figure out what's wrong with me."

A large splash rocked the water around them.

"Nothing is wrong with you," said a deep voice.

Nora spun around so quickly, she smacked Gabriella's legs with her tail. Eric peered down the side of the ship, and Ariel let out a surprised little squeak. It was a man floating upright in the water a few feet away. A long tail of emerald green undulated in the ocean beneath him.

"This is perfectly normal," he said. "Children of both worlds possess the ability to live in both worlds."

"Children of what?" Nora asked, voice breaking. "Who are you?"

"My name is Malek," the man said, considering her. "Your parents—one was human and one was merfolk."

"No offense, but I don't know you," said Nora, and she started moving toward Sauer with Gabriella. "Forgive me if I don't take you at your word."

The man tilted his head to the side. His deep black skin was salt flecked and cool toned, bring out the teal sheen in the scales running along his green tail. His dark braids were neatly gathered into a bun at the top of his head, small shells decorating the strands. A blue glass bead dangled from his left ear. He squinted his black eyes up at them as if unused to the sun, and nodded, laughing slightly.

"Of course you shouldn't," he said. "I'm sorry. I've gotten ahead of myself."

He looked real enough, and he sounded real enough. They were dealing with a witch who routinely tricked people, though.

"Where did you come from?" Eric asked. "How do we know you're not working with the witch?"

"With her?" Malek practically spat the words. "She has kept me hostage here for years!"

"The cave," Gabriella muttered.

Malek nodded. "Yes, when she left me alone in the island, she kept me in a cave beneath the lagoon. I am assuming one of you broke something or fiddled with her things? Disrupting her magic set off the island's defenses and allowed me to escape."

Sauer glanced up at Eric. "Do we have time to consider this?"

"Not really," Eric said. "Unless you know any test to determine if someone's a sea witch."

"How about I come aboard?" offered the merfolk. "I would be at your mercy, essentially."

"Unless you're magical," said Sauer.

"I assure you, I am not, or else I would've gotten free of that cave much sooner." His voice was the low rasp of grains of sand tumbling over each other in the tide. "I will tell you everything I know about the witch if you help me escape from this cursed place."

Sauer nodded. "Nora, let's get you up first."

She looked back at Malek, asking in a whisper, "Are you sure I'll go back to being human?"

"You will," said Malek. "You should've been taught how to control the transformation so that it became as natural as breathing. Most children part human and part merfolk transform every time they leave or enter the sea, but it can very much be controlled. It is supposed to be a choice. Simply leave the water. You'll see."

No one could get away from the Isle of Serein fast enough. Eric and Vanni helped Gabriella climb back onto the ship while Nora watched anxiously from the bottom of the rope. She circled in the ocean until Sauer straightened out the ladder, lowering themself into the water so that she could hold onto their shoulders, and a nervous hush fell over the ship once Nora's tail was on full display. It wasn't some trick of the sea or a tangle of colorful eels. Malek kept nervously glancing back at the island. Ariel threw down another rope for him.

"I was in trousers," muttered Nora as Gabriella

pulled her from Sauer's back and over the rail. "Where'd my clothes go?"

Sauer chuckled. "Someone grab a blanket for Nora, please."

Nora curled her tail up and touched the tip, running her fingers along the thin webbing.

"Well, you're set if we wreck," said Eric. "And it's quite lovely. Don't you think, Gabriella?"

"Graceful." Gabriella sunk to her knees next to Nora and wrapped a large blanket around her. She gave her a soft smile. There was a look in her eyes that Eric hadn't seen before. "Thank you for diving in to save me, but please don't do it again."

Nora hummed and pulled the green scarf from Gabriella's neck. "I haven't decided if it was worth it yet, anyway."

True to Malek's words, Nora's legs returned once the last drops of seawater fell from her body. They could see the tip of her tail that peeked out from below her blanket. The scales molted off like feathers from a bird and revealed her bare feet beneath. She shook her legs out, running her hands up and down them. Ariel watched, transfixed by the transformation.

Sauer checked on Nora one last time and went back to the rail. "You're Malek, yes?"

"I am."

"We could lower a boat and let it take on water," said Sauer. "Or you are welcome to come up."

"Thank you. I will come up, but unlike Nora, I will not possess legs. It will be ungainly." Malek grabbed the ladder and began to climb. "Your concern, though, is kind."

The crew steered clear of Malek, everyone caught between awe and fear, and soon enough, Sauer had the ship heading back into the fog. Sauer brought Nora a change of clothes and ushered her into the captain's quarters, and after a few minutes, they herded Ariel, Vanni, Gabriella, and Malek inside. Eric hesitated, damp and confused, and took a few breaths to clear his head.

"Can't tell if this voyage was cursed or blessed," muttered the barrelman, throwing himself back against the rigging.

"Nora will put in a good word for us with the sea," another replied. "Get up there. I'm done with this place."

Eric leaned against the door to the captain's quarters. Done. What a good concept.

He joined the others in the cabin. Malek had settled down next to the little half balcony off the back of the ship, the spray of the sea at his back. Nora sat half reclining on the bed and staring at her legs. Vanni, too, was gaping at them.

"None of us could be secretly merfolk, right?" he asked.

Eric shook his head.

Sauer pulled a chair close to her and sat backward on it. "What can you tell us about the Isle of Serein and the witch who lives there?"

"Quite a bit," said Malek. "I've been trapped there for the last seven years."

"Seven?" Gabriella sat on the table and planted her feet in the chair. "Why?"

"I was—am, until the contract runs out or she dies—retribution for a bargain my sister, Miriam, and her partner, Andrea, broke with the witch." He laced his fingers in his lap and squared his shoulders, a pose Eric saw constantly in Grimsby. "He was human and she was not, but they loved each other. He sailed out to see her every day for twenty years, and then one day, he decided he wanted to join her beneath the waves. To do so, he had to make a deal with a witch—he would become one of the merfolk, and her price was a single soul, a debt which she would call in at a later date."

One of Ariel's hands fluttered to her heart. Eric

understood that. It was such a romantic story, a desperate deal made for love. It was the sort of story Eric used to cling to.

"And the soul was you?" Nora asked, confused.

Malek shook his head. "It was my niece, their first-born, but Miriam and Andrea ran away with her. All magic comes with a price, and that price must always be paid. When it's not, magic will take its price. Andrea was a clever man, and he thought that since he could read and write, unlike most merfolk, he would be able to make sure his contract with the witch would be in his favor. All of her deals are written contracts, you see. He was wrong, and he was killed while helping Miriam escape. Miriam, from what the witch told me later, was captured near land. The witch decided to teach Miriam a lesson by killing her daughter instead of taking her soul."

Eric swallowed. And what a show of force it was—her soul meant so much to Miriam and so little to the witch that she'd go ahead and kill if it meant causing more pain.

Then what was his mother's ghost if this witch worked with souls?

"If the witch couldn't have my niece, no one could," said Malek. "But Miriam broke free long enough to get my niece ashore, where the witch couldn't touch her. Miriam was killed for that. I was regaled with the story often after I was trapped when I stumbled upon the witch years later while looking for my sister."

Sauer stared at Nora, their face inscrutable. "That's quite the story."

"I didn't realize the witch could transform people like she did Andrea," said Eric. "Is that common? Making human into merfolk?"

"Common enough," said Malek. "Less so now that most of us have left for deeper waters. Transformation is a costly magic, from what I've learned these last years, and does require a level of skill most witches do not have. She is arrogant, but it is not entirely unearned confidence."

Ariel snorted and waved off the odd looks she got. The sour expression on her face was enough for Eric to guess that she reluctantly agreed with Malek's assessment of the witch. Malek stared at Ariel.

"You look familiar," he said, and Ariel stiffened.

"I'm sorry." Sauer held up a hand and took a deep breath. "This witch could transform people into whatever they want, but instead she's not doing that for money for some reason? You know how many people would take her up on that?"

"Yes, but she doesn't want to help people," drawled Malek. "I would not say kindness is one of her strengths. The prices she charges are generally things out of her reach and far more than what anyone could or would reasonably pay, and she takes a great deal of pleasure in using souls, given how that horrifies others. For someone who hates how society stifles her, she loves trapping people in a deal. Curses, too, she's very fond of. They're rare, though, since they allow the cursed a chance to escape. She mostly saves them for nobility so that she can extract a better payment from them later when they break down and beg her to remove the curse. There's only been about five of those."

Ariel winced.

"How do you know all of this?" Vanni asked. "Does she sit around chatting like some villain in a play?"

"Yes, regularly," said Malek flatly. "I suspect she's lonely, and a person incapable of disagreeing with you is very good company. The only other people on the Isle are the souls she's trapped there, but they cannot communicate. She keeps them in the form of polyps and only releases them as ghosts when she needs more souls. Prettier that way, she says."

Eric took a steadying breath and let it out slowly. This was a lot, and none of it was good. The witch was worse than he'd thought, charging people exorbitant prices for things she knew would be life changing and saving. She could've gotten rich if she had accepted normal payments, but she seemed to be after a different sort of power. He was right to want to stop her.

He was wrong for thinking it would be easy.

"The witch," said Eric. "She's one of the merfolk, isn't she?"

It seemed obvious now. The Blood Tide, the Isle, and her obsession with gaining power on land.

"Yes, she is," Malek said in the same tone Carlotta used for Max. "So far as I can tell by her constant reminiscing, she was quite fond of the human world growing up and learned to read and write. It's not a skill merfolk have and is why she is so successful."

"I got some questions still." Nora cleared her throat and wiggled her toes. "So one of my parents was one of the merfolk?"

"Yes, they must have been," said Malek. "Do you not know them?"

"No, I don't," she said, avoiding his gaze. "My mother and I drowned in the Blood Tide, you see, when I was young, but I was pulled ashore and revived."

Malek stared at her. "You don't know either of your parents, and you drowned in the Blood Tide."

Dear, Lost Children

"I'm twenty-four years old, I think," said Nora. "If that helps."

Malek took a shallow breath and covered his face with his hands. "Did a woman save you? Breathe for you and refuse to return you to the witch, getting cursed for her good deed?"

"Oh, no." Nora shook her head. "I mean, yes, a woman saved me—I'm named for her, even—but I don't know if the witch was there or if anyone was cursed. I was just told I couldn't go back into the sea or the Blood Tide would kill me for escaping."

Eric looked up as she finished her words. It felt like having the breath knocked out of him or his chest hollowed out. He couldn't believe how narrow-minded he had been. The answer had been in front of him the whole time, and he had been too focused on the witch to see it. Nora wasn't even a common name in Vellona or Riva, but *Eleanora* was.

"Kill you?" Malek laughed into his hands. "No, the witch was saying she would come for you if you ever entered her domain. The Blood Tide can't kill you. It's just a path." He lifted his head and wiped the tears from his cheeks. "You might not be my niece, though. She's ended and ruined so many lives. I'm getting ahead of myself."

"You're not," said Eric. "Right before I was born,

my mother saved a child's life up north, and a witch cursed her child."

Eric had . . . what was it Grimsby always said? He had missed the ocean for the waves. If he had stopped to think, he might have noticed that Nora was one part of the puzzle he wanted so desperately to solve.

"Your mother what?" Nora nearly screamed.

"Saved a child from a witch, and the witch cursed her unborn child as revenge." Eric took a deep breath and said, "'If that thing in your belly ever kisses someone without a voice as pure as their spotless soul, someone who isn't its true love, then'—"

"'Then it will die, and I will drag its soul to the bottom of the sea,'" finished Malek, staring at Eric. "The witch is quite proud of that curse. Said it was her first foray into land politics. She never explained why."

Deep in his stomach, beneath the fluttering panic and disappointment, was hope. He had found the Isle. He knew where the witch would be.

"My mother dragged you from the sea, gave you the kiss of life, and refused to return you to the witch who wanted you," said Eric.

And for once, the fact that others knew he was cursed didn't terrify him. He wasn't alone in the witch's terrible schemes.

"Oh." Nora leaned back, fidgeting with her hair. "That's why you did all of this. That's what you were doing when we found you the first time. You were looking for the witch who—"

She stopped, and Eric could see the fact that he was cursed hitting her. Beside him, Ariel let out a soft whine.

"I'm cursed," said Eric. It wasn't the ideal way to tell Ariel, but it was best she learn now. "Only a few people know. My mother vanished while looking for the Isle of Serein, and when I found her notes about it, I went looking for it, too. She was always overprotective. If the witch told my mother she'd be after you if you went in the sea, I bet my mother told Edo to keep you out of it completely."

Nora narrowed her eyes at Eric, opened her mouth to speak, and then shook her head. Ariel stared at Eric in horror, the first look of utter grief he'd ever seen on her.

"She's not all-powerful," Malek said, "though she pretends otherwise, and I would say that she has woven this net around far too many fish for her to be able to drag it in."

She wasn't all-powerful. She could be outrun and outsmarted. This new knowledge about the witch had sharpened Eric's focus. The world was bright and clear, like a book seen through newly fitted glasses. It was all connected by one terrible, powerful witch at the center of this monstrous web, and that witch wanted his soul.

"Look, I'll deal with your part in this mess"—Nora waved at Eric—"in a second, but how did I drown if I'm one of the merfolk?"

"She forced you to change into a human while you were still in the sea." Malek sighed, his shoulders slumping. "She thought it would hurt Miriam the most to watch you drown and be able to do nothing to help."

"Well," mumbled Nora. "I joined Sauer to find my family, and I guess that worked out. Sort of."

Sauer raised their head and nodded at her. "This witch isn't leaving Cloud Break alive."

"If you want a family, I would be happy to be that for you. To show you where your mother was from and our family," said Malek, going over to Nora and offering her his hands. She hesitated but took them and nodded, and Malek smiled. "Knowing you're alive is worth these last seven years. To be one of *her* souls is to be little more than livestock or coin—good for fuel or trade. It's the most depraved sort of magic, the use of souls. But the sea can only offer her so much. She was ostracized after the depths she would go to for power were discovered, and now she has set her sight on drier crowns."

"She wants to rule the land," Eric said, taking in Malek's words. "But if her magic is weaker there, she knew she would need more souls and the sort of power humans exalt. That's why the ghosts appeared and started manipulating people into giving up their souls, and that's why she made deals with different kingdoms for land and titles. But how are we supposed to stop her? How do we break her curses?"

Malek shot him a solemn look more befitting a funeral. "My apologies, but there are only three ways to break a curse—do as it demands, die not doing as it demands, or kill the witch responsible."

Eric had lost his chance to catch her unaware and kill her. He worked a knuckle into his temple, a headache blooming in the back of his eyes. He would have another chance, especially if she was heading for Cloud Break. She would hurt no one else.

A knock on the door startled them all.

"Captain?" the navigator said, poking their head in. "Could you come look at this?"

"I'll be right there," said Sauer, and they squeezed Nora's shoulder as they left.

"I've got a lighter question." Vanni looked at Malek and mouthed the words a few times as if testing them out. "If merfolk can't read, how do they agree to contracts?"

"By not reading them," Malek said.

Ariel groaned and covered her face with her hands.

"Desperation makes the details superfluous." Malek shrugged. "Some days, listening to her stories, I couldn't blame her for the deals. People signed them far too readily. She is evil, certainly, but she is not irredeemable. This is the only route to power she feels she has, and so far as she is concerned, she has earned that power."

"I'll take your word on it, but I won't be the first in line to offer her redemption." Eric felt stretched out and thin, as translucent as his mother's ghost.

"I'm sorry. I can't let this go," said Nora. "You were cursed because your mother saved a child's life from a sea witch, and you didn't once think it was worth mentioning?"

"I didn't think it was you!" Eric raised his hands in surrender. "What is the chance of that? I figured it was a coincidence!"

She narrowed her brown eyes at him, the mirth in them glowing like a ship's deck under the summer sun, and clucked her tongue. "I guess."

"I have one last question, Malek," said Eric. "This witch. You've never said her name."

Dear, Lost Children

Malek swallowed. "No, I haven't. She's a bit of a legend in sea-dwelling circles—exiled for her plot to steal the throne, her use of souls as fuel, and her rather unscrupulous means of acquiring those souls. She's a cunning one, that Ursula."

17
If Only

URSULA wasn't a particularly witchy name. It was like any other name of any other person, except Ursula had ruined a half dozen lives in the pursuit of power.

Eric glanced around the room—Nora was muttering the name to herself like a bitter prayer, Gabriella and Vanni were staring at Eric, and Ariel had one hand clenched over her heart as if the name itself had hurt.

"But why do this?" asked Vanni. "So many cons, all of them long and complicated."

Malek nodded. "Power is a heady thing. Ursula is a strong witch, but because she uses souls, she largely goes unrecognized. To manipulate the soul is a terrible thing. It is a violation of a person's self at the deepest level and a field of magic most avoid. I suspect she started studying it after being wronged several times, but she was never specific when discussing what had happened, only that it had, and that she had been in the right and unfairly treated."

Ariel snorted.

"She was unfairly treated?" Gabriella asked. "So what? She gets to mistreat the rest of us?"

"Not anymore," Eric said. "Any advice for when we do deal with Ursula again? Does she have a weakness?"

The promise of seeing her soon still made Eric's hair stand on end.

"She only told me the stories in which she was the victor," Malek said and shook his head. "Most of her power comes from deals, and she thankfully hasn't managed to acquire the magical artifacts she's been after yet. She is not some sort of god who can only be killed with a specific weapon or by striking her heel. I believe she can be killed like any other person, but getting close enough to do that would be the difficult part."

Malek smiled apologetically at Eric.

The door to the quarters opened, and Sauer stalked in. "I need everyone on deck to see what I'm witnessing and tell me if it's the witch."

Everyone rushed out. Eric and Vanni helped Malek navigate the dry deck when he asked, and Ariel draped him in a water-soaked blanket once they reached the prow. The ship and sea were washed in the golden light of late afternoon. The sun was no longer stuck on high noon as it had been on the Isle of Serein, and a smear of fog lingered on the horizon behind them. Ahead of them, with the first portents of night behind the hill, was Cloud Break Bay.

"That's impossible," Eric said with a gasp. "We left at dusk and were gone for hours. We shouldn't have reached it this quickly."

Sauer nodded. "We didn't hit the fog till we were farther away, too, but when we emerged from it, we were here."

Eric used a hand to shade his eyes, trying to see as much of the bay as he could. Max slunk out of the hull with a huff and sat himself between Eric's feet.

"Hey, coward," Eric said and reached down to pet him. "Does that look like home?"

Max let out a soft *woof*, and Eric pointed toward the docks.

"The ships are all docked in the same order as they were when we left," he said. "No time has passed."

"Yes, this is how the fog works," said Malek, hauling himself up on the railing to see. "It transports you to exactly when and where you were when you first set out for the Isle of Serein. Ursula got tired of spending so much time traveling and finalized that trick about three years ago, I think. The years are a bit of a blur."

"Imagine what else Ursula could do if she tried," muttered Nora as they came into port.

Eric scowled. "She's trying, but it's all only for herself."

The ship docked beneath the castle where no one would see them. The hull was covered in odd scratches and smudges of eel ooze. A few scorch marks from the electricity marred the wood, and most of the crew seemed desperate to sleep without interruption before dealing with people. The privacy was good for Malek, too, and he would be staying near the ship to spend time with Nora.

"I have told you what I know about the witch since your accident led to my release, and because of Nora," he said to Eric before leaving to speak with his niece, "but I only escaped her through pure accident, and I will not subject myself to such danger again. She stole seven years of my life from me. I won't throw this new life away for you."

Which was more than fair.

Eric lingered near the back of the ship to think. Surely it would be obvious when Ursula arrived to Cloud Bay, the conqueror finally laying claim to the land they had attacked from afar. She seemed the sort to enjoy fanfare.

If he did nothing, Ursula and Sait would wear Vellona down eventually.

If he did anything, Ursula would kill him or whomever he sent. Snatch them away as easily as she had his mother.

Thinking of his mother left an ache in Eric's chest. Leaving her on the Isle had been like losing her all over again. The realization that her ghost was being puppeteered by Ursula had taken the smoldering coal of his grief and rekindled it. He sniffed and rubbed his face, exhausted by the scent of salt. He would do anything for his mother to be with him now to tell him what he should do next.

Footsteps padded down the deck toward him. Eric lifted his head and patted his cheeks, trying to look less panicked. It was only Ariel, though, and she beamed when he met her gaze. Eric smiled back and thanked his nearly two decades of propriety training for keeping him together. She sat down next to him.

Despite her smile, her body was tense. Eric laughed.

If Only

"Do you want to ask about my curse?"

She nodded.

Of course she did. He would have if their roles were reversed, and he had sprung it on her rather suddenly. It felt right, revealing it on the ship, and he didn't regret it. He just wished it were less relevant. Less painful.

"I was never supposed to talk about it. Only Mother, Gabriella, Vanni, Grimsby, and Carlotta have ever known about it, but I don't think I can hide it anymore," he said. "I always have to be careful, always have to make excuses, and always have to separate myself from the people around me without an explanation, and it's exhausting."

He felt lighter, as if he had been carrying his curse around his shoulders and speaking had divvied the weight between them. He wasn't alone.

Ariel made a gesture he understood as *thank you*.

"You deserve to know. You risked your life going on this voyage with me. We wouldn't have survived without you." He shrugged. "So, questions?"

She brought her hand up to her mouth and kissed her fingertips. Then she tapped him four times.

Eric smiled. "No, no kissing at all. I can't kiss anyone or let them kiss me. The curse was vague, so we were never sure if it was a kiss on the lips or any sort of kiss at all. I stayed clear of anything that could be considered a kiss."

Ariel's face fell and tears gathered in her eyes. Eric stifled his confusion at the sudden reaction, patting her on the shoulder. She was kind and loving, so of course she was upset about him not being able to kiss anyone or find love. It didn't help that they'd gone through an odd, dangerous experience. Even Eric felt all over the place.

But dealing with Ariel's emotions was much better than facing his own.

"It's fine. Don't worry about me," he said. "Kissing's not the end-all, be-all, and now we're closer than ever to breaking the curse. It is what it is. But I guess now you can see why I was a little awkward after the, uh, lagoon incident earlier."

Ariel let out something that might have been a hiccup or a laugh and covered her face.

"Everything hitting you at once?" asked Eric, rubbing her back. He was eager to move away from any more talk about kissing. "It's been a wild few days, and you only washed up here yesterday."

The whole of Ariel seemed to deflate. She closed her eyes, shoulders slumping.

"Is there something wrong?" he asked.

She nodded, cracking one eye open, and blew the last strand of hair from her face. It flopped right back down.

"Do you want to talk about it?"

Her nose wrinkled.

"Ariel," he said and tucked the strand behind her ear. "I hid my curse from everyone my entire life. It would be extremely hypocritical if I demanded you tell me all of your secrets on our second day of knowing each other."

She smiled, albeit sadly, and blew him a kiss.

"See, that's safe," he said. "I can kiss Max, too. Whatever it is that's bothering you, I promise that I am fine. Don't worry about me."

She made a talking motion with one hand and peeked up at him, pointing to herself and then her heart.

"Ah, you got to be emotional, so now it's my turn?'

She nodded, and a shot of affection ran through him when he saw her stretching out her bare toes. Talking was helping, but it wasn't making his choices any easier.

"I need to get married, but I have kept myself separated from others for so long that I don't even know how to begin to care for someone else," he said, and after the first few words, it all came tumbling out of him. He had never discussed his fears about this with his mother.

She had made up the rules to keep him alive; he couldn't bear to make her feel guilty for that. "Love terrifies me. The concept of it. The reality. Every part of it. How can I find it, enjoy it, want it, when my expression of love is warped by this curse? I know not being able to kiss someone doesn't make me lesser, but still . . . the fear is always there."

Ariel made a few gestures he couldn't understand and huffed. She chewed on her bottom lip.

It warmed the cold part of him that felt separate from the rest of people that she was trying to understand and not fix him, though.

"Don't worry," he said. "You're thinking of an idea, right? That's why you can't draw it?"

She nodded and stared up at the sky. Then she covered her eyes with one hand and pretended to dive into the sand. Of course—why couldn't he do the brave thing and love anyway? He wasn't sure he could take a leap of faith he was always warned would kill him. She had so much more courage than he ever had.

"I would love to be brave," he said, "but I admit to not knowing what that entails."

What was the point of bravery if it killed him? He was supposed to be brave—that was what propriety and history and myth said. It was demanded of men over and over, but he didn't want to be brave like that, closing his eyes and diving headfirst. He wanted to live.

What was so wrong with that? Why couldn't everyone else be patient?

He took a deep breath. "I don't know if any of this will even matter if we end up fighting Ursula. I don't want her to take my choice away from me again. If we kill her, I'm free to choose whoever I want. I can exist without the threat of dying or the worry of choosing wrong. I heard her once, my true love, after she saved me when I was shipwrecked. It's part of the curse. A true love with a voice as pure as her soul. How am I supposed to be happy not knowing her?"

Ariel's head cocked to the side, and her hand drifted to her throat.

"I didn't know about that part of the curse before. My mother never told me," he whispered. "It already feels so personal. I'd know her voice anywhere. Is that selfish of me?"

It was his choice, but it was Ariel's opinion he wanted. It was her he—

Eric shook his head. He couldn't go down that path; not yet.

"Trust," she mouthed.

Ariel took his face in her hands and turned him to

look at her. She flicked his nose. Then, gently, she laid her hand over his heart. Eric nodded and covered her hand with his.

He could learn to be brave.

Eric and Ariel joined the rest of the crew on the quarter-deck a short while later. Most were staying on the ship—Nora was camping on the beach so that she could talk to Malek—and Vanni and Gabriella were eager to return home. Knowing that Ursula was on her way, everyone wanted a nice night of peace before whatever new issue the next day brought. They all planned to meet the next morning at the dining hall, and Eric wandered up to the castle with Ariel to tell Grimsby what happened. Carlotta swooped in and took Ariel away, insisting on a bath and a physician to look at the scratches left by the eels. Grimsby followed Eric to his quarters.

Their conversation lasted the better part of two hours, drifting from Ursula to the Isle to what had happened with his mother's ghost, and it left Eric feeling far less confident than his talk with Ariel had. Explaining to Grimsby that he hadn't killed the witch and that now she was heading toward the bay made him feel like a

If Only

child again. At least he had all the letters and contracts from the Isle of Serein to back up his claims. They had plenty of evidence now that Sait was behind the storms and raids.

"I told you no good would come of this," muttered Grimsby. "Do you know how to kill her, at least?"

"She can die like anyone else," said Eric, looking away from Grimsby. "And I think evidence of Sait breaking our deals is good enough."

"We'll see." The man scowled.

Eric had never even truly met Ursula, and yet she dictated so much of his life—how close he could get to his mother, how intimate his friendships could be, his love life, and his ability to serve Vellona. He had lived in fear for so long.

"It was always her, Grim." Eric closed his eyes and turned back to his adviser. "Everything was her. Sait is paying her to ravage the coast with storms to weaken us, Altfeld promised her land if she could ensure they conquered Riva, and Glowerhaven is paying her to weaken Imber and us. Imber stuck by its deal with my mother, but how long will that last? She's pinpointed what every kingdom wants and is giving it to them while also supporting their soon-to-be rival. No matter what happens to Vellona, she is set to ruin and rule these lands."

"It is hard to imagine that there was a single person at the center of all of our troubles," said Grimsby. "That everything she did from afar affected us so deeply."

Eric stared out at the hushed night that had fallen over the bay. Even the birds were quieter, their calls warbling in the dark. Or perhaps Eric's pounding headache was drowning out the normal bustle of the castle. The horizon was blessedly dark, filled with flickering lights and the soft glow of the lighthouse down the coast, and only Ariel's windows were still the dim gold of candlelight. She flitted about behind the curtains for a while, dancing to some tune only she could hear. Every now and then, she leapt.

"Do you think the pure voice mentioned in my curse is literal?" Eric asked, more to himself than to Grimsby. Eric had not thought much about his mystery savior while out at sea. Before, he had been so excited to believe that his destined true love was out there, but now her existence felt like another weight for him to carry. He raised his flute to his lips.

The first few notes were sharp and sweet, but this time, he played his savior's song. Grimsby's shoes shuffled against the floor behind him, and Eric resisted the urge to turn and watch the unflappable man pace.

Eventually, he came to rest next to Eric against the banister. Eric didn't stop his lament of a song.

"Eric, if I may say—far better than any dream girl is one of flesh and blood, one warm and caring, and right before your eyes."

He patted Eric on the shoulder and left Eric alone. Across the courtyard, Ariel paused her dancing before her window. She stared out over the bay, smiling, and slipped back through the curtains. The candlelight in her room faded. Eric let his song die.

What if he couldn't kill Ursula? Or what if he did kill her, but his curse remained? Would he be stuck forever trying to find his dream girl? Wouldn't making a decision now be the bravest thing he could do?

Hang the curse and hang true love. He shouldn't have been forced to question himself every waking moment and to live his life within the bounds of his curse. If he chose someone despite his curse, wouldn't that be love? True love? No force—political or magical—could take that choice from him. He wasn't even sure his savior was real.

If she was, she hadn't stayed.

Eric backed up and took a running leap, tossing his flute as far as he could into the sea. He couldn't let something that had happened to him before he was born dictate how he lived anymore.

Ariel had been brave. It was his turn.

If she would have him, together they could find a way to break the curse in another way, kill Ursula, or live as happily as they could. Together, they—

A voice echoed out across the rocks, high and clear as a bell. The tune of his song, his savior's song, broke through the crash of the waves against the beach, and all thoughts of speaking to Ariel slipped from his head.

18
Her Voice

ERIC RACED from his quarters to the beach. The back stairs were slick with drizzle, and his boots slipped down the stone until he stumbled onto the beach. It took five minutes at most, but it felt like there were hours between the first note hitting his ears on the balcony and his feet sinking into the sand. He ignored his exhaustion and confusion, intent on finding the source of the voice. The melody was exactly the same as it had been the day of the accident.

Thick fog blanketed the beach. All he could see was the shadow of the waves against the sand, and all he could hear was the song. His legs carried him after it on their own accord, each step bringing him closer. A pale golden glint caught his eyes.

"Hey!" He trailed after the voice, but the singer kept just out of sight. "Wait! Please!"

He could barely make out a figure in the fog. She

sang endlessly, never pausing for breath, and Eric stumbled after her.

"Please stop," Eric said. "Where did you learn that song?"

Finally, the figure paused and turned to face him. She was a young woman, and through the fog Eric could see that her white skin was pale and even, not a single scar or freckle marking any part of it. She had curls of dark hair that twisted in the ocean breeze. Beautiful violet eyes met his.

"It's an old family tune," she said. She looked at him, her gaze filled with catlike curiosity. "I'm sorry. Do I know you?"

Eric hesitated, taken aback. Most people in Cloud Break Bay knew him, but he didn't recognize her, either. "Eric. You can call me Eric."

"Vanessa." She inclined her head slightly and took a step toward him, offering her hand in greeting.

"It's lovely to meet you, Vanessa," he said, and moved out of her reach. It was like a dream, meeting her. He feared his hand would pass right through her and she would vanish if they so much as touched. "This is an odd question, but were you singing on this beach yesterday?"

His voice wavered, and Eric took a deep breath, trying to brace himself for the answer. For either answer.

"Oh!" Vanessa's voice was clear as a bell, and her questioning tone struck a chord in his chest. "You're the boy from the beach? The one who nearly drowned?"

"I am," Eric said.

He searched her face, waiting to feel a spark or flutter, anything to confirm what he already suspected— that Vanessa was his true love with a voice as pure as her soul—but he felt nothing. Was it only because he didn't know her yet?

His thoughts drifted to Ariel and the way his soul came alive at the sight of her on the rock. How her smile broke through his fear. How passionately she acted without a care for what others thought.

"If not for that song, I would never have recognized you." Eric shook his head and forced himself to smile. He shouldn't be thinking of Ariel now. "Why didn't you stay?"

"I was scared, to be honest. I didn't know if you were alive or who you were, and I'm not even from here, so I didn't know who to go to," Vanessa said, and laughed. "Strange girls found kneeling over corpses are rarely believed. I'm surprised you even remember me."

"Of course I remember you. You saved my life," said Eric.

"I was simply doing the right thing," she said. "What anyone would have done."

Vanessa reached for him, and Eric leaned away, the hair on his arms standing on end. She pulled her hand back and touched the shell necklace at her throat. She had to be his true love—a voice as pure as her spotless soul.

"Would you like to talk about it?" she asked.

Talking. Yes, that was good. Eric had spent a whole day with Ariel before realizing how much he had enjoyed her company. Maybe he just needed to get to know Vanessa, and that would make his path forward clear.

"Talking is an excellent idea," he said. "Perhaps we could get to know each other better? It would be nice to know more about the woman who saved my life."

Vanessa peered up at him with a thin half smile. "I would like that very much."

This time, when she tried to touch him, Eric let her. She was cold, cold as the sea when you dove too deep and too dark. Her fingers, smooth and soft, slid across his palm. She paused.

It took him a moment to realize she was waiting for him to kiss her hand. A traditional greeting. A sign of affection.

Something he could do with *her*.

But Eric didn't. It was so intimate, and he had never

been able to do it with his friends whom he trusted and loved. How could he with a girl he barely knew, even if she was supposedly his true love?

"There are stairs leading up to the castle just over there." Eric pointed in the direction he had come from. "We can talk in my study."

"The castle?" she questioned. "Don't tell me you work there?"

"You could say that," he said with a small smile. Vanessa truly didn't know who he was, and that, at least, he liked. He bowed his head and offered her his arm "May I?"

Vanessa took his arm without hesitation and pressed against him. Eric held back a flinch.

So far, this didn't feel like the stories.

". . . one is a zither, and they're completely different," said Eric, setting down the instrument he'd just used to play her song. He was rambling. He hadn't stopped rambling since walking her up the stairs. They had made it to his study nearly half an hour ago, and he still didn't know what to say. She kept asking about his life, but that wasn't something Eric ever talked about with strangers. Speaking to Vanessa wasn't coming as easily as he expected talking to his true love would.

Vanessa hummed and touched the instrument, pressing her body against his side. "I didn't know there was so much to know about the zither."

Eric took a step away. It had also been an excellent shield between them.

"Forgive me," he said. "I could talk about music endlessly."

Vanessa laughed. "I noticed."

Explaining who he was had been easy enough. It was obvious by how the guards welcomed him into the castle and the portraits of him on the walls that he was Prince Eric. Vanessa had explained that she was Rivan and visiting family in Cloud Break Bay, helping her brother care for his ailing daughter. But all he had truly learned about her was that she liked walks on the beach.

"Do you enjoy music?" he asked, and could have hit himself for how silly of a question that was. "Other than singing, of course."

Vanessa laughed without smiling and said, "I fear learning an instrument was always beyond me."

She walked around his study and touched the tip of the sword displayed on his wall. Since entering the room, she had eyed everything around her with calm interest. The edge of the sword was still sharp, but she didn't wince. Eric cleared his throat.

"Music has always held a very important position in my life," he said. This was the moment he had been waiting for—finding and confessing to his true love. It wasn't as easy or joyful as he had thought it would be. Revealing something so private to a stranger didn't feel right, but time was not on his side and he needed to break his curse. He had to tell her. "Only one other thing has been as important to me in my life, but before I can tell you about it, I need you to understand that it must remain a secret."

"A secret?" Vanessa turned and arched one brow. "And you feel you must tell me? Why?"

"I do," he said, "and it will be clear why once I tell you."

She gave him her full attention and nodded.

"I'm cursed." Saying it didn't make him feel better. "If I kiss anyone who isn't . . . who doesn't have a voice as pure as their soul, I will die."

He couldn't bring himself to admit to her that the person with a pure voice was supposed to be his true love.

"Cursed?" Vanessa gasped. "Well, that is a lot to spring on a girl. Is that all?"

"Thankfully," he said with a laugh. "But when you saved me and I heard you singing . . ."

She caught her bottom lip between her teeth and leaned back against his desk. "So you think—"

"That you could break my curse."

Silence reigned while they started at each other, her eyes narrow slits of amethyst, and Eric gestured to his desk.

"I have letters from my mother to prove it if that would help," he said, shoulders tight with anticipation.

"I believe you." Pushing herself from his desk, Vanessa approached him slowly, like a sea snake stalking its prey, until she was mere inches from his face despite his attempts to not meet her eyes. "Princes do not approach strange girls and admit to being cursed and needing to kiss them unless they are serious."

Her closeness was making it hard to breathe, but not in the way that it had been when he was with Ariel. There was something uncomfortable about the way she appraised him. The curse might claim she was his true love, but what if she didn't want him? What if he didn't want her? Shouldn't he want her?

"How can you be sure it's me?" she asked. He could feel her breath on his face. "Do you want me to sing again for you, Eric? To be sure?"

Eric shook his head. "No, I couldn't forget your voice if I tried."

Her song, so clear in his memory, was the only part of her that struck the strings of his heart. Vanessa stretched out her hand, and her fingers brushed his cheek. His skin didn't warm or tingle. He had no desire to lean in to her touch. Was he expecting too much of true love?

His first few frustrating hours with Ariel had been more pleasing than this, and, now that he thought of her, every moment had been more . . . everything. Vibrant. Fun. Comfortable.

Vanessa raised her brows. She seemed to sense that his mind had wandered.

"Sit, Eric," she said, and took both of his hands in hers. "You look like you've seen a ghost."

"I have, in a way. I was uncertain if I would ever find you." He pulled away from her.

"Sit," she said again, gesturing at the chair. "Tell me whatever it is that's bothering you. You can trust me."

Eric sat but couldn't bring himself to say anything.

"I have a proposition for you," he said finally. "I would like for you to break my curse."

"You want me to kiss you?" she asked, standing over him. "And then what?"

Eric swallowed. "I could pay you if you would like,

or I could help you acquire a job in Cloud Break if you want to live closer to your family. Your brother and niece, even, I could help them in some way. Freeing me of the curse would be doing a great service to Vellona. You could have anything you wanted."

"It's not much of a curse—killing you if you kiss someone without a pure voice," she said, and sat on the arm of his chair. "But there is something you could do for me."

"Well," he said, and cleared his throat again, leaning back in the chair.

She leaned with him, and Eric stared at the wall over her shoulder. She was so close and so enclosing. He couldn't stand up or gesture without unseating her. Ariel would've at least asked first.

Ariel—she had told him to be brave and trust himself. Wasn't that what he was doing? He had been right; his true love had saved him that day on the beach.

So why did he feel so uncomfortable? She was his true love, yet he didn't want to tell her that. He didn't want her at all.

"What do you want?" Eric finally asked.

"What do I want for breaking a prince's curse?" Vanessa cupped his face in her hands, her smile never faltering. "I want to marry the prince, of course."

Eric felt as though someone had sucked all of the air out of the room.

"Could we, um, could you get up, please?" He shifted and slipped out from under her, nearly dumping her to the floor. "I'm so sorry, Vanessa, but you want to marry me? You don't know me."

And he didn't want to marry her at all. This wasn't a choice; it was expectation and unhappiness. There was nothing true about this.

"I could get to know you," she said, and clutched the shell necklace at the hollow of her throat. "Shouldn't you want to marry your true love?"

Eric frowned at the last two words.

"Vanessa—"

She surged forward and pressed a finger to his lips, dragging it down his mouth to take his chin between thumb and forefinger. Eric held his breath.

"From what I hear, you are long overdue for a marriage, and Vellona is in desperate need of security," she said. "I'm offering to be your savior twice over."

Eric reared back.

"Why did you call yourself my true love?" he asked.

She smiled and tilted his head down to look at her. "Because I am."

"But how do you know that?" he asked. "I didn't tell you that part of the curse."

She pursed her lips. Her grip on him tightened. "It was obvious you were holding something back. You've never married. You've never kissed. You nearly swooned when you heard me singing. And I've never heard of a curse so vague. I understand you, Eric. You're lying to protect yourself. It's fine, but it's not required anymore. You found me. What else is there to know?"

All Eric had wanted for so long was for someone to understand him. He wanted someone who knew all his flaws and quirks and still adored him. He might have known Ariel for only two days, but he knew what she meant with only a gesture and sometimes felt like she knew what he meant even when he couldn't find the words. It felt as if the last two days had been two decades, and Eric wanted that every day. He had struggled to repress it, to drown the part of his soul that wanted Ariel, but no matter how deep it sunk, it always returned. His feelings had always returned, and he would always return to her. No matter the depths. No matter the distance.

"I don't believe you!" he said and stepped away from her. "And I'm not marrying you."

"It sounds like you have to," she said, and reached for him.

Fury washed over him. No love of his would disregard someone's boundaries so casually.

"I don't have to do anything!" Eric said.

Eric had always believed the best of the curse, no matter how much he hated it. He had clung to the idea that he had a true love, that he was destined for one person decided by fate, but that wasn't hope. It was lies. The idea of true love setting him free kept him from living his life. He deserved to make his own choices and to have loved ones who respected those choices. His destiny was his alone.

All he had to do was be brave.

"I'll keep the curse," he said. "If you are my true love, I want nothing to do with you or it."

Vanessa's expression darkened, almost unrecognizable in the dim light of the room.

"You *want* shackles," she said, voice low and eyes narrowed. "You *want* to be alone." He stepped back, and she followed. "Abandoned when your true love dies. Exhausted by the realities that strike when true love is over. True love. You romantics are all so gullible."

She laughed and took Eric's face in her hands before he could move. She was strong, far stronger than he, and her eyes glowed gold as she leaned in close. Shoving him back, she pinned him between herself and his desk. He tried to pulled away.

"Oh, Eric." Vanessa's fingers stroked delicate lines from his temples to his throat. Her nails dug into his neck. "So pretty, yet so little going on in there."

She flicked the side of his head and backed away.

"I mean, I get it," she said, and looked him up and down. "The redhead's got good taste, I suppose. Pity you're so handsome. Such a waste."

Eric ground his teeth together so tightly they creaked, and he tasted blood. Rage, still and calm, kept him in place as he recognized what was happening. This was not the wild anger that had taken him on the Isle of Serein but something deeper.

"Hello, Ursula," Eric said, reaching for the penknife on his desk. Her name tasted of brine and metal. "How nice to meet you in the flesh."

"Well, someone's flesh, certainly." She grinned and ran both hands down her sides. "So kind of you to believe me so easily."

"Why not just kiss me and get it over with?" Eric asked.

"I might if you try to stab me with that little knife you're reaching for," she said. "You need to learn how to think bigger, lover boy."

Eric huffed, too furious to think clearly. "You need me alive for something?"

"Oh, Eric," she said, and patted his cheek. "Once we're married, no matter how much I lie to you now or how quickly you die after, I'll be the heir to Vellona on paper, and what's on paper is all that matters. Contracts are my specialty."

"The kingdom will hate you," said Eric. "They'll fight you every step of the way. You may rule Vellona on paper, but you will never truly have it."

"Oh, I don't want it. Not forever." She scrunched up her nose as if there were something foul in the room and waved a hand. "Plenty of other shortsighted humans want it, though, and they can have it—for a price. Until they pay me that price, I'll control your navy, your army, your treasury."

Eric growled and lurched for her.

"Sit." She tapped the shell at her throat.

The shell flashed, and Eric's body obeyed despite his protests.

"So I'm to die on my wedding day," he said. "Seal the marriage with a kiss that kills me?"

"A marriage is sealed with a kiss, regardless of how the kiss turns out." She laughed. "Why? Hoping to kiss your quiet little girlfriend? It's insulting you're still after her when I'm right here. She's not even flirting like I told her to. That advice was for free, you know.

Rare I do that. I should've known better than to bother."

A shiver of fear shot through Eric, but whatever hold Ursula had on him kept him from moving.

"What did you do to Ariel?" he asked. "Whatever deal she made, I'll—"

Ursula held up a finger, and Eric's mouth snapped shut. He couldn't reopen it no matter how hard he tried.

"There is nothing you could offer me that would compare to what her deal will eventually get me," said Ursula. "She didn't even want you, you know. She wanted adventure on land. I just thought this"—she waved a hand at him—"would be impossible. It doesn't matter, though. I am finally going to get what I deserve."

Eric felt the magic keeping his mouth shut loosen, and through gritted teeth, he said, "You deserve nothing."

"Oh, sweetling," Vanessa dropped her hands and clutched her shell necklace. "I deserve so much more than you can give me, but you'll do for now."

Then, eyes glowing as brightly as the shell at her throat, she sang.

19
Bridge

*E*RIC SLEPT strangely that night. He dreamed of drowning and not being saved, sinking into the quiet depths of darkness that lurked beneath the sea. He wasn't alone, but he couldn't see the others being dragged down with him. Flashes of red in the gloom and cold hands slipping from his fingers interrupted his descent. He tried to swim and grasp at them. Panic pounded in his chest.

Eric jerked away.

"Good morning, sweetling." Vanessa's voice washed over him like the sea and dragged him from his dreams. "How are you feeling?"

"Fine," he said, but there was something wrong with his voice. Did he always sound so flat? "What are you doing here?"

Vanessa, already dressed in a light day dress of pale blue and white, was perched on a chair beside his bed.

Her dark hair was twisted into a crown atop her head, and one of the family rings rested on her hand.

"I couldn't sleep a wink," she said and smiled. "I'm far too excited for the wedding."

Max growled at her, and Eric nudged him with his foot.

"Yes, the wedding. Of course," said Eric. He could hear the words coming from his mouth, but he had no control over them. It was as if he was still drowning like he had been in his dream, and his emotions were muffled beneath the waves. His heart beat faster, but it could have been joy or fear. He could *feel* neither. "We need to start preparations."

"Let the staff worry about that," Vanessa said, and patted the top of his head. "Get dressed quickly so that we can go speak with Grimes about the marriage contract."

"Grimsby," he corrected on instinct, and nodded. "Of course. I'll get dressed now."

He must have been sore from his recent trips, because moving was exhausting. Max whined the whole time he was getting dressed. There was a dull ache in the back of Eric's head, as if someone had sewn a string into his mind and was tugging it every few minutes, and he couldn't hold back his groan when Vanessa sent him back into his quarters to put on something more befitting of his station. She was right, of course, but the jingle of the gold buttons and insignia on his coat made his headache worse. Max wasn't behaving, either.

"Get off!" Vanessa shrieked as Eric emerged from changing.

Max was raised on his hind legs, front paws on Vanessa's shoulders. He nipped at her necklace, and she twisted away from him. One hand smacked his snout.

"Eric!" She stumbled away and climbed onto a desk, barely out of Max's reach. "Get him away from me!"

Eric whistled twice, and Max dropped to all fours. He kept barking at Vanessa. The sound pierced Eric's brain. He rubbed his head.

"Max, quiet, please," he muttered.

Max let out a soft woof and padded over to Eric, twisting around his legs. He nosed Eric's side.

"You can come down now," Eric said to Vanessa.

She sniffed. "I will not. Lock him in your room."

He laughed.

"Eric," she hissed, and the glint of her shell necklace caught his eye. "Take that little monster and lock him in your bedroom."

Pain clouded Eric's mind. He'd meant to say something, but he couldn't think of it now.

"Come on, buddy," he muttered to Max, and led the dog away. "I'll come see you later, all right?"

His headache only eased once the door to his bedroom clicked shut.

"Much better. Now, let's go find your man and draw up the proper papers," Vanessa said, brushing her dress off and looping her arm through his. "I had one of the servants go find him and tell him to meet us in the entry hall. After that, I'm getting a dress fitted and will be on the wedding ship, so I'm depending on you to take care of everything else."

"I will," Eric said. "Whatever you want."

"That's what I like to hear."

Vanessa led him to the entry hall. Grimsby was already there, straight-backed and curious. The castle was bustling with activity, people carrying flowers to and fro and seamstresses carting fabric down the halls. Vanessa had been busy while he slept.

"Eric," said Grimsby, meeting them near the bottom of the stairs. "What is going on?"

"Grimsby, it is my great pleasure to introduce to you Vanessa, my true love." Eric presented her left hand to him, and there was no missing the ring on her finger. "I found her, and she agreed to marry me."

"Yes, you mentioned it last night," said Grimsby,

looking no worse for wear despite the early hour at which Eric had woken him up to confess to finding Vanessa and their planned matrimony. It had been too late for proper introductions, of course, but Vanessa had helped Eric practice exactly what to say. Grimsby inclined his head to Vanessa and looked her over. "It was quite the surprise."

"It's so wonderful to meet you, too," Vanessa said, holding out her hand. "Eric and I can't wait to be married."

"So he said." Grimsby brushed his lips against the back of her hand and glanced at Eric. "Thank you for rescuing Eric the other day on the beach, but I must ask: why did you leave?"

"I was so overwhelmed by it all, and I didn't know who he was." Vanessa pressed herself more closely against his side and laid her hand on his arm. "I wasn't even aware he was my true love until last night, but we get on so well. It's only natural."

"She saved my life, Grimsby," Eric said. The man's full name felt odd on Eric's tongue, but he couldn't bring himself to call him by any other name. "She is my true love."

The words hurt in a way he couldn't understand.

"Well, Eric . . ." Grimsby gave them both a slight bow, and Eric thought he saw a frown. "It appears I was mistaken. This mystery maiden of yours does, in fact, exist, and she is lovely. Congratulations, my dear."

Vanessa squeezed Eric's arm.

"We wish to be married as soon as possible," said Eric.

Grimsby fiddled with his cravat and said, "Oh, yes, of course, Eric, but these things do take time, you know."

"This afternoon, Grimsby." Eric hadn't meant for it to come across so harsh, but the words were already out and he didn't know what else to say.

Grimsby opened his mouth as if about to protest, but seemed to stop himself.

"Oh, very well, Eric," said Grimsby, narrowed gaze dropping to Vanessa's grip on the prince's arm. "If you're sure this is what you want."

A flash of red caught his eye on the stairwell above them. Ariel had overheard their conversation. The moment he heard her sharp gasp and fleeing footfalls, Eric lurched forward, but he couldn't discern why.

"I want Ari—"

The ache in his chest snapped. Eric jerked, opening his mouth to yell for her. Vanessa's fingers tightened on his arm, and she hummed the same song she had sung when she saved him. It drowned out his thoughts and washed them away. He couldn't move from her.

Vanessa interrupted him with another low hum.

Bridge

"We want to ensure Vellona is in good hands as quickly as possible."

Ah, yes. That was what he wanted.

Grimsby leveled a look at Vanessa. "Is there anyone we should invite to the wedding for you? Family or friends, perhaps? And where should we send our congratulations?"

"I'll take care of that," she said, staring right back at him.

"Well, you must allow me to help in some way." Grimsby gestured for one of the servants waiting by the door. "Be a good lad and deliver any messages Lady Vanessa needs to send as quickly as you can today."

The boy nodded and waited next to Vanessa expectantly.

"Thank you," she said through gritted teeth, and Eric was sure he had missed something, but had no idea what it could be.

"Perfect," said Grimsby with a bow. "If you need assistance, you only need ask."

"Now, Eric, sweetling, work on the marriage announcements and make sure you sign the wedding contract," Vanessa said. "I'll see you again on the ship."

"Yes, Vanessa," Eric said, still trying to remember what he had meant to say before she interrupted him.

She slipped from Eric's grasp and down the hall, and Eric couldn't pull his gaze from her until she was out of sight. Grimsby watched her with barely contained suspicion.

"How fortunate for us that she appears now," muttered the man. "A quick marriage is not something I would have ever associated with you."

"Her voice is perfect, you know, and her soul is just as spotless. She risked her life to save me—a stranger— from a storm. Exactly as the curse described." Eric's hand shot out and gripped Grimsby's wrist. "Help me with the announcements to the rest of my family and court?"

Grimsby took Eric's hand and pried it off him. "Of course, Eric, but what's gotten into you?"

"I found my true love, Grimsby," said Eric. "Is that not reason enough to be excited?"

Grimsby only frowned, showing no enthusiasm, but Eric paid him no mind. He needed to get everything done just as Vanessa had asked. Her explanation last night had made perfect sense, but Eric couldn't quite recall all the details now. So long as he wrote out the announcements and made sure he was ready, she should be pleased, though. All he wanted was to please her.

Bridge

They walked in silence. Grimsby's quiet anger unsettled Eric, leaving him unsure and on edge. Grimsby took in the odd disarray of Eric's study with little more than a flare of his nostrils, and Eric sat at his desk with a sigh. He pulled a sheaf of papers from a drawer. Announcements were easy enough. All he really needed to do was draft a few letters to the different lords and then use those as a basic template for the others.

Grimsby paced before Eric's desk and watched him work through the first letter before he asked, "Does your Vanessa have a family name?"

"Of course she does," said Eric, setting aside the first letter. It was to Brackenridge and was hopefully contrite enough, all things considered. So long as he ensured they wouldn't protest Vanessa as Vellona's ruler if anything happened to him . . .

"What is it?"

"What's what?" Eric asked.

"Eric." Grimsby groaned and pulled a chair up to Eric's desk. They were sitting next to each other, but Eric still felt seas away. "Eric, you've spent months trying to convince me that a quick marriage is neither the answer to our problems nor what you want. Did you not say that there were more important issues facing Vellona? Was Ursula not on her way here yesterday?"

"All the better to get married as soon as possible, make sure I cannot be killed by a kiss, and secure the support of the court members upset at my lack of betrothal so close to my coronation." Eric signed his name on a letter for Glowerhaven and let his quill rest away from the paper. "She's the one, Grimsby. Wait until you hear her voice. I'd know it anywhere."

"Then get betrothed!" Grimsby threw up his hands. "Kiss her and get it over with, but marrying her this quickly?"

"She wants our first kiss to be at the wedding," said Eric. "It will be more romantic like that."

Grimsby narrowed his eyes. "What are we to do about the Isle of Serein?"

Eric startled. "What?"

"The Isle of Serein. Your mother. The ghost ship. What will you do about them?" Grimsby crossed his arms over his chest. "You do remember that Vanessa can't solve all of the problems threatening you, don't you?"

"Don't be ridiculous," said Eric. "Of course she can. Vanessa knows what she's doing."

"How? Who is she?" Grimsby narrowed his beady eyes further. "And what about Ariel?"

"What about Ariel?" Eric, vision suddenly spotty, rubbed his eyes and frowned at the tears smeared on his hands. He wiped them on his trousers.

Grimsby dragged his chair closer to Eric and pressed the back of his hand to Eric's forehead. "Are you well? Just last night you were ready to court her."

Eric pulled away. "It doesn't matter if I was taken with Ariel. She's not my true love. Vanessa is."

Eric tried to smile at Grimsby to reassure him that he knew what he was doing, but from Grimsby's answering frown, Eric wasn't sure it had worked. He turned back to the rest of the letters, ignoring Grimsby's hemming and hawing. The man would come to terms with it all eventually. Vanessa would sort him out.

The door to his study slammed open, and Eric spilled a bottle of ink across his desk. Grimsby yelped and leapt to his feet. Vanni stood in the doorway.

"Wedding?" he practically screamed, cheeks pink, and pointed at Eric. "You're getting married?"

Gabriella poked her head over Vanni's shoulder and nodded at Eric. "We heard about it through the bay's rumor mill, and we're upset we didn't know first."

Eric mopped up the spilled ink with the ruined blank

pieces of paper and glared at Nora, who entered the room behind Vanni and Gabriella. "Have you come to be angry at me, too?"

"No, she started running," muttered Nora, and gestured to Gabriella, "so I followed. Figured it was something interesting and not wedding stuff."

Vanni waved her comment off. "The most important part is why today? You and Ariel just met."

Another headache bloomed in the back of Eric's head.

"What does Ariel have to do with it?" Eric asked.

"He's not marrying Ariel," Grimsby said, and gathered up the letters Eric had been working on. "He's marrying Vanessa."

"Who?" asked Gabriella.

"Yes, that was my question last night when he told me," said Grimsby. He read over the letters Eric had written and blanched. He cleared his throat and then handed them to Gabriella with shaking hands. "Vanessa is Eric's true love, whom he found on the beach last night."

"You make it sound like some sort of nefarious plot," murmured Eric. "She was on a walk."

"I would hate to imply anything untoward," said Grimsby. His lips were pursed, and an unhappy furrow split his forehead. He gave Gabriella and Vanni an imploring look. "Vanessa is quite *enchanting*."

Next to Grimsby, Gabriella tensed as she read the letters, her fingers clenching the pages far too tight. Nora read over her shoulder and glanced at Eric. Gabriella handed the letters to Vanni.

"I trust that each of you will help us with this wedding in any way you can," Grimsby said, looking at them each in turn. "That is what Eric wants, isn't it, Eric?"

Vanni stared down at the letters, raised his eyes to Eric once, and handed them back to Gabriella. "Of course. Whatever you need."

Eric laughed. "Are the announcements really so bad that everyone needs to read them?"

"No," said Gabriella with a tight smile. "We're just all amazed you're doing paperwork."

"Save your wit for the dinner speeches," said Eric. "We will need food and musicians, and anyone in the bay who should be invited will have to be informed."

"Vanni and I will take care of the food and alerting the guests." Gabriella passed the letters back to Grimsby. "Let us know if you need anything else."

"We will. There will be quite a few political aspects to deal with," said Grimsby. He turned his attention to Nora. "I am certain your captain would be very interested to know that once Eric is married, Vanessa will be set to inherit Vellona, along with any contracts he has with pirates or the like, should anything happen to him."

"They would," Nora said, and stuck out her hand to Grimsby. "I'll pass on the message and find you a crew for the wedding ship."

"Why would she even want any of this?" whispered Vanni.

Nora snorted. "Decadence? Pleasure? If you're going to poison a man's dinner, no reason not to enjoy your own."

"Please keep your upsetting metaphors to yourself," Grimsby said, the letters flapping in his hands. Eric couldn't figure out what they could be talking about.

Someone rapped sharply on the door, silencing the others, and Eric leaned back in his chair. He would get nothing done this morning. The door creaked open, and Ariel slipped inside. Her eyes were bloodshot and watery. Eric gripped the edge of his desk.

"Ariel. Lovely," said Grimsby, shooing the others out the door. "Come in. Eric has something to talk to you about."

Eric stared at Grimsby in a panic. He had nothing to say to Ariel. He looked at her and his mind went blank. His chest felt empty.

Bridge

"Eric," Grimsby said, the letters dangling from his hands. "Talk."

But Eric was too distracted by the announcements in Grimsby's hands, where he could see his messy handwriting. There were only two words on the page.

Help me.

Eric couldn't remember writing that. It wasn't what Vanessa had asked him to do at all, but Grimsby darted out the door before Eric could look closer.

Ariel approached Eric's desk cautiously. The hesitation hurt, but he couldn't bring himself to comfort her. It was like the need to do it was there but buried under all his other responsibilities. Vanessa would be furious if he didn't get everything done, and thoughts of her potential displeasure clouded everything else.

Ariel let the silence stand. She rocked on her heels before his desk, twisting her hands before her. Her nervousness seeped into him.

"I want you," he said, and his jaw clenched shut. His exhaustion and excitement mixing, surely. Eric rubbed his face. Where had that come from? "I mean, I want you at the wedding. Please. It would mean a lot to me."

Ariel took a deep breath, a look of pain flickering across her face, and she tapped twice against the table.

Eric flinched at that answer. "Ariel, you don't understand. I was going to talk to you, and I found . . ."

His throat cinched, as if a hand had curled around his neck, and Eric gritted his teeth. His headache surged.

"She was singing," he said, and tried to describe how enchanting her song had been. He needed to explain how compelling Vanessa was. He needed . . .

Ariel raised both of her hands to stop him. She motioned at him, made the gesture for "want," and then waved to the world around them. Eric swallowed.

Speaking was like swallowing glass.

"I want to spend the rest of my life with my true love," he said in answer to her question, and his voice broke. His skin was too tight, too hot, as if there were suddenly two Erics sharing his flesh and neither was pleased about it. The pain pitched, and Eric mumbled, "I heard Vanessa. She's my true love. She's all I can think about."

Ariel worked her mouth as if trying to speak and nodded. She pointed toward the sun.

"Time?" Eric asked and smiled when she nodded. "We're getting married at dusk."

She paused at the words, seemingly deep in thought. Then she pointed to herself and then at him, letting one hand drift up from his chest to his face. Gently, she curled his lips into a smile.

"You want me to be happy?" he asked.

She nodded.

He tried to say he wasn't. He tried to peel his tongue from the back of his teeth and force out, *This won't make me happy*. Only a strangled gasp escaped.

Singing echoed outside in the hallway, and Ariel's brows pinched together. Everything Eric meant to say vanished.

"I am happy," he said. "More than you can imagine, and I would like you there to celebrate with me."

Ariel inhaled sharply, tears gathering in the corners of her eyes.

Eric reached out to brush them away, and his thumb touched her skin, and—

A school of memories—red hair like dawn spilling across pale shoulders, strong hands tight around his wrists as they tugged him from harm's way, and the shuffle of unsteady feet through warm sand—flickered beneath the surface of his mind. They had nearly kissed in the lagoon, and he hadn't been afraid at all. He had been so certain that—

The door to his study crashed open.

"Eric!" Vanessa glided into the room, coming between him and Ariel. "There you are. I've been looking everywhere for you."

The fog in his head cleared at the sight of Vanessa. Eric took her hand as she made her way next to him. The world was sharp and clear, and the uncertain haze that hung about Ariel was completely gone. She wasn't important. She wasn't anything.

"I was working on the announcements and informing my friends of the wedding," he said, his full attention on Vanessa.

He wasn't sure how it had ever been anywhere else. It was as if there were a string tangling her with him, and if he turned away, it would strangle him.

"Very good, sweetling." Vanessa glanced over her shoulder at Ariel. "Run along . . . I'm sorry, who are you?"

Ariel fled the room, and every remaining thought Eric had of her vanished with her.

20
Dead in the Water

*T*HE REST of the day was a blur. Ariel didn't return to speak with him after Vanessa scared her away, and Eric knew it should have bothered him. Ariel was his friend, and Vanessa had cast her aside like trash. It was upsetting.

Except no part of him felt upset.

He felt empty, hollowed out, and he couldn't ever recall being full. He knew there were things he was forgetting—things he had meant to do, things he should be doing, things he shouldn't be doing. It just all felt so inconsequential.

It was easier to smile and nod when Vanessa spoke. She told him to focus on getting ready for the wedding and little else while walking him to his quarters. After that, he was in Carlotta's gentle care, and he bathed and got dressed slowly. Carlotta asked about Vanessa and the wedding, hemming and hawing with each of Eric's answers, and he frowned. He didn't have many answers, but that wasn't odd. Vanessa was a private person.

Late afternoon, an hour before dusk, Grimsby pulled Carlotta aside and whispered to her as Eric smoothed the wrinkles from his coat. Gabriella and Vanni came to walk him to the wedding ship before he could ask Grimsby what was going on.

"Grimsby's got a plan," Vanni whispered to Eric as they left him at the back of the deck behind the guests. "Don't worry."

They were standing near the stern, where Vanessa would join Eric soon. One walk down the aisle—that was all that separated him from being married.

"I'm not worried," Eric said. "Why would I be?"

Vanni only shot Gabriella a look before they moved to their seats.

Waiting for Vanessa to appear so the wedding ceremony could begin, Eric tugged at the uncomfortably tight collar of his state clothes. He took a breath and looked around the ship. Columns as white as whale bones rose up from the deck, green vines and pale pink flowers twining up them, and the evening's ruddy light spilled out over the bay. At the prow, the Vellona crest rested beneath great curtains of ocean blue, gilding glittering in the sun. A crown sat above it all.

The sun touched the horizon. Music swelled. The wedding guests shifted in their seats, the familiar forms of Vanni and Gabriella twisting in their chairs to look at him. Gabriella's expression was tense, the green scarf holding back her hair wrinkled from constant fiddling, and Vanni hadn't even dressed up. That should've bothered Eric, and he knew it. He couldn't bring himself to care, though. That couldn't be good.

Soft footfalls neared, and the guests rose.

Finally, he was marrying his true love, but there was no lightning strike of excitement or flutter of love. Maybe he simply had to spark his own happiness.

Vanessa glided next to him, and her white-and-pink skirt rustled against his trousers. The peachy sky began to darken to a red-stained orange.

"Ready, sweetling?" Vanessa asked. She did not take his arm. "Walk."

Eric couldn't move his head from staring straight ahead, not even when he heard Max whimper.

The altar was no more than two dozen paces away or so, but each step was an eternity. The guests looked on with the same somber expressions. Sauer was the only one who didn't look like they were at a funeral, and that was mostly the red coat's fault.

Eric and Vanessa reached the small altar before the

even smaller priest, and the crown of Vellona loomed over them. The blue curtains were dark against the backdrop of the setting sun, and Max tugged against his leash at Grimsby's side. Eric wanted to pull away and comfort him, but Vanessa would hate that.

Eric hated that she would hate that. He hated that he didn't even try to pull away and calm Max.

"Welcome!" said the priest, and his voice was barely loud enough for Eric to hear, much less everyone else. "Dearly beloved, we have gathered here today to see these two lovebirds bound in matrimony."

The priest droned on and the sun sunk lower.

". . . you, Eric, take Lady Vanessa to be your lawfully wedded wife for as long as you both shall live?" the priest asked finally.

Eric paused. True love should not feel underwhelming or mediocre or whatever this empty emotion was. It was supposed to be all-encompassing and passionate. He should have been happy.

When was the last time he had been? Last night? Before he met Van—

Vanessa squeezed his arm, nails digging through his sleeve, and Eric spoke without thinking. "I do."

A gull squawked. The priest paused, looking up. Eric longed to look and see what was happening, but

Dead in the Water

Would Vanessa approve? kept repeating in his head. He didn't move, and Vanessa turned away from him. A flock of birds tore across the bow, forcing Vanessa away from Eric. The priest ducked behind his podium.

Wings and webbed feet raked over Eric's shoulders, but he still couldn't move. The flock swooped again, dropping half-eaten fish and seaweed on the deck. Vanessa shrieked, and the guests scattered back toward the stern. Water splashed against the ship, rocking it. The ship listed severely.

"Eric!" Vanni called.

Eric couldn't even answer him. His arms trembled as the world became a swirl of white feathers. He forced himself to move, letting the tilt of the ship drag him to the side and spin him around. The scene played out in a shuddering blur, birds sweeping guests from the deck and crabs scurrying with military precision. A pair of sea lions barreled through the crowd, sliding across the deck and into Vanessa. Vanni and Gabriella herded some of the guests into the captain's quarters. Nora looked anxiously over the rail.

"Why didn't we plan for this?" asked Grimsby.

"We prepared to fight a witch!" Sauer ripped a starfish off their shoulder and flung it at Grimsby. "Why would anyone ever plan for this?"

A sea lion slammed into Vanessa and threw her into the cake. She screamed, flinging buttercream and salt water from her face. Her legs tangled in her sodden dress.

"Eric!" Gabriella helped Vanni away from the other sea lion. "Come on!"

He wanted to. He needed to. His feet shuffled, each movement painful and slow. The wedding guests were scattered and panicking, overrun by the rampant sea creatures. Everyone was trying to find a place to hide or just trying to stay upright and on the deck instead of being knocked overboard. Vanessa's eyes rolled to Eric and narrowed, and she used one of the frightened guests to help her stand. She tossed them aside once she was done.

"Don't you dare lea—" A wave swept over the side of the ship and smacked into her back.

Hair red as the setting sun caught Eric's gaze. And then there was Ariel, gasping for breath and soaked to the bone, crawling onto the deck through a scupper hole and stumbling to her feet.

Noticing the girl, Vanessa lurched toward Ariel, but a scraggly gull caught her necklace in his beak and pulled her back.

"Oh, you little . . ." Vanessa grabbed the gull by the

throat and twisted. "You think a ball of feathers can stop me?"

Max growled at Grimsby's side. The dog whined at Eric and then ripped his lead free of Grimsby, launching himself at Vanessa. His teeth locked down on the back of her leg. She screeched and dropped the gull. It ripped the necklace from her neck, and the golden shell fell to the ground. It shattered at Vanessa's feet.

A golden mist rose from the pieces, bright against the dark scarlet of the sunken sun beyond the ship. The tendrils twined together, and the distant hum of a familiar tune rocked through Eric. He closed his eyes, the sound reaching deep into his soul as his savior's song echoed over the deck. It was beautiful and otherworldly, and he couldn't believe he had thought it Vanessa's. The voice was kind and certain in a way Vanessa wasn't. She hadn't even bothered to learn Carlotta's name, for Triton's sake. Eric opened his eyes.

The golden glow of magic warmed the air and drifted to Ariel like dandelion fluff on a breeze, and her beaming smile matched the clear, bell-like tone of the voice. Ariel held up her hands, and the magic moved eagerly to her. She clutched it, pulling the voice to her throat. It settled into her skin.

One final note rang out, and Ariel's skin, the air, the world, glimmered with magic.

The haze in Eric's head cleared. Whatever hold Vanessa had over Eric broke, the tightly strung tension in his body fading. The near-constant headache vanished, and he tried to reach out for Ariel. His shaking hands moved easily through the air, and he could move again. He fell to his knees, unable to take his eyes from Ariel. She smiled and gestured at the sea lions. They lay down at once. Max danced around her in joy.

"Ariel?" he whispered, finally free to speak.

She smiled and said, "Eric!"

It was the first time her voice had been hers, and it was glorious. He was back on the beach, drowning and exhausted, and her voice was the air in his lungs. It wasn't bells in winter ringing out over the icy waves. It wasn't like anything he'd heard before. His name on her lips was everything.

Max leapt up on Ariel, licking her face. She laughed, not the silent one he was used to but beautiful all the same, and patted his head. Eric stumbled to her.

"Ariel," he said again, and took her hands in his.

"Eric! No! Get away from her!" Vanessa yelled. Her voice, lower and rougher, raked at his ears.

Eric put her off for one more moment and pulled Ariel close. "It was you all this time."

"Oh, Eric," she said, and the words struck him like an arrow. "I wanted to tell you."

It was if they were back on Sauer's ship with the Blood Tide seeping across the sea before them, red and terrifying, and Ariel diving from the ship, except this time, he dove with her.

Eric bent to kiss her.

"Eric!" Vanessa howled. "No!"

But before his lips met Ariel's, she flinched away from him. The bloody red light of the fully set sun washed over her, and she crumpled and clutched her legs. A gasp of pain and an unsettling crack silenced everyone. Her legs shimmered and fused together. Green scales burst from her skin.

A mermaid's tail thrashed where her legs had once been.

Shock froze him in place. Ariel's tail knocked against the deck, iridescent and glittering in the falling light. A stranger wrapped in nothing but sailcloth appearing on a beach with no knowledge of the kingdom or written language and an endless curiosity focused on things commonplace to most kingdoms—he should've known from the start. His savior had rescued him from the depths of the sea during a storm and swam him all the way to Vellona's safe shores. Of course she was a mermaid.

He moved to tell her it was fine—she was right not to tell him, since she had no way to know how he would react—and reassure her, but a roiling cackle cut him off.

"You're too late!" cried Vanessa.

Eric spun to face her and stumbled. Storm clouds gathered over the ship, lightning webbing the sky. All of it centered on Vanessa, the flashes shadowing her face. Her skin burst at the seams, color undulating across the once-pale flesh in hypnotic swirls until it turned a deep purple, darkening to black the lower it went. Her legs split up the sides. They thickened and twisted, six writhing tentacles spilling out from her flesh. She ran her hands through her dark hair, and it faded to white beneath her fingers.

The remaining wedding guests screamed and scrambled away from her. Eric stepped between her and Ariel.

"Oh, sweetling. No warm welcome?" She rose up on her tentacles and smirked down at him. "I thought you would be much more excited to see me after you spent so much time hunting me."

Ursula.

Eric hadn't had time to truly consider her last night.

This was who had cursed him before he was even born, finally before him just as he had imagined so often these last few days. He had assumed he would be prepared, not reeling after being compelled into a marriage he had rejected. It was fitting; even the choice of how they met she had stolen from him. A flush of heat surged through him. He wanted to hurt her as much as she had hurt him. Offer her everything she wanted and rip it away. Make her feel worthless.

And he hated it, but he hated her more.

Ursula surged forward before Eric could move, snatching Ariel and pulling herself up onto the rail.

"You're too late!" repeated Ursula. "So long, lover boy."

Eric lunged, but Ursula dove over the side of the ship, slipping out of Eric's grasp with Ariel in her arms.

"Get the guests away," Eric shouted. "I have to go help Ariel."

He turned and found Vanni and Gabriella at his side. Grimsby was herding the guests into the quarters and out of the way, and Sauer was at the helm. The ship began to turn slowly, its lack of sails working against them. The rowers were still recovering.

Vanni grabbed Eric's hand. "You can't deal with Ursula alone. Remember what Malek said."

"I know, and I love you both," said Eric, wrapping his arms around Vanni's neck. He grabbed Gabriella by the shirt and pulled her close, too. "Help Sauer and Nora get the ship back to shore safely."

"Eric," Gabriella muttered into his shoulder, and pulled away to look at him.

Vanni shook his head, fingers still clenching Eric's coat. "No, we can go with you. Grimsby and Sauer can get everyone to safety."

"I trust you both with my life, but more importantly, I trust you with the bay. Grimsby's going to need help evacuating Cloud Break," Eric said. "And Ursula isn't here to take Vellona. She will if she can, but she's here, first and foremost, for Ariel and me. We need to be the ones to face her."

"Fine." Gabriella hugged him once more and pulled Vanni away. "But once people are out of danger, we're coming right back out to help."

If Eric couldn't defeat Ursula, he would at least get people as far away from her as possible.

The wedding ship was better equipped for battle than Eric had thought it would be, but pistols and swords would be useless underwater. Eric's friends had clearly been planning for a fight on the ship, whether or not they had realized Eric's bride had been Ursula in disguise. Eric was thankful to find two harpoons in the hold, and he tossed them into the ship's dinghy, darting between the panicking guests who were still overrun with upset birds and sea lions. Max found Eric on the quarterdeck and locked his teeth around his ankle, tugging him away from the ship's edge. Eric patted Max's head.

"I have to go, buddy," Eric said, glancing over the sea every few seconds. There was a golden light beneath the water a little ways from the ship, and he was terrified of losing track of it. How could he help Ariel when he was only human? He knelt down and pried himself free of Max. "Come on. Let me go before Grim figures out I'm leaving."

Max whined and licked his face but ran back over the deck.

Eric lowered the dinghy into the waves. He climbed down into it, the choppy sea throwing the little boat back and forth. He could still spy the glow of magic through the water, and he rowed toward it. Ursula would have the advantage, but there was no helping that. At least it had stopped moving away.

A strangled shout from the ship caught his attention. "Eric!"

He turned back and groaned. Grimsby stood at the rail, expression stricken.

"Eric!" he cried. "What are you doing?"

"Grim, I lost her once. I'm not going to lose her again!"

Eric pushed on toward the light. He would do all the paperwork in the world without complaint after this so long as Grimsby got back to shore safely.

With another dozen good strokes, Eric was atop the glow of magic. He stopped rowing and grabbed a harpoon. He dove into the sea, warbling sounds like whale calls shaking him all the way to his bones. Under the water he could make out Ursula, a golden crown atop her head and a large glowing trident in her hands. Two large eels Eric recognized from the Isle curled over her shoulders like a cape. She had pinned Ariel against a rock, jabbing the trident at Ariel's neck.

Fury ripped through Eric, and he hauled his arm back before launching the harpoon. It sliced through Ursula's arm, drawing a hazy cloud of blue blood. Ursula spun to face him, distracted, and Ariel eased away from her.

"Why, you little troll!" Ursula raised the trident toward him.

Dead in the Water

Eric spun and swam away.

"Eric!" Ariel's voice rippled through the water, otherworldly and familiar all at once. "Look out!"

Ursula whipped around and hissed at the eels. "After him!"

The eels cut toward him. Their jaws worked as they swam, teeth gnashing at his feet. Eric's chest ached, and he gasped for breath when he broke the surface. Air flooded his lungs, and his fingers scrambled for a hold on the boat. The eels wrapped around his legs and yanked. Ocean water filled his mouth.

One of the eels tightened around his chest and arms. The other twined between his legs. They pulled him deeper and deeper, and salt burned in Eric's eyes. He struggled against their hold, but their teeth nipped at his hands every time he tried to break free. A blur of blue and yellow, the same bright fish that had followed them to the Isle of Serein, flew at the eels and rammed into one's head. The eel about his legs shivered and let go. It tried to wiggle free of the crab clinging to its tail. The other released Eric to help it.

Eric drifted up, and he twisted, trying to spot Ariel. The witch raised the trident, magic sizzling at its tip, and Eric's exhausted limbs moved too slow.

"Say goodbye to your sweetheart," Ursula said.

Ariel lunged and yanked Ursula back by her hair. The magic meant for Eric struck the eels. They lit up like storm clouds, lightning coursing through their bodies. They exploded in a shower of magic and bone.

Ursula gasped and gathered up the pieces of them to her chest.

Ariel fled while Ursula was distracted. Eric raced back to the surface and gasped for air. Ariel broke the surface near him.

"Are you all right?" he asked, pulling her close.

Ariel wrapped her arms around his waist. "You have to get away from here."

"No, I won't leave you," he said, and pressed his forehead to hers. "I'm so sorry. I didn't want to go through with the wedding, but I couldn't stop myself. Her voice, well, *your* voice—it was some sort of compulsion, like the ghosts."

"It's all right." Ariel gripped his collar. "Eric, I'm sorry I—"

"You have nothing to apologize for," he said. Lying Eric could understand. It was necessary to survive, whether you were lying about your name or a curse or some other important piece of yourself. There was safety in lies. "We can talk later. *We* have to get away from here."

"She has my father," said Ariel. "He's King Triton—"

Dead in the Water

"*The* King Triton?" Eric nearly choked.

She tapped his shoulder once. "I have to get back his crown and trident, or else she'll be unstoppable."

Had she not been unstoppable before?

The water around them glowed with bone-white light and bubbled. The waves grew and ripped Ariel from Eric's arms. He struggled to reach her again, and a golden spear rose up from the water. Ursula, great and terrible, a leviathan of magic and fury, emerged from the sea. She was giant and growing larger still. Ariel and Eric clung to her crown, trapped atop her. Ariel shouted to him, but he couldn't hear her over the rushing of the sea. She pantomimed diving.

Eric peeked over the edge of the crown to the sea far below and nodded.

"One," he said.

Ariel swallowed and shouted, "Two."

They dove together, crashing into the water, and Eric surged to the surface. He looked around for Ariel, salt burning his eyes. Ariel swam up a few feet away.

"You pitiful, insignificant fools," Ursula said, cackling as the clouds swirled in a maelstrom at the tip of her trident. She was taller than Vellona's highest cliffs, inescapable and pulsing with power. "You think you can win this fight?"

Eric shook the salt water from his face. "You took everything from people for decades!"

He peeked at Ariel once and tried to keep Ursula's attention away from her.

"That's what people do. We take," she spat. "I started with nothing, and look at where I am now."

"Was it worth it?" Eric shouted. "All that pain and suffering? What was it even for? More magic? More injustice?"

"This is justice!" She sneered down at him. "Restitution! Retribution! I am taking what I am owed. I am taking what your"—she rounded on Ariel—"family has taken from me. You think Triton wronged you? Do you know what he used to do to witches he feared might get more powerful than him? Banishment! Death! And for what? Because I used a few little souls! You have no idea what true desperation is, but I do."

"Why?" shouted Eric. "What use do you have for every soul and crown and kingdom?"

"None except to rule!" She bounced a ball of sickly green lightning across her fingers and flicked it toward the bay with the trident. The water around it boiled and steamed. It slammed into the supports of a dock. "Don't worry, sweetling. I want them to bow, not die."

Ariel was only a few strokes away from him now.

Dead in the Water

"You want to reshape the world to serve you!"

"Of course I do, darling," she said with a laugh. The trident glowed in her hands. "The world was shaped by people like you and Triton. It was shaped to serve you. Why shouldn't I have a turn?"

Ariel was just about to reach Eric when a tentacle as large as a ship emerged and crashed into the water between them.

"Now I am the ruler of all the ocean!" Ursula spun her trident, magic crackling in the air, and plunged it into the water. The sea churned around Ariel, wreckage-choked eddies twisting around her. "The waves obey my every whim. The sea and all its spoils bow to my power." Ursula loomed over Ariel. "And so will you, Princess."

She said it with such venom, Eric recoiled.

His mother's journals detailing the destruction left in Ursula's wake were proof enough of Ursula's deviousness. She had stolen Ariel's voice and used it against her. She had bewitched Eric after he rejected her and stripped him of his ability to tell her no. Ursula manipulated and manipulated until people had no choice but to make impossible deals with her, and even then she removed their real choice with contracts and magic. She had rigged the game so that the only choices were hers.

But knowing she was monstrous and facing the monster were very different.

This was what she had wanted all along—dominion over sea and land and an army of ghosts to ensure her rule. Power derived from desperate souls with no one else to turn to. She must have been one of them once. She had to have been, to know exactly how to lure them.

She didn't want to shape the world. She wanted to control it.

"Eric!" Ariel shrieked.

The whirlpool pulled Eric in, sucking him beneath the waves, and the holey hull of an old ship passed over him. Eric slammed into the wood and got dragged along it. His fingers scrambled for purchase. He caught the slimy remains of a rope.

It whipped about in the storm. Eric groaned, pulling himself up to the barnacle-washed deck. He collapsed on it, pain burning in his chest and arms, and Ariel screamed again. He slipped to the rail and looked for her. A flicker of red tumbled down the walls of water to the seafloor at the bottom of the whirlpool. Ariel crawled behind a large rock.

"It was so easy," Ursula said. "What was that old man teaching you that you didn't bother to read the contract you signed?"

Dead in the Water

The shattered bones of shipwrecks bobbed in the whirlpool and smashed into each other, raining salt and splinters onto Ariel. She threw up her arms to protect herself.

What could he do? Eric searched the ship for anything—cannon, harpoon, pistol—and found nothing. The rigging was tangled in the broken deck boards and eaten through by years in the sea. The masts were broken.

Up on the quarterdeck, the wheel still spun with the rocking of the ship. Eric lurched to the stairs and dragged himself toward the wheel with the rail. The tiller ropes were still attached, so he could steer the ship. At the very least, he could get between Ariel and Ursula.

"Is this all you've got, girl?" Ursula aimed her trident at Ariel, and magic burned through the air in jagged bolts. Ariel leapt out of the way, the stone where she had been smoldering. Ursula whipped another lash of magic at her. "Where's your prince now?"

Eric spun the wheel and turned the ship to Ursula. A rage Eric had never known consumed him, and a flash of lightning struck the jagged spear of the bowsprit. Ursula had taken his life, his love, his choices, his mother, and his kingdom from him. He only had one shot.

He wouldn't let her take anything else from him ever again.

"So much for true love." Ursula laughed and narrowed her eyes. "Sweet dreams, Princess."

She raised the trident, ready to strike. Eric screamed, muscles aching at the grip it took to keep the ship steady. Before Ursula could complete her blow, the bowsprit cut through her stomach, impaling her, and the pale waters ran sapphire blue with her blood. She choked and looked down, hand grasping at the ship. The trident slipped from her fingers, and lightning struck her crown. She fell onto the ship, flipping it forward. It launched Eric into the air.

He hit the water, one last glance of Ariel safe and sound calming his heart, and it all went black.

21

Happily Ever After

ERIC CAME to on the beach. The sky was oddly bright and clear, and he rolled onto his back, then up into a sitting position. Cloud Break's streets were filled with people, none of them screaming in terror, and even from the beach he could see the distant white pillars of the wedding ship. He sighed and dropped his aching head into his hands. At least those on board had gotten back safely.

How much time had passed? If the storms had stopped and people weren't running in fear, Ursula had to be dead, but did that mean her magic was gone? Were all her deals null and her curses broken?

"Ariel?" he called out, but his voice cracked. He couldn't even lift his head.

A splash came from the sea as if in answer. Eric looked up, breath catching in his chest. Ariel rose from the waves, a dress the pale blue of seafoam clinging to her and glittering with pearls along the cloth, and walked toward him. She smiled as their eyes met and dug her bare toes into the sand.

Toes!

Relief washed over Eric. He stumbled to his feet and raced to her. Ariel laughed and smiled, holding her arms out to him. He took her by the waist as he had when they danced and spun her around. Her laughter chased the last of his worries and pains away. He pulled her close.

Eric had waited an eternity for this moment. He raised one hand to her cheek and traced the line of her jaw, and his other arm curled tightly around her waist. She grinned up at him, a little crinkle in the corner of her eyes. He had thought about it when they danced under the stars that first night on the beach, her body pressed against his and her hair tangled in his fingers. He remembered how it had felt to lean in to her when they nearly kissed in the lagoon, before his fear got the better of him. He had wanted to take her in his arms when she dove off the ship after his mother and gone with him onto the Isle of Serein. He had always wanted her and been too afraid every time. This time, he'd be brave.

Eric kissed her.

Ariel tasted of salt and smoke and triumph. She gripped the back of his neck and moved her lips against his hesitantly. They were full and warm, and the whisper of her breath against his mouth blotted out his thoughts. He never wanted to part from her again, not for the sea or curses or politics or magic. This was his choice. Ariel was his choice for as long as she would have him.

Ariel broke the kiss first, gasping and pressing her forehead to his. Eric licked his lips, tasted the sea, and kissed her once again. She giggled against him.

"We did it. Ursula is gone." Her fingers curled around his hair. "And I think I owe you a story."

"Only if you want to tell it," Eric said. "Although it would be nice to know more about you, and I certainly wouldn't mind learning how you ended up in Cloud Break with no voice."

"I'll give you the short version, I think," said Ariel. Her smile softened and she squeezed his hand. "For now, anyway."

Eric's heart skipped a beat. *For now* meant that there would be a later. They had time now.

"I'm the youngest of seven," Ariel started. "I love my family, but they don't understand me at all. I always wanted to be human, and I saw you on the ship before the storm."

"You were near the ship?" he asked, trying to remember that night. "Oh no, did you see that statue?"

Ariel grinned. "I kept the statue after it sunk . . . At

least, I kept it for a while. I used to collect human things—pipes and forks and statues—and then my father banned me from venturing to the surface. I was supposed to be perfect. A good singer, obedient, and decidedly unadventurous. It made me feel like a something, though, not a someone. When he found my collection, he destroyed it. So I went to Ursula, knowing she was a witch."

Eric's heart broke. "You went to Ursula to escape him?"

"Not exactly. I had always dreamed of what it would be like to live on land. When Ursula made me her offer, it seemed like the right choice," she said. "I should've figured it was a trap. She just wanted to use me to get to my father."

Eric squeezed her hand to keep her from wading into other thoughts, and Ariel took a deep breath.

"My deal with her was that in exchange for my voice, I would be human for three days, but if I didn't convince you to kiss me by sunset on the third day, my soul would be hers," she said.

"She played us like fiddles." Eric groaned and leaned his forehead against hers. "She knew I would never kiss you because of my curse."

"And the worst part," Ariel whispered to Eric, "is that I didn't even consider reading the contract."

Eric couldn't help laughing.

"Laugh all you want. Your books turn to nothing in the sea." She poked him in the shoulder and turned, laying her ear over his heart. Suddenly, her face fell, and she looked down at the ground. "Eric, with Ursula gone, you're no longer cursed. There's no way to know if I'm your true love or not."

"I don't care." Eric kissed her again and relished how her heart thrummed against his chest. "It doesn't matter if you were my true love or if you weren't. You're who I want. You're who I am choosing to love. And I do love you."

Ariel yanked him back down to her. Eric laughed against her lips, unable to stop. She smiled against him.

"I won't swim away this time," said Ariel.

"If you do, I'm following," he said, and spun her around again, memorizing the sound of her laugh. He kissed her again—he would never tire of the feeling of her lips against his—and pulled her into a tight embrace.

Grimsby's raspy voice echoed over the beach, and Eric pulled away from her.

"I think we have to stop hiding," he whispered.

Ariel laughed into his chest. "Were we hiding?"

"We are never not hiding from him." Eric took a deep breath and shouted, "Over here, Grim!"

Grimsby rounded one of the larger rocks. He looked better than he had after the *Laughing Dove* wrecked, and his only wound was a spectacular bruise shaped like a starfish on one cheek. He raced to Eric, tackling him in a hug. Eric barely stayed standing and returned the grip with a laugh.

"Grim," he said, "is everyone safe?"

"Safe as houses. Not a single casualty," said Grimsby. He pulled back and clasped Eric's shoulders. "Never again, lad. Never again. Vanni and Gabriella are at the docks. We've been looking for you and Ariel all night."

Eric sighed, and the last tension in his sore muscles leaked out from him. "I promise I won't make this a habit."

"I must say," Grimsby said, peering around him to Ariel, "terribly sorry about your having to swim to the ship. We rather thought you wouldn't want to be there, but I can't say anything we were planning at the wedding went as we thought it would."

"What exactly were you planning?" Eric asked. "You cut those vows close."

"We figured Ursula must be involved somehow, given how powerful the magic over you seemed. We were hesitant to act too quickly and risk losing others to her magic or losing you completely. The plan was to wait until you said 'I do' and her guard was down to act. Most of the guests were Sauer's crew, and we figured there would be a fight once she was challenged. But Ariel and her squabble of gulls arrived before we could enact our plan." Grimsby drew himself up and clapped Eric on the shoulder again. "It's over now, though, thanks to you two! We'll need to contact the Vellonian council and the other kingdoms, of course, but without Ursula's storms and with the evidence Sait was conspiring with her, we should have some leverage to work with now."

His gaze caught on something behind Eric and Ariel, and Eric turned.

At the edge of the water, a tall, imposing figure with a powerful blue tail and a golden crown atop white hair rose from the waves. He held the trident Ursula had taken with practiced ease. Eric took a few steps forward until the waves lapped at his toes and bowed.

"Thank you, King Triton," said Eric.

Grimsby choked and bowed.

Triton inclined his head to Eric. "So you're the human my daughter's been chasing after."

"I wasn't chasing him," muttered Ariel.

"I recall a statue," Triton said, and Eric winced. That was not an ideal first impression.

"Daddy, be nice. He saved my life." Ariel took Eric's hand and led him into the surf. "Eric, this is my father, King Triton. Daddy, this is Prince Eric of Vellona."

Eric bowed again, deeper this time, and said, "It's an honor to meet you."

"And you," Triton said after Ariel narrowed her eyes at him. "Thank you for helping my Ariel."

"Of course. She helped me first. I don't think I'd be alive without her." Eric glanced at Ariel. "She's wonderful."

"Well," Triton said, clearing his throat. "I haven't always trusted her opinions on the human world, but I was clearly wrong. You've both saved many lives today."

"I'm glad." Eric straightened up, Ariel's hand still tightly gripped in his, and braced himself. "May ask a question about Ursula's magic?"

Triton nodded.

"The souls Ursula trapped as ghosts or fuel or polyps or whatever it was her magic did—can they rest now?"

"That rather depends on them," Triton said, lips twisting up to reveal a smile identical to Ariel's. "They're not ghosts. The souls Ursula used were not gathered from the dead but the living."

Something deep and dark in Eric broke, and he

tensed. That couldn't mean what he thought it meant. Ariel laced their fingers together.

"The ghosts, whatever they are, they're not dead?" Eric asked.

"Not at all. Once she died, their souls—the ghosts— would have reverted back to how they were before Ursula's magic took hold of them. They're wherever she kept them prisoner, I imagine," said Triton.

"It was an isle out in the middle of the sea," Ariel said, glancing at Eric. "But we had to use her magic to get there."

"Ah, she still used that old place?" Triton swept his trident through the sea. "I believe I can be of some help, then. Consider it a thank-you and an apology."

Magic bubbled in the water. A thin line of red shot out across the waves, vanishing into the north. It widened and split until dozens of little paths led from the horizon to different parts of Cloud Break. Triton hummed and nodded.

"That should do it," he said. "Ways for those stuck on the Isle to return home. They'll follow their own path."

With a shaky breath, Eric asked, "The ghosts will return home?"

Triton didn't bother to answer. He moved aside, and

Eric saw a figure walking across the waves toward Cloud Break. They were still far out at sea, but even from here, Eric could tell it wasn't a translucent ghost but a real person. And it wasn't just them—more people began appearing out at sea.

"Eric," Ariel whispered and kissed his cheek, her eyes full of understanding. "Go."

He took off running. The roads were crowded with people all eager to find out what had happened. Eric shoved through everyone, not even stopping when he passed Gabriella and Vanni trying to explain what had happened to a group of folks on the docks. There were more and more figures walking across the sea, and people were taking notice. Eric pushed on, catching sight of a single person sprinting down a blood-red path of magic that led to the beach beneath the castle. Eric raced to meet them there.

The running figure was a tall woman with salt-and-pepper hair cropped short. The moment her feet touched the sand, the red path that had led her back to Vellona vanished. Eric skidded to a stop a few steps away and stared. Her clothes were waterlogged and torn, a few cuts clearly from swords, and the long blue coat hanging haphazardly from one of her shoulders still bore his family's sparrow crest. Until the fight had ripped it from him, Eric had been wearing an identical coat.

"Mother?" he whispered.

"Eric?" Her head whipped to him. Eleanora of Vellona had not aged in the two years since Eric had seen her, and the shock of her voice brought him to tears. She stared at him as if she had never seen him before, tears gathering in her eyes. "Oh, darling. I'm so sorry."

Eric's mind went blank. Not the haze of Ursula's magic but true emptiness. His mother had been dead. He had mourned her. He had recovered.

And now here she was.

Eric's knees gave way. His mother caught him and wrapped her arms around his shoulders. Eric tucked his face into her shoulder and sobbed. His fingers gripped her shirt tight.

"How long?" she asked once he could breathe again.

Eric pulled back but kept hold of her. "Two years. Two extremely long years."

"But you saved us," she said, and sniffed, brushing his hair from his face. "I remember flashes, bits and pieces, and you were there for some of them. Is Ursula dead? I feel like she must be, but we all just awoke on this isle, and . . ."

"She's gone. It's a long tale." He pulled back, overwhelmed, and laughed. "But most importantly, I had help, and I would very much like to introduce you to Ariel, my true love."

Coda

THE SUN hung low over the sea, the pink tendrils of dawn spreading out across the bay. The salted breeze scattered white petals across the deck of the ship, and the candles flickering across the rail cleared away the last dregs of night. Eric ran a hand down the ship's side, listening to the odd silence of Cloud Break Bay. There were no calls today and no swords clanging beneath the docks. There was only the sea.

"It is a beautiful day for a wedding."

Eric turned at his mother's voice. Even after three years of her being back, a part of him still expected her to vanish by the time he looked.

Eleanora of Vellona, the golden crown resting on her head and the state sword strapped to her hip, had already cried all the last evening during supper and looked to be near tears again. Eric folded himself into her arms and fought back a laugh. Her Grimsby levels of stoicism had been slipping ever since they started planning the wedding.

With Ursula gone, the storms that had ravaged Vellona had stopped, fishers were pulling in regular catches again, and the farmlands were producing more than they ever had in Eric's lifetime. It was, as most folks were saying, as if a curse had been lifted. Sait, too, had withdrawn back to their lands and quieted down. Not that they had taken credit for the mercenaries they had been paying to rough up Vellona, but the attacks had stopped the moment they realized Vellona would soon be able to fight back. No one wanted to anger the queen who had returned from the dead or her son who had defeated a witch as powerful as Ursula. The rumors about what had happened in the bay had spread to the other kingdoms. Most of them were embellished, thanks to Sauer and Grimsby.

It helped that Eric's soon-to-be wife was a daughter of King Triton, too.

"Look at you," Eleanora whispered, stepping back but keeping her hands on his shoulders. "I didn't think I would get to see this."

"You could've seen it twice," he said, and she patted his cheek. "Fine, fine. Do you promise not to cry the whole time?"

Coda

She laughed. "I'm permitted a few tears on my son's wedding day."

"So long as you don't cry on my coat," he said. "I'm afraid to even touch it in case Carlotta sees another imaginary dust mite."

"Well," she said and pulled him away from the rail, "it's bad luck to anger Carlotta, so let's see."

She brushed her hands over his shoulders. They matched, though Eleanora's state suit was far more decorated than his and a capelet with the golden sparrow of Vellona hung from her shoulders instead of a coat. Carefully, she pulled a long, thin box from her trouser pocket and handed it to Eric. He glanced around.

"We already have rings," he said. "Unless Max ran off."

"This," she said and tapped the box, "was the first gift your father ever gave to me, and it's yours now."

Eric opened the box and laughed. Inside was a roughly hewn flute.

"Sounds terrible and might not work at all anymore, but it's yours." She kissed Eric's cheek. "New songs, darling."

"New songs," he repeated, and hugged her tight, chin on her shoulder. "Thank you."

Behind her, Vanni and Gabriella waited, and Eric

beckoned them over. Vanni was taller, somehow, and he had taken to wearing his hair in a little knot atop his head to keep it out of his face. It made him look older, and Eric still wasn't used to it. Gabriella, at least, hadn't aged at all. Nora's green scarf had finally fallen apart last year, but several green threads from it were woven through Gabriella's short braids.

"I wanted you to have something of his today," said Eleanora, stepping back. She smiled at Vanni and Gabriella. "I can't imagine King Triton is any less weepy."

"He's not, but Ariel's sisters have finally gotten her dressed, and the priest is ready," said Gabriella. She inclined her head to Eleanora and quickly greeted Eric with a hug. "Well, feeling better about this wedding?"

Eric snorted. "I can't even remember the entire day I spent with Ursula. It's all a blur until that shell smashed."

"I think that's just a wedding thing." Gabriella smiled and sighed. "I was doing great for mine, then Nora walked in and next thing I remember, I'm throwing almonds at people as they leave."

Gabriella and Nora had spent the year after Ursula's downfall hunting down Sait's mercenaries with Sauer and then married a year ago on *Siebenhaut*. Once the waters were safe, they had visited Malek's

Coda

and Nora's family and returned to the bay only two months ago.

"That was me. You only threw them at me," said Vanni. "Some of them hurt."

Gabriella laughed. "What sort of wedding guest doesn't gladly accept their favor?"

"See if I ever make anything for you again," he muttered, and rolled his eyes.

He would. He had slowly taken over the bakery part of the family business, specializing in sweets now that the shop was his alone. He'd made everything except the dinner course for the wedding tonight.

"You made me breakfast this morning," she said.

Eleanora glanced at Eric, and he shrugged. As much as things had changed, *this* had stayed exactly the same.

"Are you ready, Princeling?" Vanni asked and kissed Eric twice on each cheek, pulling him into a hug at the last second. "No nearly dying this time."

"I hope not," said Eric. "I think we've all had enough of that for a lifetime."

"Well," Vanni said and pulled away, "you look happier this time."

"Immeasurably so." Gabriella appeared at his side and looped her arm through Vanni's. "We'll be with the old reaper if you need us."

"Please, Gabriella," Eleanora said. "The reaper is hardly old enough to be mistaken for Grim."

Eric snorted, and she knocked his arm.

"Come here, dear." Eleanora shooed Eric away from Gabriella and straightened out the crisp lines of her suit, realigning the cuffed sleeves and high collar. "There we go. Don't you three look good, and don't I feel old seeing all of you like this. Now, time for you to wait for Ariel, and time for us to step aside."

The three of them mingled with the guests on the deck. Eric waited near the back of the ship where he would see Ariel for the first time all day. He had seen her every day for the last three years, but that hardly mattered. They had spent most of their first two years together traveling across Vellona, speaking with everyone about Sait's mercenary attacks and helping repair the damage from Ursula's meddling. Quite a few people had returned after her death, and they had tried to find all of them to make sure no one was missing. Ariel had adored traveling over land, and it had given them a chance to get to know each other without the threats of curses and contracts. When they'd returned to Cloud Break Bay last year, Vellona loved Ariel nearly as much as it loved Eleanora. It made Eric's eventual coronation feel less stifling.

Coda

Not that he would be king soon. His mother still had plenty to teach him, and he was more than fine with that.

Eric paced, wiping his clammy hands on his trousers. This time, there was no haze or fear, and the sight of the priest taking his place at the opposite end of the aisle didn't send his heart stuttering. A platform had been placed on the deck so that the merfolk would be able to see Eric and Ariel walk down the ship to the priest, and Ariel's sisters whispered in the waves. Triton and Eleanora chatted quietly over the rail. The ceremony would begin as soon as Ariel joined him and they walked down the aisle together.

The door to the quarters below deck creaked, and silk rustled in the breeze.

"Eric?" Ariel asked.

"Ariel," he said, and turned.

His heart stopped and his breath caught in his chest. The white dress was the latest fashion in Vellona, but the crown glittering with magic was purely hers. Pearls dotted the blue hems of her dress, and her veil had the opalescent sheen of oyster shells. He swallowed and touched her face with a shaking hand. She was real.

True love *was* real.

"You look wonderful," he said.

She leaned against him and looped her arm through his. "You look much better this time around."

"Is no one going to let me forget that day?" he asked.

"Not until we've replaced it with this one," said Ariel, and she rose on tiptoe to kiss his cheek. "I love you."

Eric pulled back and said, "I lov—"

Max leapt between them from out of nowhere and licked Eric's face. His paws knocked Eric back out of Ariel's arms, sending them both stumbling. Ariel let out a loud laugh, caught Max around the middle, and pulled him back. He licked her, too, the little box that had carried their rings clacking against the bell of his collar. She kissed his nose.

"Well," Eric said, "welcome to the family."

Max scrambled out of her arms and woofed at a gull flying overhead. He chased after it, Ariel laughing as he scrambled over the deck.

"I like our family," she said, and pulled Eric close for another kiss.

Her touch was like the sea, strong and sure, washing the worries from his mind. The world around them sharpened until all he could see was her. The dawn sky was bright in her blue eyes, a new beginning for both of them.

Coda

"Me too." Eric kissed her once more and looped his arm through hers so that they were standing side by side.

Behind the priest, the quartet began to play the song Ariel had sung to him on the beach all those days ago. The music quieted down the chatter, drawing everyone's attention to Eric and Ariel. The crowd rose, and next to his mother, Grimsby tilted his head back to hide his tears, accepting a handkerchief from Sauer without even glaring at the onetime pirate. Malek and several other merfolk looked up from their spots on the rail of the ship. Eric smiled at his mother, and Ariel waved to her sobbing sisters in the waves. Together, Eric and Ariel took their first step down the aisle.

"Come on," Eric whispered. "It's time for a new adventure."